THE LAST COCKTAIL PARTY

THE LAST COCKTAIL PARTY

Elisabeth McNeill

This first world edition published in Great Britain 2002 by
SEVERN HOUSE PUBLISHERS LTD of
9–15 High Street, Sutton, Surrey SM1 1DF.
This first world edition published in the USA 2002 by
SEVERN HOUSE PUBLISHERS INC of
595 Madison Avenue, New York, N.Y. 10022.

British Library Cataloguing in Publication Data

McNeill, Elisabeth
  The last cocktail party
  1. Murder – India – Bombay – Fiction
  2. British – India – Fiction
  I. Title
  823.9'14 [F]

ISBN 0-7278-5801-7

Typeset by Palimpsest Book Production Ltd.,
Polmont, Stirlingshire, Scotland.
Printed and bound in Great Britain by
MPG Books Ltd., Bodmin, Cornwall.

ONE

December 1ˢᵗ 1969

A gentle tap on the compartment door woke her from a deep sleep.

'Come in,' she called, turning over towards the window and prising open the edge of the bamboo slatted blind with her finger.

It was a glorious dawn. The sky was streaked in colour as the train crossed a flat dry plain, dotted here and there with coarse shrubs that looked like big balls of twigs. A man in a white shirt, squatting by the railway line as he relieved himself, stared blankly at the Madras Mail tearing past on its way to Bombay. She grimaced with distaste and lay back against the pillows as her bearer unlocked the door with his spare key and padded in quietly on bare feet. On the shelf by her side he laid a battered tin tray carrying a steaming cup of tea and a separate white saucer, which was chipped round the edge and stained with yellow tannin marks.

'Good morning, *mem sahib*,' Swami, the bearer, whispered as he stepped backwards towards the door again. He was a kind looking, grey-haired man with a deeply wrinkled face.

She returned his greeting and asked, 'Did you remember my pills?'

He gestured towards the saucer on which lay two pills. One was small and white, the other was a green and black capsule.

She looked at them and made an irritated noise. 'Is that

1

the best china this train can offer? It's filthy. Go and find something better for me.'

He lifted the offending crockery without comment and took it and the pills away, returning a few moments later with a fresh cup of tea and another saucer, still plain white but cleaner than its predecessor and less chipped.

Sipping from the cup, she eyed the pills as he laid the saucer down. 'Are these the same ones?' she asked.

'Yes, *mem sahib*,' he said.

'But they were on that dirty saucer. Bring another two,' she ordered.

'There are no more of the big ones. That is the last,' he told her.

She made an annoyed noise. 'Tut! Kenneth must have forgotten to put in a spare for me, even though I told him to! It's just as well I'm nearly home now. Oh, all right.' As the old man was backing out into the corridor, she consulted the gold watch that circled her wrist. It was seven o'clock.

'Are we running late?' she asked.

'It is right on time, *mem sahib*.'

Mollified she went on, 'In that case we'll get in at nine, won't we? Bring me hot water for washing in an hour's time. Remember to lock my door when you leave.'

As he backed out, he saw her settle back into her bunk and reach out to pop the green and black capsule into her mouth.

Exactly an hour later Swami returned, carefully carrying a large enamel jug from which steam was rising. Over one arm was draped a fluffy pink towel. When he rapped on the compartment door there was no reply, so he put the jug on the floor and fished in his pocket for the key. It turned easily in the lock but when he tried to enter the compartment, he found that the door would not open. It seemed to be stuck.

Despite pushing with his shoulder, it still refused to budge. His tranquil expression did not change, but he felt irritation rising inside him as he pushed harder; straining as he did so. The opening widened a little and he craned his neck to look round the edge of the door.

To his horror, he saw her lying sprawled on the floor in her lace-trimmed pink negligee. Her feet were braced against the door and her golden head was propped against the edge of the bunk, as if she had collapsed whilst trying to get up from the bed. Her eyes were wide open in an astonished stare as if she'd been transfixed with shock. He knew better than to try to touch her, but turned and ran along the corridor calling out for help. Soon men and women were blocking the corridor outside her compartment, all talking at once, animated and excited by the drama of seeing an unconscious white woman lying on the floor.

Another woman passenger from the sleeping carriage pushed her way through the mob, ordering, 'Let me in. I'm a doctor.'

The crowd parted to allow her past and jostled each other as they fought for good viewing spaces from which to watch her hitch up her sari and kneel down beside the unconscious woman on the floor. The doctor straightened the golden head, put her fingers on the thick, white column of neck to check for a pulse, and after a short time stood up again, pulling a sheet off the tumbled bunk and laying it over the recumbent body so that it covered the terrible, staring eyes.

Without emotion she pronounced, 'She's dead. Who's with her? What's her name?'

Swami stepped forward, his face twitching and his hands trembling. 'Her name is Mrs Sonya Richards, and I am her servant Swami,' he said. Then he started to cry.

TWO

Mid-February 1990

'This is ridiculous!' Alice Richards stood in the doorway of the attic room, which her husband called his office, with an angry look on her face and her fists on her prominent hip bones. She was an immaculately dressed and made-up clothes horse of a woman with imperious features. Her carefully dyed blonde hair was lacquered into a helmet-like style that added to her aggressive appearance and her slightly crossed pale blue eyes made her look like a spitting Persian cat.

Kenneth kept his head down and did not meet his wife's terrifying stare. On the desk in front of him was a long sheet of continuous paper bearing a list of names, and a tall pile of envelopes. 'No, darling, it isn't,' he demurred mildly.

'Of *course* it's ridiculous. You could be doing something useful like tidying out the garage. Besides, all the stamps for those letters going God knows where, must be costing us a fortune. Most of the people you're sending them to are probably dead or too gaga to remember anything about Bombay anyway,' snapped Alice.

'Marian and Peter will reimburse me for the stamp money,' said Kenneth, picking up an envelope and starting to write on it. He wished she'd go away and leave him alone.

'They'll only do that if enough people buy tickets. The numbers have been falling every year and what if nobody comes to your precious Cocktail Party this year? You'll all lose money then. I said from the beginning that Marian

4

shouldn't have made a provisional booking at that fancy club. It's pathetic the way you and your friends live in the past. When you get together you never talk about anything except things that happened twenty or thirty years ago. You're fossils!' Alice's carefully powdered face grew flushed as she ranted, pouring out her resentments one after the other.

'We haven't all got your advantages, darling. We can't defy time the way you do,' said Kenneth, unable to hide the edge to his voice.

'You don't defy time, as you put it, because you're all so lazy. Keeping myself looking this good takes hard work, you know. That fat slob Peter could do the same but he's too idle and so is his butterball of a wife. As for you! It's gin that's ageing you, Ken Richards. Your kidneys are going to pack up any day now. I can tell by the bags beneath your eyes.'

Alice had worked as a nurse before she married and, although she had never completed her training, she considered herself to be an infallible source of medical knowledge and liked nothing better than diagnosing other people's ailments.

Her husband sighed. He hated being called Ken and she knew it, so she used that name when she was being particularly beastly to him, which was practically all the time nowadays. 'I drink gin because I need some comfort in my life. I'm not just on this earth to provide you with money, you know,' he told her.

'Ha! You're not even very good at that. You're stingy as hell. Except to your precious daughter, of course. You spend enough money on her and she's not even yours! What're we going to live on if your capital runs out? Marian and Peter won't be much help to you then, will they? I don't see them running along here with a nice cheque, do you?'

'Questions, questions,' snapped Kenneth, 'Anyway my capital's not going to run out. Go away and practise your yoga. That might calm you down.'

She pulled the door shut with a bang and disappeared.

A few moments later he heard the crunch of gravel on the drive and stood up to look out of the window. Rain was pouring down from a slate grey sky, but that did not worry him because she had finally gone and driven herself off in a fury.

'Thank God,' he sighed, poured himself a gin and tonic, although it was not yet ten o'clock in the morning, and went back to addressing his envelopes.

When ninety-eight of them were done, he slipped a photocopied letter into each and folded in the flaps with an air of satisfaction. 'That's a good job well done,' he said aloud and lifted the telephone to ring his friend Peter. 'Hello, Peter. It's Kenneth. I've done all the notices for the people we listed and I'll put them in the post this afternoon,' he said in a cheerful voice, expecting to be congratulated on his efficiency.

Peter's gentlemanly drawl came purring over the line, 'Well done, old boy! We can always rely on you. The replies should start coming in by the end of next week I hope. Then we'll know whether it's viable or not. We need acceptances for at least a hundred to cover the club costs.'

He always spoke to Kenneth in a tone of kindly conde-scension with a certain note of wariness which emphasised the social gulf between them. This attitude made Kenneth over-eager to ingratiate himself and he knew that when he replied he would sound like a puppy lying on its back with its feet in the air waiting for its tummy to be tickled.

'I'll let you know as soon as they start arriving,' he said, 'I'm sure it'll be all right. I've sent out ninety-eight fliers and most of them are for couples. It's the last party, after all, isn't it? People will turn out for that . . . end of an era, what?'

Peter sounded doubtful. 'I hope so. There's just one thing that worries me. Marian and I've been talking about it and we're thinking fifteen pounds a ticket's perhaps a *little* steep. What about making it ten? We'd certainly get more people then. Not all of them are as comfortable as us, old boy. I know several who're a bit strapped for cash these days, what with Lloyds coming a cropper and all that.' Peter was never strapped for cash because he was still drawing fat director's fees, and assumed that the man he was speaking to was in the same fortunate position.

With a sinking heart Kenneth looked at the teetering pile of closed envelopes on his desk. Shit! he thought. But what he cravenly said was, 'Perhaps you're right. Do you think I should change the price in the letter, then?' He was hoping the answer would be 'no' but was quickly disappointed.

'Good chap. We could make it ten pounds. That's very tactful of you,' said Peter, as if changing the price was entirely Kenneth's idea.

Four hours later, when the rain stopped, he had drunk two more gins and typed out another letter which he took to the village post office to be photocopied one hundred and ten times because he wanted a few spares.

This time he did not phone Peter again, but before he refilled the envelopes, he carefully read the communication that had taken so much time and trouble to complete:

> The committee of the annual Bombay Cocktail Party have reluctantly decided that this year's event must be the last! Falling attendees over the past two years indicate that the Grim Reaper and illness are cutting down our numbers and so we have decided to go out with a bang and make this year's event the best ever!

Kenneth was particularly fond of clichés and exclamation marks which he slipped in wherever he thought a point should be emphasised, unaware that they gave his letter a hysterical look.

> Your committee have provisionally booked this year's party for July 20th to be held in the Royal Overseas

League, Park Place, just off St James Street, London of course! Clever Marian has negotiated a very reasonable price for this superb location and we are happy to be able to offer tickets at only £10 a head! You'll all agree that's a bargain for a glass of good wine and canapés – plus the company of old friends! There will be a cash bar for those who want more than one glass of wine! We cannot be sure that we have contacted everybody who might be interested in this historic party, so please help by passing this letter on to as many of your old Bombay friends as possible.

We will confirm the date and location as soon as we hear how many of you are able to come. A list of those planning to attend will be sent out with the tickets. Cheques with acceptances please!

The letter was signed Kenneth Richards (Secretary), and gave his address as, Fir Tree House, Little Hamberton, Nr Tunbridge Wells.

It was after six o'clock by the time he finished his task; he'd eaten no lunch and Alice had still not come home.

While he was walking back from posting his sheaf of letters, the rain started pouring down again. It made him hunch his shoulders against its onslaught because he had forgotten to put on his raincoat. As he turned the last corner, Alice drove past him in their blue Vauxhall, splashing his trouser legs with water from a deep puddle around a choked drain. He was sure she'd done it deliberately.

He was right. Alice had seen him and steered towards the puddle. As she watched through the driver's mirror, she rejoiced to see the water drenching him. In a whisper she began chanting like one of the witches from *Macbeth*, 'Die, die, die. Get out of my life.'

THREE

The mail – only one letter – arrived late on a windy February day at a large white house worth several hundreds of thousands of pounds near Wimbledon Common. A sullen Portuguese maid carried it through to a drawing room that overlooked a carefully landscaped garden where frost silvered the landscaped shrubs. She put the letter on to a spindly occasional table before an enormous plate glass window.

'Why put it where I can't easily get at it? Bring it *here*!' snapped a querulous voice.

The maid, whose name was Juanita, picked up the letter and crossed the green carpet to where a thin woman with carefully set blonde hair sat in a winged armchair with a silver topped walking stick lying propped against it. Juanita held the letter out without speaking and the woman said, 'Open it, then.' When she saw her maid using her thumbnail to prise open the envelope, tearing roughly across the paper surface, the seated woman shrilled in fury, pointing at a nearby desk, as she said, 'What do you imagine a paperknife is for? We don't all live like peasants you know.'

Silently, thinking that she would like to use the silver knife for slitting her employer's throat, the maid took a single sheet of paper out of the tattered envelope and handed it across to her tormentor.

'Give me my spectacles,' she was told next and when they were handed over, Juanita was ushered out of the room with the shake of a hand.

'The last Bombay Cocktail Party . . .' read Julia Whitecross aloud, and, looking up, added to nobody in particular, 'Fancy that.' Then she lowered her head again and read the rest before she levered herself out of the chair and limped across the carpet to lay the missive down on the lowered flap of her beautiful Georgian desk. Everything in the house was exquisitely tasteful, the work of an expensive interior decorator with a showroom in Bruton Street. There was not a speck of dust to be seen because Juanita was painstaking. Only close examination of two enormous vases of exotic looking flowers on wooden stands on each side of the window, showed that every bloom was artificial, but exquisitely made out of silk by Chinese sweat shop workers in Hong Kong. Julia did not like real flowers. 'They need too much looking after because they keep dying,' she complained.

A telephone sat on the desk and Julia lifted it, swiftly keying in a number. 'Let me speak to my husband,' she snapped when it was answered. The person at the other end said something and was answered with, 'I don't care if he is busy. I want to speak to him *now*.'

As she waited, her once pretty face sank into its now habitual expression of discontent which darkened even more when James Whitecross came on the line.

'I don't care if you are busy. Your secretary, if that's what you call her – I'd suspect she was your whore if I didn't know about your peculiar tastes – told me so, but I wanted to speak to you. Yes, it is important. I've had an interesting letter in the post.' He asked what the letter said, but she swept on, ignoring his question. 'It's not as if I get many letters nowadays. Everybody seems to have forgotten all about us, but that's not surprising since we never go anywhere,' she whined. Although she'd made the call only on a whim, because of a wish to annoy him and had no real desire to go to the party, she was working herself up to a decision which she knew would infuriate him.

'What does the letter say?' he repeated.

She snapped back, 'I'm going to tell you what it says if only you'll wait. Yes, I know you're busy. You've already told me that . . .' There was another pause during which his angry voice buzzed over the line and she replied, 'You shouldn't speak to me like that. You know I'm in constant pain . . . Oh all right! The letter says that the last Bombay Cocktail Party is going to be held in the Royal Overseas League in July . . . Yes, that *is* important. I want to reply and say that we'll go. I want you to take me, to pretend that we're still happily married . . . What do I mean by *still*? How can you say things like that? *I* was happy when we lived in Bombay. It was probably the only time we've ever been happy together. I want to reply straight away so they know we're coming . . . Of course you can take me. You can set aside that date quite easily. You set dates aside for things you want to do. I'm going to phone now and accept . . .' She drew breath eventually and hung up without giving him a chance to reply.

A few moments later she rang Kenneth Richards' phone number and Alice answered.

'Sorry, Kenneth's out,' she said shortly.

Julia put on her sweetest tone and asked, 'Am I speaking to his wife?'

'Yes. It's Alice.' The tone was hostile.

'You probably won't remember me, but I remember you. It's Julia Whitecross here. I was friendly with Kenneth's first wife Sonya. That was such a tragedy. We were all so happy when he married again. You were in Bombay, too, when Sonya died though, weren't you?' said Julia sweetly.

'I was married to Mike Field at that time and I remember you, vaguely,' said Alice, not bothering to sound anything except disinterested. As far as she was concerned, the fixation of her husband and his friends with the past was ridiculous. Her only reason for attending his stupid cocktail party each year was to show herself off and feel satisfaction at how much better she was wearing than the other women present. She was vain to the point of mania and still cherished the hope of finding a third husband who could offer a better or more interesting life than pedestrian Kenneth. If only he'd die before her figure went. It was such hard work keeping it in shape.

Julia did not allow Alice's obvious discourtesy to put her off. Pitching her voice higher, she trilled on, 'I live in Wimbledon now. It's like being in the country but so convenient for town. My husband James – do you remember him? – is still working, of course, but because he's one of those captains of industry he won't give it up, no matter how hard I plead with him. Men! Kenneth will be retired now I expect.'

'I remember your husband, and yes, Kenneth has retired. He's seventy after all.' Alice was itching to finish this call and she didn't bother to sound cordial.

'Well, I'm rushing out now but I only rang to tell him that James and I will definitely be at the Cocktail Party. I'll send my cheque today. In fact I'll send something extra. I was thinking of a few hundred pounds actually, because I think the last party should go off in style. Perhaps my donation will make it possible for the guests to have two drinks each instead of only one! I remember our days in Bombay with such affection, you see.'

'Good. I'll tell him all that when he gets back,' said Alice disdainfully and hung up.

Julia was not going out but she had an object in mind. Pausing only to call for the mid-morning glass of chilled champagne, which she considered essential for the control of her arthritic pains, she rummaged purposefully in the top drawer of her desk in search of her old address book. As the drink was brought in by Juanita she held in her hands a small notebook, covered in faded red leather and with several of the pages detached or hanging by a thread.

She was so absorbed in riffling through it, that she did not notice Juanita had spilt some of the champagne onto the desk shelf as she put the glass down beside her mistress's hand. Hastily and fearfully the maid wiped it up with the edge of her sleeve, as normally such an error brought a torrent of recriminations on her head.

'Who will I call first?' Julia murmured to herself as she turned over the indented index of the little book, 'Good. Here's the Bolithos. Tom and Belle, Little Court House, Stratford-upon-Avon. I wonder if they're still there,' she said as she dialled their number. It rang out, once, twice, three, four, five, six, seven times. Disappointed, she was about to hang up when a man answered and repeated the number back to her.

'Is that the Bolitho home?' asked Julia in her sweetest voice.

'It is,' said the male voice.

'Could I be speaking to Tom?' cooed Julia.

'No, you couldn't. I'm afraid he's dead.'

'Oh I'm so sorry. I'd no idea. Are you a relative?'

'I'm his son.' Julia remembered the Bolithos' little boy. He'd been called something like Horace or Hector and was born the same year as her own son, poor Max. That would make him twenty-six now.

'This is an old friend of your parents speaking – Julia Whitecross. You won't remember me because you were only a child when we last met. Your mother's still alive I hope.'

'She is. Do you want to speak to her? Hang on and I'll fetch her, she's in the garden,' he said.

Belle, when she came to the phone, sounded just the same. Her voice was still low pitched, almost a growl. 'Hector said it was you, Julia!' she exclaimed, 'After all this time! How *are* you?'

'I'm not so good these days, almost crippled most of the time because of rheumatoid arthritis, but one mustn't complain. I try to keep cheerful for James's sake. It was such a shock just now to hear Tom's dead,' said Julia.

'Died last year,' said Belle briskly, 'liver – cirrhosis,

13

hardly surprising considering he must have drunk the output of a large distillery in his lifetime, bless his cotton socks.'

'I hope he left you comfortable,' said Julia in a concerned voice and from Belle's muttered, 'Oh yes,' she had a good idea that Tom had probably got through the family finances as well as its wine cellar.

'I'll tell you why I rang, Belle,' said Julia, changing tone and tack, 'I've just received the most interesting note from Kenneth Richards. You remember him, don't you? He was married to our friend Sonya who was found dead on the Madras Mail. I always had the deepest suspicions about that, didn't you? He had her insured for a *lot* of money . . .'

There was a pregnant pause at the other end of the line but eventually Belle said slowly, 'Of course I remember Sonya – and Kenneth. What does he want?'

'He wrote to let me know that the last Bombay Cocktail Party is to be held in London in July if they can get enough people to agree to go. I thought we should turn up.'

Belle sounded suspicious when she replied, 'Us? You and me? Why?'

'Darling,' trilled Julia, 'It's the last party! They've been holding them every year for *ages* and now they're stopping because we're all getting too old. Soon there won't be anybody left. You and I were considerable figures in society there, and we should certainly be at the last do.'

'I know they hold them every year. Tom and I went to one about ten years ago, but I haven't bothered since. I don't go to London much. It's quite a trek from here, you know,' said Belle doubtfully.

'But you must come and stay with me and we'll go together. James is keen to go, too. You won't mind that, will you? We can have a real night out, just like old times.'

Belle gave her fruity laugh. 'I think we're a bit old for those kind of parties now,' she said.

Encouraged by the laugh, Julia pressed on. 'Do come Belle. I think we ought to support this for old times' sake.

I'm going to send them a cheque for a few hundred pounds
– although the tickets are only ten each. I said to Richard's
wife – who still sounds frightful, by the way – you must
remember her, Alice Field, a skinny blonde with an eye on
the main chance. Anyway, I said to her that my donation
might make it possible to give everybody at the party two
glasses of wine each instead of a measly one.'

Belle went on the defensive again. 'There's no way I'm
sending a few hundred quid,' she said.

'Darling, you needn't send anything because I'll buy
your ticket for you. It's my treat.' Julia wanted company
because she was doubtful she would be able to prevail on
James to go.

'I still don't know,' said Belle doubtfully, 'I'm not sure I
want to see any of that old gang again really – except you,
of course.' You liar, she thought.

'Come and stay with me,' pleaded Julia, 'We'll go to the
party and remember the good times, because we did have
some adventures, you and I, didn't we?'

'That's true,' conceded Belle.

'So say you'll come. Mark the date off in your diary. It's
on July the twentieth. It'll be so interesting to see all those
people from the past and hearing what's happened to them.
You never know who might turn up.'

Life was pretty spartan and dull in Little Court House these
days and the suggestion that some of the glamour of the past
might be recaptured brought Belle to a sudden decision. 'All
right. I'll come,' she said.

Julia sounded delighted. 'Wonderful! In his letter Kenneth
Richards said we were all to put the word around about the
party so there would be a good turn-out. I'm going to ring
up some more people, but there's one or two I'd especially
like to be there but don't want to approach myself for various
reasons. If I give you the names, will you do it?'

'Depends who it is,' replied Belle cautiously.

'I have their names and numbers. If you've a pencil handy,

I'll give you them right now.' By this time Belle realised why she was being treated with such sweetness. She'd not just been rung up for the chance of her company. Typical of Julia, she thought.

'Oh, all right,' she said.

'OK, first of all there's Andy Parnell. You remember *him*, don't you?'

'Yes, he was that ship's doctor you had a thing about, wasn't he?'

'That's right. I'd really like him to be there. He's a GP these days, somewhere near Birmingham.'

'My God, is he?' said Belle, disbelievingly.

'Here's his number. Be an angel and ring him. He'll remember you, I'm sure. Do it now and let me know what he says. And here's Kenneth Richards' address, too. If Andy says he'll go, he'll have to get in touch with Kenneth and buy a ticket.'

'What others do you want to be told?' asked Belle after she wrote down the details.

'The other one I want you to contact is Tricia Keen. I don't know what name she's using now because she'll have married again, several times probably. When you speak to her don't say I gave you the number or she might not come. We weren't on very good terms when we saw each other last. But I'd really like to see how she is now . . . I'm so looking forward to the party and to seeing you again, Belle,' trilled Julia.

When she hung up the phone, Belle wondered exactly why her old friend was so pleased at resuming contact. After all, they'd been out of touch for more than twenty years and Julia had never made any attempt to speak to the Bolithos during all that time. 'She's up to her old tricks,' she told herself, remembering the perverse pleasure Julia used to take in stage managing situations that could give rise to trouble.

FOUR

The next meeting of the Cocktail Party committee was held in Marian and Peter Salisbury's lavish house in St George's Square at the beginning of March. Plump, dark-haired Marian, who looked like a busy little bantam hen, liked to do things in style, so she provided a sumptuous lunch. Pudgy Peter, whose blond hair had thinned to a cottony looking fuzz on the top of his round head, was equally hospitable and felt in his element mixing Martinis that were so strong and cold that they almost took the roofs off his guests' mouths.

Kenneth was the first to arrive, having come by train from Tunbridge Wells, and was already installed in a comfortable armchair when a taxi drove up to the front door. With much bustle and braying, Arthur Perkins was ushered into the room by Peter. Kenneth looked bleakly at the new arrival, unable to conceal his disapproval. Perkins had been one of the people he most disliked in Bombay and he'd not been alone in feeling that way. Marian and Peter were probably the new arrival's only friends.

Peter saw the expression on Kenneth's face and said breezily, 'You know each other, don't you?' Not waiting for a reply, he rushed on, 'Arthur's agreed to help us out by taking on Pip's job. You heard that Pip Leyland died just before Christmas, did you Kenneth? Such a terrible loss.'

The answer was a silent shake of the head and Marian jumped in to fill the hiatus by saying, 'We were devastated. Pip's been the Cocktail Party's secretary for years and

17

years, ever since the first one in 1960. We thought he'd be irreplaceable, but Pip's widow Merry sent us his papers – six big box files of them. He kept notes about everything and everybody, didn't he Arthur? Have you gone through them all yet?'

'Nearly, very nearly,' said Perkins in his peculiarly unappealing nasal voice. Not only did he speak as if someone was grabbing him by the balls, but he also adopted a very camp manner that gave him the air of a stand-up comedian. He was short and stout with sparse red hair that curled over his scalp like little squirming snakes. Because the day was chilly, with an iron-grey sky, he was wearing a swirling navy blue cape lined with red over a loud checked suit and a flamboyant bow tie that added to his vaudeville appearance. His shoes were dark blue suede with built-up rubber soles, cunningly designed to hide his lack of height.

Kenneth managed to collect his manners enough to feign cordiality and not abuse his hosts' hospitality. 'Poor old Pip,' he said, 'I didn't hear he'd died. He was one of the Gymkhana Rugby Club stalwarts when I first went east. He must have been in his eighties.'

'Eighty-three and as sharp as a needle to the very end. He was so looking forward to the last party. It's terribly sad he didn't live to see it,' said Marian solemnly.

'So we asked Arthur to help us out,' said Peter firmly, 'and fortunately he agreed at very short notice. It was Arthur who drew up that first guest list. The list you've sent the notices out to. It's very comprehensive, isn't it?'

Kenneth nodded, grudgingly.

Perkins smirked slightly, for he never permitted himself a genuine smile, far less a laugh. His smirks were unpleasant because they were so supercilious and his long face with its prominent nose gave him the look of a horse, and not a very well bred one at that.

Inside Kenneth fumed, angry that Marian and Peter had called in this reptile without consulting the rest of the committee, but he was too much in awe of them to voice his feelings. Not that he could have influenced the others anyway, but Perkins was a particular hate of his because for years he had made Kenneth an object of poisoned remarks to which he could never think of an adequate retort until hours later. Their enmity went back to when he'd earned Perkins' everlasting hatred by referring to him in his hearing as a 'poof'.

He guessed that Peter and Marian had been anxious to replace bluff old rugby-hearty Pip with someone whose tastes were more 'cultural', like their own. There had been too much of a heavy drinking, *gung-ho* influence in the original party committee and little by little the Salisburys had 'refined' it. Pip was the last to go and in spite of what they said, Kenneth was pretty sure they were not grief stricken at his departure.

Sensing he had his enemy on the run, Perkins swept around the large drawing room, pointedly ignoring Kenneth, and headed straight for the fireplace. 'Oooh, you've got a new picture, haven't you, darlings?' he said.

Marian beamed. 'Trust you to notice, Arthur. We bought it at Christie's in December. They thought it may be a Mary Cassatt, although it's not signed.'

The picture, painted with generous brush strokes in delightfully pale pastel colours, depicted a sweet-faced woman with two children sitting on a rock beside the sea.

'I do hope that you didn't pay too much,' neighed Perkins. He had set himself up among the Salisburys' acquaintance as an aesthete and art expert because he had several social contacts among the art dealers of Mayfair.

It was obvious from Marian's face that the picture's price had been fairly high but she said bravely, 'Oh no. It was a bargain, especially if it *is* a Cassatt.'

'Hope springs eternal, but then it always does with amateurs,' said Perkins. He could not resist being cruel, even to the few people who were on his side.

The deflated atmosphere that followed this jibe was lightened by the arrival of the final committee member, chartered accountant Alex Macdonald, a beaming, chubby, dark-haired and pale-faced bachelor in a too tight, dark blue, pinstripe business suit and horn-rimmed glasses.

He was considerably younger than the others, but he'd attached himself limpet-like to their middle-aged circle when he was only in his twenties, and now looked like a grown-up Billy Bunter. He hated being thought of as young and since the age of eighteen had longed to become a senior citizen so he could be taken seriously. Although he was a man totally devoid of humour or enterprise, Marian thought he was 'reliable', and so he was. It would never enter his mind to be anything else. He'd never married because he was terrified of women and had no idea how to approach them, but he was, and had been for many years, desperately in love with his hostess, whom he worshipped like a dominating goddess. Sensing her power over him, she used him mercilessly.

Perkins raised one eyebrow quizzically as he coldly watched Macdonald coming into the room. 'Still dressing like a geriatric, I see. How old are you now?' he said spitefully.

'Hello Arthur. I'm forty-five,' said Alex, who seemed to be aware of Perkins' elevation to the committee, although Kenneth had not been.

Relieved that her most forceful guest's malice had been diverted from her putative Cassatt, Marian interrupted by clapping her hands and announcing that lunch was ready, taking care to seat Perkins between herself and her husband. She and Peter were about the only people in Bombay society who were ever able to tolerate the man, because they admired his considerable theatrical talent, and in a way felt sorry for him.

He was a complex mix of hang-ups and frustrations. Rejected for National Service, and a sexual misfit at a time when homosexuality was against the law, he'd been packed off to India to work in an insurance company by a disapproving clergyman father who wanted such an embarrassingly camp son out of his sight.

In fact he missed his true vocation for he should have become a professional actor, and would have if he'd been born into a different family. He was incredibly talented and had the ability to become someone completely unlike himself whenever he stepped on to a stage. The only time he was ever happy was when he was running the Bombay Gymkhana Amateur Dramatic Society, and he would brook no opposition when doing so. Marian was one of the few people with enough nerve to stand up against him.

She was an adversary worthy of his steel, but other people he crossed were repelled and intimidated by his ability to hurt with cruel jabs and adroitly directed put-downs. He always knew where to hurt the most, especially because he had an obsessive interest in gossip and collected it like a magpie. No fact was too trivial to be ignored by him, no individual too lowly to be beneath his notice, and his memory was phenomenal.

When he took over Pip's archives, he was delighted to find that the old boy had noted every single person who'd ever bought a ticket for the Cocktail Party, and often made notes beside their names, detailing who they were, who employed them and what they were like. Perkins would have paid good money to get his hands on such information, and when it was handed to him on a plate, so to speak, he couldn't believe his luck. He spent hours poring over the names and comments, much of which was scurrilous or slanderous because Pip never expected anyone but himself to read them.

While they were tucking into their smoked salmon, Perkins directed his gaze at Kenneth for the first time and asked, 'So you sent out my first mailshot, did you? Had any acceptances yet?'

Kenneth looked up and said, 'Some, but it's early yet.

They only went out five days ago. Twenty or thirty people have phoned already though.'

'Twenty or thirty? I do hope you're keeping strict notes,' said Perkins in a school-masterly voice.

'Twenty-seven up to this morning actually,' Kenneth snapped back, 'A woman called Julia Whitecross even rang yesterday to say she was sending an extra donation of three hundred pounds so people could have two drinks each instead of one.' Julia had gone over the top in order to impress.

'How very generous,' said Marian soothingly, 'If we were to hit the two hundred figure that'd make it the best-attended party ever. I've one or two names on my own list who weren't on Pip's, but I'll contact them myself. I hope you'll all do the same if extra names occur to you.'

'I have a couple I need to chase up,' said Alex who was quite impervious to the tension in the atmosphere. Marian smiled sweetly at him.

Perkins said sharply, 'Then get on the telephone to them tonight.'

Marian's face was glowing as she said, 'We *must* see that the party goes with a bang. It's up to us.'

They all agreed and went on eating and drinking with added gusto, as if to fortify themselves for the task that lay ahead.

'Since you've been sending out the notices, I expect the cheques will be sent to you. Do make sure that every payment is noted.' Perkins leaned across the table to address Kenneth.

'Of course I will,' was the defensive reply.

'Hmm. Just as well to have a counter check.'

'You don't imagine I'll be peculating, do you?' Kenneth was stung into protest.

'Why not? There must be some reason why the old boys in Bombay used to cut you dead, mustn't there?' Perkins smiled as he delivered the insult and Kenneth felt the blood drain from his face. Any pleasure he'd been experiencing from the delicious food and plentiful drink disappeared. Seeing he'd struck his adversary to the quick, Perkins followed up with, 'Pip's notes are so interesting. He was a terrible old gossip, wasn't he? Nothing missed him and he seems to have been a very good judge of character.'

Then he leaned back again and let that sink in. None of them said anything but Kenneth's face visibly whitened and for the rest of the lunch he sat silent and miserable.

They left separately. Alex went first in a haze of delight at winning Marian's smiles. When Perkins said goodbye he was smug at having needled a man for whom he felt particular dislike, and Kenneth, though he acted cheerfully as he said his farewells, was actually deeply depressed and miserably wondering if he was ever going to be allowed to cast off his past.

It's not bloody fair. It's so long ago and I was just a boy but I'm never going to be allowed to forget it or to live it down and I try so hard! he thought. He was close to tears as he rode in a taxi to the station.

FIVE

The habits of a disciplined life were hard to break and, although he was seventy years old, retired Detective Inspector Tommy Morrison of the Bombay Police rose and showered in cold water at six o'clock every morning and drank his first cup of tea at six fifteen. He was still spare and fairly spry, although rheumatic pains slowed him up before his pain killers took effect.

He breakfasted cheerfully on a March morning, and his bearer Prakash, who had looked after him devotedly for many years, settled him in a chair on the peeling verandah of his old-fashioned bungalow near the Afghan Church in Colaba. A few moments later the *Times of India* and a small sheaf of mail were laid on a table beside the old man.

Tommy adjusted his spectacles on his nose and lifted two letters. One was from his eldest son in Australia, so he opened it first and a cheque fluttered out on to the floor.

'Dearest Papa,' the letter said, 'Please use this money to buy a ticket to Perth. My family and I want you to come and stay with us. There will be no problem with entry visas or anything like that because I have influence in high places. It grieves my heart that you are living so far away, all alone. My brother and sister and I plead with you to come here, to this wonderful country where we will be able to take care of you and make you very comfortable.'

Tommy fished the cheque off the floor and smoothed it between his fingers. It was not the first time that his son, an even higher ranking policeman than his father, had sent

24

him money to pay his fare to Australia. As usual the cheque represented enough money to buy a first-class air ticket, fit himself out for the journey and generously pension off Prakash, but he knew he wouldn't use it. Bombay was his home and he cherished an enormous emotional link with the city.

He intended to die in the house where he had spent his married life and brought up his children. They, however, did not share his love for the teeming, cacophonous city and had all gone away to recreate themselves and cast off the odium of being born Anglo-Indian. He sighed, laid the cheque down and picked up the second item of mail.

This was a large brown envelope with two blue airmail stickers on it – the sender was obviously anxious that it reach him as soon as possible. His address was printed in large block capitals in black ink. He examined it curiously and noted that it had been posted six days ago in London SW1. There was no sender's address on the back.

Inside the envelope were two sheets of paper. The first was a leaf of flimsy lined paper with a serrated edge that looked as if it has been roughly torn out of a school jotter. Letters cut from newspaper headlines were pasted onto the sheet and the message it bore was stark:

SONYA RICHARDS WAS MURDERED 1.12.1969. DO YOU KNOW WHO SHE WAS?

Throughout his career in the Bombay police force, Tommy had received several anonymous letters, usually tipping him off to various crimes, real or imagined. It was a favoured method of communication among Indian informants or people with a grudge, but this was the first time one had been sent to him from abroad – especially from London SW1.

He smoothed the sinister sheet out on the top of the table beside him and noticed that the letters had been cut

25

from different newspapers as the print styles, paper and ink were varied. Probably about five papers had been used, he decided. Someone had taken a lot of trouble.

At first he couldn't remember anyone called Sonya Richards and wondered why the message had been sent to him. It was unsettling and made no sense. Perhaps the second sheet of paper in the envelope would provide a clue, he thought. When he unfolded that, however, he found it was a photocopy of a communication announcing the plans for the Last Bombay Cocktail Party on July the twentieth. His brows furrowed as he read it. Then he snorted and laid it down. The first thought that came into his head was, Someone's playing games. It's a joke, like modern advertising or some sort of parlour game, using sensation to whip up interest for their cocktail party.

He had never attended any of the London-based cocktail parties held annually by old Bombay expatriates, although he'd heard all about them. He was not in social contact with, or on the mailing list of, the kind of people who went to such nostalgic – and to him ridiculous – events. But someone wanted him to know about this one. Why?

He lifted the second letter up again and held it against the light that came shafting under the half-dropped chick blinds that hung round his verandah. It was then he noticed that the signature at the end of the letter had been underlined in pencil: *Kenneth Richards*.

Kenneth Richards. Sonya Richards . . . 1969. Of course! His memory sparked into life and he was taken back to a cool morning twenty-one years ago when he was summoned to Bombay's Victoria Station because a white woman had been found dead in a first-class sleeping compartment of the incoming Madras Mail.

His superiors often assigned Tommy to cases involving expatriates not only because he was an Anglo-Indian who spoke perfect idiomatic English, but also because he could pass for one of them and be accepted on almost equal terms.

He was the trainer of the police rugby team, something expatriate men respected, and was also tall, pale skinned, aquiline featured with light brown hair. The only things that gave away his mixed origin were his sharp, slightly hooded brown eyes and a sing-song way of talking that made some people take him for a Welshman.

Sonya Richards, he thought. Of course! The woman on the train. He remembered seeing her body lying slumped on the floor by the bed in a glamorous pink lace wrap, with tendrils of blonde hair fanned out around her sheet-covered face. He'd had to shove his way through a chattering crowd to kneel beside her.

'Get them out of here,' he'd snapped to his constable who set about driving off the crowd by thumping them with his night stick.

'Who found her?' asked Tommy when he lifted the sheet and revealed an ashen, staring face. She'd been a handsome woman, he noted.

A shaking old servant in a white cotton uniform and black pork pie hat was pushed towards him. 'I'm Swami her servant but I didn't kill her, I didn't kill her,' the old man gabbled. Like all respectable poor people he was terrified of the police.

'Of course you didn't,' chimed in a young Indian woman from the compartment doorway, 'It's obvious she's had a heart attack.'

Tommy looked questioningly up at her and she told him, 'I'm a doctor. I tried to resuscitate her but she's definitely dead. A heart attack, I'm sure.'

'Take the servant to the station to make a statement,' Tommy told his constable, adding sternly, 'And don't beat him, he's an old man.' The caution was necessary because police methods of taking statements usually involved violence unless the person being questioned was rich or powerful. Afterwards Tommy regretted not going to the station with Swami.

Kenneth Richards was the name of the dead woman's husband who turned up within minutes because he'd been waiting on the platform to collect his wife off the train. He swayed and had to be supported when he saw her body on the floor, immediately starting to wail like a child. His cries had been truly terrible.

'Oh Sonya, Sonya, Sonya,' he howled, covering his face with his hands. At the time Tommy thought it odd that such a heartbroken man made no effort to hug or touch the body, or even get close to it. Their relationship was probably fraught, like so many British couples in the city, he thought.

'She's had a heart attack,' said the officious little doctor who was enjoying her role in the drama. It was obvious that to her this event was a highlight in a rather humdrum life. The cotton sari she was wearing was cheap and drab and she peered at the scene through round, metal-framed spectacles that made her look like a schoolgirl.

The husband took his hands off his face and nodded in agreement, 'You're right. Her heart is – *was* bad. She has to take pills every day. I was afraid this would happen but she insisted on going to Madras to visit her friend. Oh Sonya, Sonya, Sonya!'

Tommy had not liked the look of Kenneth Richards but was sufficiently experienced to know that his likes and dislikes were irrelevant to the matter in hand. The woman had died in dramatic circumstances. The first thing he had to do was arrange for the body to be taken to the morgue where a cause of death would be determined. About this he was inclined to agree with the young doctor. The corpse was well nourished, and a half-full bottle of Parry's gin, with a lipstick-stained glass beside it, stood on the shelf beside the bed. There were several empty tonic water bottles in the dustbin. A hardened drinker obviously. The ashtray in the compartment contained several cigarette stubs, also lipstick stained. Tommy counted them – twelve. A lot for an overnight trip. It was obvious that Mrs Richards had not stinted herself on the good things in life.

The investigation was perfunctory. Later that day the police doctor reported that Mrs Sonya Richards, aged 35, expired from a heart attack. She'd recently been diagnosed with a heart ailment and was under medication for it. Nothing more need be done; there were no suspicious circumstances. The body was released to the grieving husband and cremated the next morning. Tommy wrote out his report, closed the file and other concerns filled his mind – until now.

'Prakash,' he called and the bearer appeared with a questioning look on his face.

'Bring in the telephone,' said Tommy and it appeared at his elbow, on the end of a long cord.

'Get me my special notebook,' was Tommy's next order and Prakash did not need to be told that the book needed was a precious, pocket-sized black Rexine book that contained the record of a lifetime's contacts. Some of the leaves were loose and the writing faded but every address and phone number in that book was important and had served Tommy well in the past. He turned the pages slowly with his knobbly fingers till he came to the one he wanted. 'F for Figueras,' he said. Pedro Figueras had first been entered in the book when he was a superbly intelligent detective constable living in the police lines at Thana. Today he was Deputy Chief Commissioner with a good flat in the Fort.

Tommy's hands hurt too much in the morning to dial the number, but he showed it to Prakash who rotated the dial for him. A woman answered, and in response to Tommy's request to speak to her husband, she gave an exasperated 'Tttch' before she called his name.

'Pedro,' said Tommy when he picked up, 'I need your help.'

Figueras, one of the few senior Indian officers who had never disdained Tommy because of his mixed birth, said it would be his pleasure to help his old friend in any way he could.

'I want the file on the death of a woman called Sonya Richards, who was found dead on the Madras Mail on the first of December in 1969,' said Tommy.

The other man sounded doubtful. 'It's a long time ago, Tommy,' he said.

'I know, but we might be lucky. Will you try to pull it out for me?'

'I'll try but I can't promise anything. You know what those filing clerks are like. If rats or silver fish don't eat the files, they often get lost,' was the reply.

They were lucky however. That afternoon a constable turned up at Tommy's bungalow with a parcel wrapped in brown paper. Tommy unwrapped it eagerly and found a tattered looking pink cardboard file that turned out to contain the reports of all fatalities in Bombay for the first week of December 1969.

A report on the death of Sonya Richards, in Tommy's own writing, was filed on page five. He had summarised how he found the body and appended the police doctor's report. This made interesting reading. There had been no autopsy because the dead woman's doctor certified that she suffered from a feeble heart and was taking medication for it. The pills prescribed for her were noted. One was a tranquilliser and the other was Digoxin for her heart, a low-dose capsule to be taken twice a day.

In a note, the doctor wrote, 'I cautioned Mrs Richards that she must never take more than her prescribed dose because too many capsules could cause heart failure. I felt it was necessary to point this out because sometimes, especially at night, if she'd taken too much to drink, she tended to be forgetful and might take her pills twice. She was also advised not to drink tonic with her gin because quinine can suppress the action of the heart. Her husband knew about my warning and was careful to supervise her drinking and her pill taking.

Her death, although premature, was not totally unexpected, however. She suffered from a very irregular heartbeat and tended to ignore advice.'

Appended to the page with a rusting paper clip were other notes saying that Sonya Richards, aged 35, was the wife of tobacco company employee Kenneth Richards, 49, of Bhulabhai Mansions, Nepean Sea Road. She married her present husband in 1963, but had previously been married for twelve years to insurance executive Ralph Redmond, also of Bhulabhai Mansions, Nepean Sea Road. That marriage ended in divorce, but the couple had one daughter, Laura, born in 1952. After the marriage broke up the child remained in the custody of the mother.

What brought Tommy up in his seat however was a photocopy of Sonya Richards' birth certificate. It told him she was born in the Carmelite convent in Poona in 1934, and given into the care of the nuns at birth. At the age of six weeks, she was passed on to a British couple called Captain William Walker of the Indian Army Medical Corps, and his wife Barbara, who later adopted her. Tommy remembered the waxy, ivory-coloured skin of the dead woman and her tousled yellow hair, which didn't really match her complexion. If she was a foundling, she might have been Anglo-Indian like me, he thought. Mixed race children were often given up for adoption and he'd known many who successfully passed for English and denied their origins. In Sonya's case her very fair hair was probably produced by a bottle of dye.

Tommy had never been ashamed of his ancestry as so many were. In fact he was proud of his mixed heritage because his mother was descended from Henry Hodge, one of the legendary characters of Indian history, an Englishman who raised his own private army and fought on behalf of various rajahs at the end of the eighteenth century. Hodge had married an Indian princess and had many handsome children who in turn scattered their seed up and down the subcontinent.

But why had someone taken the trouble of telling an Anglo-Indian ex-policeman about the suspected murder of a fellow Eurasian? Was that what was meant by the phrase: *Do you know who she was?* It did not make sense. Yet his informant must have known he'd been involved with the case at the beginning, and thought he would still be interested. Tommy laid down the file and sat back in his chair with his hands clasped behind his head and wondered, Why alert me to this case again so many years later? It was closed. There were no suspicious circumstances. He leaned forward again and once more picked up the sinister, anonymous letter.

Could the person who sent it be the woman's husband? His name was on the party notice – and underlined so it would not be missed. If the husband was not the sender, someone else was anxious that Tommy should know about the party and that Mr Kenneth Richards would be there.

Why?

SIX

For several days Belle Bolitho kept deliberately for-getting to do as Julia had told her, but eventually she knew she'd have to follow instructions, so she forced herself towards the phone. The number she'd been given for Dr Andy Parnell was answered by a woman, who sounded very old and feeble.

'He-llo?' she quavered doubtfully as if she distrusted the whole telephone system.

'I'm trying to find Dr Parnell,' said Belle sweetly.

'He's dead, dear,' said the old voice.

'Dead? But he was so young!' Belle exclaimed in genuine surprise. Andy would only be in his late forties or early fifties at the most now, she reckoned.

'Quite young. He was only eighty,' said the woman at the other end of the line.

'Oh, then that's not the Dr Parnell I want to speak to. Is there another one?' Belle asked.

'You must want my son but he'll be taking his surgery now. He'll not be able to speak to you. Goodbye,' the woman was about to hang up.

'Wait!' cried Belle urgently, 'If I ring you later will it be possible to speak to him?'

'He doesn't live here any more. He lives thirty miles away.'

'Can I have his phone number there, please?'

'Oh all right, hold on,' and the line went dead for what seemed like an interminable time. Belle was about to hang up in despair when there was a crackle and a cough announcing the return of Mrs Parnell senior. 'Are you still there?' she asked. The suspicious note was even more evident now.

'Yes, ready and waiting,' said Belle sweetly but quickly found it was a mistake to say more than was absolutely necessary.

Mrs Parnell snapped, 'It's not so easy getting about at my age, you know.'

'Sorry,' said Belle humbly, 'Did you find the phone number?'

'Of course I found it. Surely I know my own son's phone number.'

It was difficult to retain the pretence of good temper, but Belle knew that, despite the frustration of dealing with the old woman, it would be worse dealing with Julia if she failed in her mission. So she said nothing and was rewarded by the quavering voice reading out a number.

'That's the surgery, and you'll need the home number too . . . here it is.'

Mission partly accomplished, thought Belle as she hung up.

At one o'clock, when she reckoned surgery would be finished and Andy might have gone home for lunch, Belle rang his private number and was answered by the man himself – she still recognised his voice with its soft Scots burr.

'Hello, Andy, this is someone from your past – Belle Bolitho, Julia's friend,' she said.

He was guarded. 'Really?' was all he said.

'Julia asked me to ring you and tell you about a gathering of ex-Bombay people that's being planned. She wants you to go.'

Andy sounded very brisk and businesslike. 'I don't take professional calls at home. Please ring me at the surgery – I'll be back there at half past two and able to take your call then.' And the line was cut off. Obviously he did not want to speak for fear of being overheard. Belle remembered Julia's delight in their old games of subterfuge and cover-up. Life was so boring nowadays compared to the past, but the reappearance of Julia, who dragged trouble around with her like a cloak, could be guaranteed to spark things up.

At thirty-one minutes past two, Andy answered his surgery phone himself after only two rings so had obviously been waiting for the call. Belle went straight to the matter in hand and told him about the party, adding at the end, 'As I said, Julia wants you to be there.'

'Why didn't she ring me herself?' he said.

'I don't know, but you must remember what she's like. She makes mysteries, she likes dabbling and causing confusion.'

'So, she's not changed then?'

'I don't think so. I haven't heard a word from her in twenty years – not even a Christmas card – and then the other day she rings up, eager for us all to meet at this party. She must have some reason,' said Belle.

Andy laughed, 'Normally the last place I'd choose to go would be to the Bombay Cocktail Party, but with Julia pulling my strings, I'm curious.'

'Me too,' agreed Belle, 'I've already said I'll go because I'm sure she's planning something.'

'What did you say the date was?'

'July the twentieth.'

There was the sound of turning pages and Andy said, 'That's a Friday. Strangely enough I'm booked to go to a conference at Guy's that day. I could stay over or get the late train home. I'll think about it.'

Obviously he was not going to tell his wife, if he had one, about his plans.

'You could bring your wife,' Belle said sweetly.

'I don't think she'd want to go. Our youngest is at school, you see. When I talk about Bombay she gets rather bored anyway,' he said airily.

I bet you don't talk about it much, thought Belle. She

gave him Kenneth's address so he could buy a ticket and finished her call by saying, 'Hope to see you there then.'

She made her second call that evening – at cheap rate time. Julia never had to think about the expense for anyone carrying out her orders, but Belle was not in that happy position. A man with a Cockney accent answered the phone and when she asked for Tricia, he said, 'She's in Portugal.'

'Permanently?' asked Belle.

'For the winter. She goes there every year because of her bad chest. I'm her brother and I look after the house for her when they're away.'

Her brother! With a voice like that! Belle was instantly intrigued for she had always wondered about Tricia's background. It was very difficult to pin her down and she never talked about her childhood. Come to think of it, her very precise diction had always had an artificial sound to it.

Belle turned on charm that seeped over the telephone wires like honey. 'I'm an old friend of Tricia's from Bombay days and I've only just discovered her English phone number. I'm very keen to see her again. Do you think you could pass on a message for me?' She certainly did not want to have to phone Portugal.

'Yeah. OK.'

'Tell her that the very last Bombay Cocktail Party's being held on July the twentieth in the Royal Overseas League, St James's. The organisers are very keen to get as many of the old crowd together as possible for the last time and Tricia was *so* popular with everybody, it wouldn't be right to have the party without her. I'll give you my number and she can ring me if she wants more details. It's Belle Bolitho calling – she'll remember the name. I live at Stratford-upon-Avon now. Where are you exactly?' Julia hadn't passed on Tricia's address with the phone number and Belle was curious.

'Virginia Water,' said the brother.

'Lovely,' said Belle, thinking, Tricia always landed on her feet.

She did not really expect to hear anything, but was surprised a few days later when she received a phone call from Portugal.

After the exchange of pleasantries and enquiries about each other's health, Tricia said, 'What's all this about a cocktail party, then?'

'A lot of the old crowd get together every year in London. Haven't you ever been to one of their parties?'

'Yes, once or twice, years ago. I didn't know they were still going on.'

'After this they won't be. This one's the last. They want as many people as possible to go to it. After us there weren't many English people being sent out to India and they didn't party like we did – we were the last of an era I expect and now we're dying off.'

'Some era!' said Tricia and it was difficult to discern whether she was being nostalgic or sarcastic.

'Well, there were a lot of good times. I don't think anybody who lived in Bombay for any length of time in those days wasn't changed by it. You went out one sort of a person and came back another,' said Belle seriously.

'That's very true,' agreed Tricia, 'I often wonder what would have happened to me if I'd never gone.'

You might have been living in Stepney now instead of Virginia Water, thought Belle. In her mind's eye she saw the Tricia she'd known long ago – tiny and bird-like, trim as a dancer, with flowing brown hair and a face like a wicked pixie, heart-shaped and with slanted eyes. When she chose to turn on her charm, she was irresistible. No wonder Bertram Keen, although a confirmed bachelor and twenty years her senior, had been bowled over by her.

When he was killed in that air crash over Switzerland in early 1968, everyone expected Tricia to go straight home after the funeral, but she'd stayed on in their company flat, defying his employers to throw her out. She'd hung on for over a year and during that time had lived it up and had a ball – earning herself the nickname of the Merry Widow. Belle shook her head at the memory of those wild times.

'I'm not entirely sure I want to go to the party. There's nobody I particularly want to see again,' said Tricia.

Although Julia had said not to reveal that she was particularly anxious for Tricia to be at the party, Belle decided to flout her instructions.

'I feel much the same, but I'm curious because Julia contacted me with the details and more or less talked me into it. She's terribly anxious that we all get together there,' she said.

'Julia Whitecross? She wants me to go?' Tricia sounded disbelieving.

'Very much. She asked me to ring you up for her, you and Andy Parnell, the ship's doctor. Remember him?'

'Indeed I do. Randy Andy. He had his wicked way with lots of the girls but Julia thought she was going to ride off into the sunset with him, didn't she?' said Tricia.

'She did, but I suspect that although he acted silly, he had too much sense for that. I can't work out what she's after, trying to get us all at one party again.'

'Mischief. You may be sure she's up to mischief. Is James still around?' Tricia asked.

'It seems so. She threw his name into the conversation,' Belle told her.

'Most of her old escapades were directed against him. This might be, too. You never know with her,' mused Tricia quietly.

Belle agreed. 'It makes me curious, though,' she said.

'Me too,' said Tricia, 'I'll think about it, but tell Julia that I said I wouldn't be going. Then we'll be able to surprise her if I do come. I'll not buy a ticket in advance but pay at the door – they'll take my money, I'm sure.'

SEVEN

The fields around a villa, perched on a Spanish cliff top overlooking the golden-coloured Roman ruins of Claudio Baelo at Bolonia and across to North Africa, were a paradise of spring flowers, wild orchids, irises and narcissi. From early morning, a pale sun glittered down, turning the sea the colour of emeralds. The wind coming off Africa, that could be seen rising like a battlement on the other side of the Strait of Gibraltar, frilled the water's edge with flurries of white spray that looked like deep flounces of lace. The long curving beach far below the house was deserted, except for a few people exercising horses because it was still too cold to swim, and even the most intrepid wind surfers, who camped out there all summer, were not yet in evidence.

Dee Carmichael emerged from the bedroom, yawning and pulling on a blue bathrobe as she padded barefoot across the terrace to a table in the sun where Algy was taking breakfast.

'You're such a dormouse,' he said looking up. 'The day's half over by the time you appear.'

She ruffled his hair fondly as she passed and replied, 'I haven't your energy. What time were you up this morning? I never heard you go.'

He consulted his watch. 'It's a quarter past nine and I was up at six. Since then I've written fifteen hundred words, my ration for the day. Not bad, eh?'

Her admiration was genuine. 'You really amaze me,' she told him as she poured out her first cup of coffee.

'Discipline, that's all it takes,' he said smugly.

She laughed, 'You sound like an old schoolmaster. If I didn't know better, I'd think you were some sort of saint.'

He rustled his two-day-old *Daily Telegraph* and said, 'But don't you realise that I am, Saint Byron, that's me. One of these days they'll be carrying my effigy around Tarifa and taking me up to the hills for my summer vacation.'

She laughed again. 'I can just see it. You'll be leaning down from your throne telling them how to carry you. "Watch out for the next bend," you'll be saying.' He was a terrible passenger in the car if she was driving, so terrible that she had given up and left the driving to him. She was as good a driver as he was, but he liked to think of her as scatty and irresponsible so that he could look after her, and she played his game. He'd always enjoyed looking after people – some people – and she had to admit that being looked after appealed to her too.

'Has the post come yet?' she asked.

He lifted the binoculars he kept on a shelf beneath the table and peered down the hill. 'The van's on its way up now. Are you waiting for something?' he asked.

'I sent off an idea for a travel book a month ago and I haven't heard anything yet,' she said.

'You don't need to write a book. This place'll be like a word factory if we're both hammering away,' he said.

'It'd be all right. I miss not writing. You can work in the early morning and I'll work at night,' she said.

'To hell with that. I like having you beside me at night,' he said and they both laughed again.

When the mail was carried in by the maid, Maria, there was nothing about Dee's travel book but there was another letter for her. It had been re-addressed from her home in Scotland and looked rather battered. The postmark showed that it had been a month in transit.

She examined the envelope carefully and said, 'I don't recognise the writing.'

More examination, and more musing, 'It's postmarked Tunbridge Wells. I don't know anybody in Tunbridge Wells.'

Algy lowered a magazine which had come for him and said, 'Open the thing for heaven's sake.'

After reading for a minute or two she looked up and told him, 'They're holding another Bombay Cocktail Party and it's going to be the last.'

He laughed. 'The Bombay Cocktail Party? You're kidding. I thought that was a joke. Who goes to something like that?' he asked.

'Old Bombay hands. People who call themselves *Koy-ay-his*. That's Hindi but I don't know what it means exactly. They all go to the party, get drunk and talk about old times. They flirt with each other, ask who's dead and who's suffering from what. It's getting to be quite sad really.'

'They must all be about a hundred and fifty,' he said unfeelingly.

'Yes, they're growing old – like me and you, although you're wearing better than most. The trouble is I'm so incorrigibly curious that I can't resist the chance to catch up on people from the past. I keep remembering names and wondering what happened to them. It's a bore having to go to London and I'd like it best if I could be transported through the ether and eavesdrop on the party as a spirit, or a fly on the wall,' she told him.

'In other words you want to go,' he said.

She nodded. 'Why not come with me? You were in Bombay, too, for a bit.'

'For about three months and I hated every minute of it. The British people out there were the pits, I thought.'

'Oh come on, not any worse than they are in other places,' she protested.

He shook his head. 'You're wrong. They were the most decadent bunch I ever came across, all sleeping with each other and drinking like fish. Except you, of course!'

'Tell me, are you descended from John Knox by any chance?' she asked jokingly. For someone who had lived like him, he was amazingly conventional.

'You know what I mean,' he said and went back to his magazine.

'So I take it you don't want to go to the party,' she said. It amazed her how fond she was of this curmudgeon. They had started living together less than a year ago without any discussion and their relationship seemed to flow easily from the start, as if it had been an undercurrent in their lives for ever.

They'd first met when they were in their early twenties and had gone through various marriages and relationships since then, but she'd never felt so easy and relaxed with anyone in her life until she moved in with him. She'd reached harbour at last.

'Right first time. I don't want to go to the party,' he said. In fact she knew that even if the party had appealed to him he couldn't go anywhere near London. She wasn't able to get him to travel any farther than the south of France. He'd found refuge in Spain when he broke his links with the CIA and had his reasons for suspecting that old enemies would track him down if he ever showed up at Heathrow airport security.

'Do you mind if I go?' she asked.

He looked straight at her. 'I don't mind at all so long as you come back.'

'It's not till July – if they hold the party. It'll only go on if there's enough people interested,' she said.

'If everybody's as curious as you, it'll be on. That's fine by me but you'll miss the hot weather and the good swimming here in July,' he said.

She looked at the letter in her hand as she said, 'But it's still good in August, too. This letter says they want everybody to contact friends and try to swell the numbers. I think they intend to go out with a bang.'

'Unfortunate way of putting it,' he said jokingly.

'Whenever I've gone to the party in the past, I've usually asked Colin Andrews to go with me. I'll contact him and see what he says,' she mused.

Algy's grin faded. 'Who's he?' he asked.

She was surprised at his reaction. It had never occurred to her that he might be jealous and in a way she was pleased. 'Oh, he's gay, but he's been a good friend of mine for years. Didn't you ever meet him in Bombay? You'd like him.'

He relaxed. 'Gay? That's OK then.'

'I promise I'll bring you back lots of gossip that you can recycle for your books,' she told him. He wrote mystery novels under a brace of different names and made quite a bit of money because of his industry and his burgeoning imagination.

'Good idea, I need some new villains,' he said.

'I'll look out for one especially,' she said and walked around the table to kiss him, adding, 'And don't worry. I'll miss you every minute I'm away.'

She rang Colin that night and as the phone rang out she could visualise his elegant flat in St John's Wood with its cream upholstery and modern paintings. Colin had exquisite taste which he'd picked up by osmosis despite being born into a working-class family in Salford. Once he had qualified as a pharmacist and shaken the dust of his home town off his feet, he had accepted that he was homosexual. After that he blossomed and succeeded brilliantly in the pharmaceutical industry. She admired him and liked him tremendously.

'Darling!' he carolled when he heard her voice. It pleased her that he was able to be as camp as he liked when they spoke to each other now because, at the beginning of their friendship, when homosexuality was illegal, he'd been much more reserved. When she told him a few years ago that she'd always known about his sexuality, he was genuinely surprised.

She told him about the cocktail party and said, 'Would

you like to squire me again? They say it's going to be the last time they hold it.'

'The Last Bombay Cocktail Party! It sounds like a novel,' he said.

'Yes, it does, doesn't it? It'll probably contain the plots of several novels in it as well.' She thought of her promise to dig up anecdotes for Algy. The party should be a fertile field.

'Yes, I think we should attack it together. You must dress up in something glamorous – with a turban – so you look like a French film star and I'll wear my new cream silk suit. I bought it in Hong Kong at Christmas and it's divine!'

She giggled. With Colin beside her she always felt confident enough to go over the top with her clothes and make-up. 'I'll go to Harvey Nicks and have my face made up,' she told him.

'Lots and lots of eye-liner,' he said, 'and very high heels. I won't go with you otherwise. You'll stun them. They're all so middle class.'

'And I'm not?'

'You're utterly bourgeois darling and you know it,' he said.

'Will we go then?' she asked.

'Of course. I can hardly wait. Where are they holding this party?'

She consulted the paper in her hand and said, 'Royal Overseas Club, Park Place.'

'That's St James's,' said Colin. 'Let's push the boat out and meet at the Ritz at five o'clock. The party'll start at six or six thirty, it always does. You'll know me by the silk suit,' he joked.

'OK. I'll buy the tickets and you buy the drinks. I'll post the cheque today. Even allowing for the Spanish post it should reach them in plenty of time,' she said.

'You're in Spain?' he asked curiously.

'Yes, I live here most of the year now,' she said.

'Alone?'

'No.'

'I'm so pleased for you,' he said and it was obvious that he meant what he said. She knew how for years he'd searched for the ideal companion but never found him, and in the past she'd confided her own feelings of loneliness to him.

'It just happened, out of the blue. It can happen like that you know,' she told him and he sighed, 'I hope you're right, darling.'

'Maybe your fate's waiting for you at the cocktail party,' she suggested.

'You never know, do you?' he said.

EIGHT

Laura Gomez was helping her husband and sixteen-year-old son, Lance, to load a skittish bay mare into a horse box with the legend GOMEZ RACING painted on its walls, when a girl groom came running out of the office shouting, 'Laura, Laura, phone!'

'Damn and blast,' snapped Laura, handing the halter rope of the mare to her husband. 'You get on with it. I'll be right back.'

Roly Gomez, a wiry, compact ex-National Hunt jockey who was almost eight inches shorter than his wife, took the rope without comment and quietly led the mare up the slope of the loading ramp. Then he led her into a stall and softly patted her on the nose. His touch with horses was much gentler than Laura's but the training licence was in her name because, two years ago, he'd been warned off for taking part in a complicated betting coup. Roly could never resist a wager.

Walking at a fast clip, Laura, a thin, taut woman in a zip-up blue windcheater and tight jodhpurs, headed for the office and lifted the phone off a desk littered with paper. 'Hello!' she snapped.

'It's Kenneth,' said a voice.

Her shoulders relaxed and her voice softened. She loved her stepfather.

'Hi, Kenneth. We're a bit busy at the moment. We've a horse running at Doncaster today and she won't go into the box,' she said. As she spoke she looked out of the

46

little window and saw that, thankfully, the loading had been safely completed so she pulled out a stool with her heel and sat down.

'Oh I'm sorry. I didn't realise you were racing today. I'll phone later tonight. Will your horse win?' said Kenneth apologetically. He was always very deferential to his step-daughter and really admired her courage and skill at running a racing stable.

Laura laughed, 'We hope so. We decided to send her at the last minute because the going's soft which she likes and so she's a good chance. She's worth backing each way because she's standing at twenty-five to one. She's called Lucky Strike and she's in the three thirty. I'll really have to rush though. Roly's waving to tell me to come. Why did you phone though, Kenneth?'

Roly *was* waving and she waved back.

'It's not important,' he apologised and a note of irritation came into her voice as she said, 'Oh, spit it out. It must be. You never ring at this time of the day unless it's important. Put me out of my misery.'

Kenneth, who had rung her number on impulse because he was so pleased with the huge response to his mailshot about the party, now felt rather stupid. 'I just wanted to tell you that the Bombay Cocktail Party's to be in the Royal Overseas League in St James's on July the twentieth – it's the last one that'll ever be held and I'd really like you to come. I'm on the committee and I'm sending two tickets up for you and Roly. What I wanted to know was, do you think Lance'll come too?'

She gave a snort, 'No chance. He hates all adults at the moment. He's at that age. Thanks for our tickets though. We'll try to come but I must go now. Bye!' In fact the thought of going to the cocktail party appealed to her as little as it would to Lance.

And she hung up, but before she left the office she stared at the Injured Jockeys' Fund calendar on the wall in front of her. 'July the twentieth,' she said aloud and leaned across to flip over the pages of the calendar. There was a meeting at Newmarket the next day. If they had to go to London for Kenneth's sake, she and Roly might be able to combine the cocktail party with a trip to the races where there was a chance of meeting potential clients, which were much needed at the moment. Lying in a wire tray beneath the calendar was a pile of bills – from the farrier, the feed merchant, and her credit card company – all of them overdue.

A shout from the yard reminded her of the business in hand. Roly was keen to be off, so she ran from the office and climbed up into the box beside him. 'You're in charge today. Don't do anything daft,' she shouted to the grinning Lance from the open cab window.

'I'll just sell the lot and run away to Australia,' he yelled back with his thumbs up, 'Good luck!'

Laura leaned back in her seat and looked at Roly. He was Irish with a slightly crooked, broken nose, deep-set eyes and a curling, good-natured mouth. His whole life was given up to horses. She'd first seen him when he rode a storming finish in a three-mile handicap steeplechase at Doncaster and won by a nose. She was eighteen, already horse mad, and had gone to the races with an equally enthusiastic school friend who lived near the course.

Roly was twenty-two and had been racing for seven years. He looked like a hero to her when he vaulted, mud spattered, out of the saddle in the winner's enclosure and threw his arms round his mount's neck. No wonder he was so pleased! Although she didn't know it at the time, he'd just won himself two thousand pounds, as well as his race fee. Jockey Club laws against jockeys betting were completely ignored by Roly, and that proved to be his undoing.

'Listen,' she said firmly to him now. It was always essential to keep things simple when talking to Roly, for he didn't deal in nuances.

'I'm listening,' he said, steering the big box on to the motorway. Their yard was near Malton and they had long drives to the northern courses where they entered most of their runners.

'We must win something soon,' she said.

'Don't I know it,' he agreed.

'Do you think Lucky Strike'll pull it off today?' she asked.

'She's bursting out of her skin but she's up against some heavy stuff. That big chestnut gelding, Brigadier, from Ackerman's yard is due for a win and he's carrying the same weight as she is. I think we should tell Macready to pull our mare and I'll put a wad on Brigadier,' said Roly.

Laura groaned, 'Oh God, will you never learn? If we were caught pulling another horse I'd be warned off too and what'd we do then?'

'Everybody does it,' said Roly innocently.

'Not everybody, only some. And if we told Macready not to try he'd probably blab, you know what he's like.' Her voice was weary. Macready, their stable jockey, was Irish and irresponsible – like Roly.

'Yeah, he's a bit loose-tongued,' agreed her husband.

'Loose-tongued? He's brain dead,' she said. 'He's fallen off on to his head too often. Ask him a question and he answers with the first thing that occurs to him. We'll have to find another jockey soon I think.'

'Lance is old enough,' said Roly who'd started his career at fifteen, but Laura bristled. 'No way. He's staying at school. I don't want him flogging himself to death for nothing a week like we do. He's a clever boy. He can make something of himself. Anyway he's going to be too tall.'

'He's good on a horse though, and he may be tall but he's skinny. He can make the weight,' said Roly.

'So he's good on a horse! He can have a pleasant hobby. He can hunt at the weekends and be a gentleman. For a career I want him to join a bank and become a manager, or he can go to college and study accounting! He's good at maths,' said Laura.

Roly looked astonished as he said, 'A bank manager? An accountant? If he's good at maths why can't he become a bookie at least? That wouldn't let us down.'

She groaned. Both of them knew that it was absolutely essential for one of the Gomez Racing horses to win a race soon, or more owners would bail out and the bank was already making nasty noises about their overdraft. Laura was the worrier of the family and she frowned, pressing her fists against her forehead.

Roly looked at her with concern, 'Who was that phone call from?' he asked, thinking it was the cause of her anguish.

'It was Kenneth, inviting us to a cocktail party,' she said.

'Oh.' That shouldn't make her behave as if the bottom had dropped out of her world, he thought.

'Will we go?' he ventured after a bit.

'We might have to. He really wants us to be there. I hate to do it but I think I'll be forced to ask him for another loan. I hope that woman he's married to doesn't get to hear about it because she'd not let him lend me a penny.' Laura and Kenneth's second wife, Alice, had very little in common and never spoke to each other if they could help it.

'It might not come to that. Lucky Strike'll pull it off,' said her ever hopeful husband.

But Lucky Strike ran third and Brigadier won. As they gloomily loaded the box for the return journey, Roly permitted himself to say, 'You should have let me put a couple of hundred on Ackerman's horse after all. We wouldn't even have had to pull our mare to be in profit.'

She turned on him like a tigress. 'Shut up, shut up! You make me sick. Where would the money come from for the bet? We haven't got a couple of hundred pence far less a couple of hundred pounds,' she yelled. She was miserable because as soon as Lucky Strike was pipped at the post she knew there was nothing for it but to touch Kenneth for another loan.

NINE

The doorbell of an elegant house in London's Hans Place rang out and Barbara Carlton-Grey went to the surveillance system to peer through at whoever was outside. On the doorstep stood a dumpy, dark-haired woman wearing an expensive looking long trench coat with a mink collar and a matching mink hat.

Barbara activated the microphone and asked, 'Who is it?' As far as she knew, the caller was a stranger, probably collecting for some upper-class charity or canvassing for the Conservatives, for she looked like a right-wing political volunteer.

The woman on the step pushed her face towards the security grille and said, 'It's Marian Salisbury. From the old days in Bombay. Is Mrs Carlton-Grey at home?'

At first Barbara had not a clue who Marian Salisbury was, then, after a second or two, she remembered. Of course! Married to Peter Salisbury, both of them eager social climbers and pillars of the Bombay Gymkhana Amateur Dramatics Society. They had never been close friends, only acquaintances of beautiful Barbara and her husband John. What on earth did she want?

Innate good manners, and immaculate social training honed by the very best girls' boarding and finishing schools, made her voice sound cordial as she said, 'How lovely to see you after all this time! Wait a moment and I'll open the door.'

'One can't be too careful,' agreed Marian's voice through

the intercom, 'Peter and I live in St George's Square and we're always on our guard nowadays, too. So sad.'

She's making sure that I know she has an expensive house as well, thought Barbara sceptically, but she was beaming hospitably when her unexpected guest stepped into the hall.

'How nice to see you again,' she said, hiding her surprise as she helped Marian out of the all-enveloping coat, which she saw was lined with mink as well as having such an opulent collar. Fur coats may not be worn openly on the street nowadays but there was no rule against using mink as a lining if you could afford it.

'It's so cold out there for March, but lovely and warm in here. What a nice house,' said Marian looking appraisingly around, her dark eyes eager and calculating.

'We spend more time here now that the children are grown up. The house in Wiltshire seems so empty without them,' said Barbara apparently artlessly. The flicker that crossed her visitor's face told her the Salisburys had no country residence. Marian was a doughty fighter however. 'We like London, too, but it's pleasant to get away from time to time isn't it? We have a little place in Greece where my family come from and we go there as much as possible,' she countered.

Leading the way into the sitting room, Barbara enthused, 'You're so lucky. I love Greece. Where's your house?'

'In the Pelion peninsula. There's some very substantial merchant houses there. My brother and I inherited one from our grandfather and we share it now.'

'How lucky,' said Barbara again.

They sat down facing each other in an elegant sitting room with what looked like eighteenth-century family portraits on the walls, and Barbara said, 'Do have a sherry.' Marian accepted the offer and while sipping the amber liquid, she at last got to the point of her visit as she said, 'You must be wondering why I called.'

When Barbara smiled in silent assent, her visitor said, 'It's because of this.' She opened her crocodile-skin handbag and produced a sheet of paper, which she handed over. Barbara took the paper and smiled vaguely. She couldn't read it without her spectacles and she was not sure where they were.

'What is it?' she asked, wondering if she was about to be approached for a charitable donation after all.

'It's about the Bombay Cocktail Party,' said Marian.

'Oh yes? Do tell me.'

'Peter and I are on the committee and it's been decided that this has to be the last party. Everyone's getting too old or losing touch. Only fifty people came last year and quite frankly we lost money. We always like to find a good location, you see, and that costs quite a lot.'

Barbara agreed with a consoling murmur. By this time she'd wearily decided that she was about to be asked for a donation towards launching the party.

Marian was plunging on, 'So this year we've decided to make a tremendous effort to alert everyone and tell them that this is the swansong. They must either come this time or never again! We're sure lots of the old gang will respond. Bombay was such an important part of our lives, you see.'

In an instant Barbara was carried back to her Bombay days. She'd spent five years of misery there and still quailed at the memory, but she smiled encouragingly at Marian and nodded her head in encouragement. What a curse a training in good manners can be sometimes, she was thinking.

Marian went rattling on, 'So we've booked a large reception room at the Royal Overseas League in Park Place, St James's. We considered the Travellers' but their charges were a little too high. St James's is all right though, isn't it? We're contacting all the people who we think will be interested in coming and I was passing by so I thought I'd ring your bell and tell you about it.' Then she sat back and sighed, having got her mission off her chest.

Barbara wondered how Marian knew where she lived, but what she said was, 'How kind of you to remember us. John and I will be very interested. When is it and how much are the tickets?'

'It's on July the twentieth and they're only ten pounds. Kenneth Richards – do you remember him? He's the one whose wife died on the Madras train – he's on the committee too – and he wanted to make them fifteen but Peter and I thought that fixing them at ten was more tactful. Quite a few of our old friends are living on fixed incomes nowadays and are feeling the pinch, especially after the Lloyds debacle. It's not kind to flaunt one's own good fortune, is it?'

'Certainly not,' agreed Barbara wondering how she was going to avoid going to the party. The easiest thing to do was to buy tickets and just not turn up, she decided.

'Put us down for two,' she said firmly.

'That's wonderful! You've no idea how many people we're contacting. All the old theatrical crowd, the rugby people, the tennis club lot, the yacht club coterie, even some members of the Willingdon. You'll know so many of the people who turn up. It'll be quite like old times,' gushed Marian, delighted at her success in ensnaring Barbara who had always been a remote but beautiful presence on the edge of Bombay parties. Barbara had great social cachet because of her family connections but it was John who'd been the party animal, not his wife.

'It'll be lovely to see John again as well. He was the life and soul of so many parties, wasn't he? Everybody will remember *him,*' said Marian.

She was not to know that remark was to change Barbara's mind about attending the party. In an instant she decided that she and her husband would go after all. That should provide an opportunity for publicly demonstrating her hold on him, and making him atone for the shaming hell he'd put her through during their years in Bombay.

Marian, in high spirits, stayed chatting for an hour.

She'd called on Barbara on impulse, but for years she'd known where the Carlton-Greys had their town flat because she'd always admired cool, elegant Barbara intensely and followed their progress in the post-Bombay years. They had not been close friends and she'd never had an excuse to pick up their acquaintance back in London so this was the perfect opportunity. She already envisaged inviting the well-connected Carlton-Greys to dinner and introducing them to her other London friends.

Barbara was a desirable addition to any dinner party. A complete contrast to dumpy, motherly looking Marian, she was tall and slim, with a still beautiful face and a mane of glittering hair. Now as before, she moved around as if surrounded by a different atmosphere than everybody else. Her clothes were always immaculate, and even in the hottest weather she'd never seemed to sweat; when she played tennis the red dust of the Bombay courts never stained her pipe-clayed shoes while other people's ended up looking as if they'd been dusted with paprika.

Marian remembered the Carlton-Grey children as two pretty girls who were also always immaculate, never rumpled or food stained. Like their mother they were well bred and beautiful which was not surprising considering that they were the offspring of such a lovely mother and a spectacularly handsome father, for John had the same caddish good looks as the film star Rex Harrison.

It was at parties that Barbara was most impressive. Everyone in their Bombay set knew that John was an inveterate womaniser, picking up any woman who was susceptible to his drawling line of chat and his heart-stopping looks. He was particularly partial to young girls, the 'fishing fleet' daughters of Bombay-based parents who turned up from their boarding schools or university courses during the holiday season. He seemed to consider it one of his missions in life to initiate those girls into the mysteries of sex and most of them had been eager to learn.

He'd been quite blatant about it. Walking into a crowded room, he'd pause at the door and survey the gathering before heading for the female of his choice. Barbara would immediately be left to her own resources. She invariably retired to sit chatting with her few friends while her husband whirled past on the dance floor, oozing seduction.

'How can she bear it? How does she manage to look so calm about the way he behaves? It's shocking really,' whispered the gossips.

In fact Barbara was not a bit calm, but was seething inside with hurt pride and impotent fury. Her training as a lady however forbade her to demonstrate her true feelings in public, so she sustained the impression of being either unaware or uncaring. When the flirtation reached the stage of the couple disappearing into a bedroom or a locked bathroom – which frequently happened – she would rise to her feet, gather up her handbag and silk stole and go home.

What was said between the couple in private was never known because she had no close confidantes. Memories of those parties, and the shame they caused her, came surging up in Barbara's mind as she rummaged in her handbag for two ten pound notes to give to her unexpected visitor.

Marian was in high feather when she reached her home in St George's Square, delighted at having bagged two high-profile guests for the party. They lived in considerable style because her husband Peter, having first made his mark in India, soared through the management ranks of a large shipping company until he was appointed to a position on the board at home. Before he retired he had ended up as one of the major business figures in the country as well as the recipient of an honour from the Queen, and a considerable power behind the scenes in the Tory party. He was the Bombay set's major success story and Marian, who had backed him magnificently throughout his entire career, was extremely proud of him.

'I called on Barbara Carlton-Grey this afternoon and told

her about the party. She was really keen to come and put her name down for two tickets,' she said flopping down in a chair beside her husband who was watching racing on the television.

'Well done. They'll add a note of class to the proceedings. She's niece to the Duke of Adlington, you know. And that handsome swine of a husband of hers is well connected too, although she's the one with the money. We must let everyone know they're coming because that'll encourage some of the stand-offish set to turn up as well,' he replied.

John Carlton-Grey's success with women, his languid accent and the fact that he had attended one of the country's best public schools and Oxford University, always made plain Peter deeply envious, for he was the product of a minor educational establishment, the sort of 'public school' that made those in the know smile pityingly at the mention of its name. He'd worked his way up from the bottom, starting as an office clerk – 'Like Clive of India,' Marian always said – but even from his present pinnacle of success, he still felt inferior to Carlton-Grey.

When Marian left the Hans Place house, Barbara took up her embroidery frame to calm her nerves but her hands were shaking too much to wield the needle. Jumping up again, she walked across to a magnificent grand piano in the window alcove and tried to induce a calmer frame of mind by playing a piece by Beethoven, but with her foot well down on the forte pedal. She did not hear the door open behind her as her husband came in.

'I could hear you playing outside in the street,' he said in surprise.

She whirled round on the stool. Her hair, greying now but still luxuriant, had worked itself out of its velvet Alice band and was tumbling round her face, making her look almost as lovely as she had been when young. He, on the other hand, had lost his sexy dash. He still looked elegant but very thin and his expression was careworn.

'I don't suppose Beethoven will cause too much complaint among the passing populace,' she said and turned back to the keyboard, finishing the piece with a huge flourish before bringing her hands down on the keys in a discordant crash.

His surprise became astonishment. 'What on earth's the matter with you?' he asked. She wasn't given to such extrovert behaviour.

'Nothing. I had a visitor this afternoon and she made me remember things,' she said, getting up and shaking out the skirt of her pleated blue skirt as she got up from the piano stool.

'Oh yes, what things?' he asked, heading for the brass-handled butler's tray and putting his hand on the silver top of a crystal whisky decanter.

'Things I'd rather forget. I don't think you should start drinking whisky yet,' she said.

He paused and stared at her, 'Who came? Who was it?'

'Do you remember a couple called Salisbury who were big stars in that dramatics society in Bombay? His name was Peter and hers was Marian. I don't think you ever made a pass at her, did you? She was rather too old and dumpy for your taste – still is.'

He furrowed his patrician brow, ignoring the crack about Marian's shape. 'Salisbury? Oh yes, he worked for a shipping company, didn't he? Or was it tobacco? They were very good on stage. I seem to remember them tackling a play by Arthur Miller and making a pretty good job of it. They were friends with that beastly queen Perkins, weren't they?'

'Peter Salisbury was in shipping and his wife tells me he's ended up very important. He's on the board of several companies, so the money must be rolling in. She was wearing mink this afternoon.'

He raised his eyebrows, 'She's a brave woman then.'

'Not obviously. It was in the lining of her coat.'

'Humph. What did the mink-swaddled wife of a business tycoon want with us?' he asked.

'She came to invite us to a party.'

He eyed her cautiously, 'Are we going?'

'I think we might. I bought two tickets anyway.' Barbara's eyes sparkled as she watched him.

'She was *selling* tickets for her party?' He sounded incredulous. He and Barbara were not the sort of people who turned up at glittering events where the tickets cost hundreds of pounds each.

'It's the last Bombay Cocktail Party. Some of the people who were out there at the same time as us have this party every year – nostalgia, I expect. This year's will be the last one and Marian Salisbury said that they are hoping to attract as many people as possible to turn up and talk about the past.'

'So that's what upset you,' he said, obediently but ostentatiously replacing the stopper from the whisky decanter.

She glared at him and said, 'Shouldn't it? I don't think you should have a drink yet. It's only a quarter to five. Wait till six at least.'

He withdrew his hand at once and said meekly, 'All right, darling. Now, tell me. Exactly what's the matter? We don't have to go to that party even if you have bought tickets. Nobody'll care.'

'I'll care! I want to go. I want to show people like the Salisburys that we made it. I bet they all thought you'd run off and leave me eventually. I want them to see that I've tamed you.'

He flinched. 'All right, we'll go,' he agreed. She knew she had him on the run and went on, 'It's not just that stupid party that's upset me. I got a bill from your tailor today. Did you really need a new suit?'

'You said I could have one. You were with me when I ordered it,' he protested.

'It'll have to do for some time then,' she warned. He said nothing to that because both of them knew very well that every penny of the money that sustained their lives was Barbara's. In spite of his glittering university career (a first in History), and being one of the young golden boys of an international oil company, his career nose-dived after they left India, driven out by his company's switch-over to Indianisation. He'd never had a decent job after that and for the last fifteen years had been unemployed.

What compounded his problems was that he came from a family that was brilliantly clever, and well connected, but not rich. His father, a Cambridge don and a distant descendant of Darwin, was still alive, although wandering in his mind and using up his remaining capital in a discreet old people's home.

Bit by bit, coming home dejected from unsuccessful interview after unsuccessful interview, John's pride and confidence had been sapped. For a long time he still looked dapper and handsome; still talked in the same flippant, upper-class way when in company, but he grew hollow inside. Barbara, who for years had nursed deeply burning resentment of his cavalier treatment of her, seized her opportunity to take revenge. It became the secret motive of her life, unacknowledged even by herself.

Her strength was that she was fabulously rich. The heiress of a vast and long-established fortune, she could have lived a millionaire's lifestyle on the interest of her money alone, but she came from the sort of family that is almost ashamed of its wealth. She considered ostentation vulgar and was capable of petty penny pinching, scrutinising her household accounts intently and forever looking out for possible economies. Nothing pleased her better than a bargain.

The collapse of her husband's career was a double triumph for her. She dispensed with their household staff and put him to work, turning him into a butler/driver/general factotum. Never for a moment did she let him forget that she controlled the purse strings. She even augmented his father's nursing home expenses, which she did graciously, but signing her cheques in front of the nursing home management with a flourish that left them in no doubt about who controlled the purse strings. John paid over and over again for each infidelity he had ever committed. His pocket money was doled out weekly and their small circle of friends were in no doubt about his position.

If people came to dinner, the food was cooked and served by him. 'John's hobby is cooking,' said his wife sweetly. He was not even allowed the consoling luxury of indulging in too much of their vintage wine because she was not above reminding him that it was purchased for their guests and not for him. When they held dinner parties, she stopped allowing the men to sit over their port, and forced them upstairs with the women. 'In this age of women's liberation, it's so much more modern,' she said.

When she refused him the consolation of an afternoon whisky, he turned back towards the sitting room door and said, 'I'll go and make tea. Would you like some?'

Her smile was radiant and her tone sweet when she replied. 'Yes, darling, China, I think. Where have you been this afternoon?'

'Shopping for food,' he said wearily.

Her expression sharpened, 'What did you buy?'

'A leg of lamb and all the trimmings. The girls are coming to dinner tomorrow, aren't they?'

Barbara nodded, 'But they would be perfectly happy with one of your nice curries – so much cheaper.'

He consoled her, 'There'll be enough lamb left over to do another two meals for us.'

'Where did you buy it?' she asked.

'I put it on your account at Harrods Food Hall,' he said.

Her mood changed back in an instant. '*Harrods*! On the account! What a stupid thing to do. You could have got it for half the price in one of the shops behind Victoria. You are a fool, John. I'm not made of money. I suppose it was too much trouble to go as far as Victoria when Harrods is just over the road.'

But she was berating an empty space because he'd gone off to make the tea. When he returned she was still fuming, but less furiously. The strength of her anger had gone inside again like a concealed weapon, the way she usually hid it.

He poured their tea through a silver strainer and when they were sipping it, he said cautiously, 'Nevertheless I'm surprised the idea of that party appeals to you.'

She glittered. 'It appeals to me tremendously. And it should be the same for you. Just think! You're sure to meet some of your old flames there, darling. There were so many of them after all! Won't that be exciting?'

He put his cup down and stared at her. 'Leave it be,' he said quietly.

'Why should I? I thought it would be fun for you to go to the party with me and see all those people from the past.' Her hazel eyes were again alive with excitement and malice.

'It's over. It's past. I'm sorry,' he said.

'I know! I want us to go to the party so people can *see* you're sorry.'

He sighed. There was no way he was going to be able to avoid the humiliation she planned for him.

TEN

The sheet of paper bearing the sinister message: 'Sonya Richards was murdered! 1.12.1969. Do you know who she was?' had been stuck up on a peg board behind Tommy Morrison's writing desk and every time his eye rested on it, he frowned. The few facts he'd gathered about the dead woman stayed in his mind but did not appear to be sufficiently significant to give rise to the peculiar message, especially since his only connection with the case was that he'd been the police officer sent to look at the body.

After a few days he almost succeeded in persuading himself the letter was either a hoax or the work of a poison pen writer. Yet he didn't take it down from the peg board. Something told him to leave it up there.

He lived in a leafy area of Colaba, one of the few places not yet redeveloped in Bombay. On a warm late April morning he was promenading slowly past the Afghan Church on his way to his favourite tea house to meet some of his few surviving cronies, when a yellow and black taxi drew up alongside him and a turbaned head poked out of the window. The taxi driver bawled a greeting.

'Good morning my old friend. Would you like to be driven anywhere?'

Tommy paused, leaning on his walking stick, then slowly grinned. 'Good morning sergeant. What are you doing driving a taxi?' he asked.

'It is my own taxi. I've left the police. Let me give you

a free drive, old friend,' was the reply from the handsome, bearded and grinning Sikh behind the wheel.

Tommy shook his head. 'But I'm only going to the tea house. It's no distance. I can see it from here.'

'No, no, I insist. I'll take you to *my* favourite tea house on Malabar Hill. Get in. This is a new taxi, very nice and clean.'

It was indeed immaculate with loops of orange marigold flower heads interspersed with silver foil hanging against the inside windscreen and the back window.

When Tommy commented on the garlands, the driver, Raj Singh, said, 'This is my first day as a taxi driver. It's a lucky omen for me to see you and give you the first ride. Such an old and reliable friend as you will bring me good fortune. You always did. Don't you remember saving my life once in a riot at Chowpatti? You hauled me away from a gang of *goondas* who were going to tear me into little pieces.'

Tommy smiled because he did remember the riot and rescuing the foolhardy young Raj Singh who'd rushed into the throng without waiting for backup. He could not refuse to ride in the taxi now that he'd been told that story, or Raj Singh would think his luck was blighted. Besides Tommy had always got along well with Sikhs.

They went to the top of Malabar Hill and drank fragrantly spiced tea in a little hut near the Parsi Towers of Silence. On top of the tower walls, a line of bare-necked vultures roosted, beady-eyed and waiting here for their next meal because the sinister fortress-like structures were where the Parsi dead were laid out to be eaten.

Tommy eyed the birds and said, 'I'm glad I'm not a Parsi. If I was, I'd be looking at those birds and wondering which one of them was going to have the pleasure of tearing me apart soon.'

Raj Singh scoffed, 'Not soon! You are still in good health. Cheer up, stop thinking like that.'

'I'm seventy,' said Tommy.

'Hah! My father is eighty-five and he's going to Amritsar next week. Then he says he is going to Madras to visit my brother,' Raj Singh replied.

'I haven't been out of this city for years,' said Tommy, recognising the truth of what he said with surprise.

'Where would you like to go if you did take a trip?' asked the Sikh.

'My children want me to go to Australia, but I know they won't let me come back if I do. For myself, I wouldn't mind going to Poona . . . That's about it. I haven't any great ambitions to travel.'

'So, Poona! My taxi and I will take you to Poona. We will take you on Sunday. I will call for you at five o'clock in the morning and you'll be in Poona before midday.' Raj Singh's eyes were sparkling at the thought of the excursion.

'I'll only go if you let me pay your fare like a real taxi driver,' said Tommy.

'We'll come to a price for that then. You can buy the petrol and the *khana*. It's a long time since I was in Poona. I had a lady friend there at one time, a very fine looking woman. I might look her up. Who will you go to see there?'

Tommy grinned. 'I had in mind to visit the nuns in the Carmelite convent,' he said mischievously.

Raj Singh groaned. Convents and nuns were not good reasons for visiting Poona as far as he was concerned.

On Sunday morning the shining taxi drew up at Tommy's gate at exactly two minutes to five and the old man was put into the back seat with several cushions and a lunch box prepared by an anxious Prakash. Another cold box full of iced beer was loaded into the boot. Beside Raj Singh in the front passenger seat was a young lad with a fluff of beard growing on his chin and enormous, trusting golden eyes.

'This is my youngest son,' said Raj Singh proudly. 'He is still a student but he wishes to join the police, too, so I have brought him along to meet you. I have always told my children about Inspector Tommy who was so clever and so brave.'

The boy, whose glossy black hair was coiled on top of his un-turbaned head in a loose bun, looked shyly at Tommy and brought his folded hands to his brow in greeting. Tommy bowed gravely back. 'He will make a fine policeman one day,' he said to the boy's father.

It was quicker and easier to get to Poona than it had been in the old days, and the taxi roared along, overtaking bullock carts and pony *tongas*, heavily loaded lorries and family cars packed to the roof with people and bundles. They swooped up the corkscrewing *ghat* road, with Raj Singh tooting the horn and waving gaily every time he passed a vehicle driven by another Sikh. He was enjoying himself hugely.

Once on the vast plain that stretched across the heart of India, he stopped under a grove of trees and they all got out to relieve themselves and drink their first bottle of cold beer. When they returned to the car, the boy was carrying a long spray of purple orchids, which he reverently draped along the fascia of the car, gently handling the exotic flowers as he did so. 'They are very beautiful,' he said almost apologetically to Tommy.

The road into Poona was thronged with traffic, but Raj Singh was not content to creep along and set about over-taking slower vehicles with only paint-scraping margins, jostling idlers out of his way and into ditches. He'd obviously researched the situation of the convent and drew up at its gate triumphantly at five to twelve. 'I said you'd be here before noon, didn't I?' he crowed.

The boy pulled a bell rope that hung alongside a wooden door set in a high stone wall and after a bit it was swung open by a woman in a long fawn robe and white wimple. She peered suspiciously at them and said, 'If you've brought a baby, put it in that basket.' A wicker basket lay at one edge of the step and they all looked at it, shaking their heads.

'No baby,' said Tommy, 'I would like to speak to your Mother Superior.'

The nun looked at him with sharp eyes set in a wrinkled brown face. It was impossible to tell her race or nationality. 'Who are you?' she asked in English.

Raj Singh stepped forward and said, 'This is Detective Inspector Tom Morrison of the Bombay Police – retired – a very important man. Please treat him with the respect he deserves.'

His solemnity impressed the nun who stepped back, opening the door wider as she gestured to Tommy to enter. Raj Singh told him, 'I will return for you in two hours, sir. I'm sure I can trust the holy sisters to treat you with great hospitality.' This was said loudly with a sharp eye on the hovering nun.

Inside the wall was another world. No dust and sand here but a luxuriant garden, full of trees and vegetables. Mango trees and banana palms were growing round the perimeter, with smaller shrubs and bushes clustered in the middle. Profusion ruled because the garden provided the vegetarian community with most of its diet. Tomatoes hung in scarlet swathes and grape vines were trained up the trunks of citrus trees. Spears of maize with ripening yellow cobs showing between their tall spikes filled one corner – the pre-monsoon harvest season was almost upon them.

Here and there were clumps of flowers, mostly purple asters, scarlet geraniums, pink petunias and yellow marigolds like the ones that decorated Raj Singh's taxi. At the far side of the garden, a few women with their habit skirts looped up between their legs like coolies could be seen labouring away in vegetable beds where lettuces and beans grew alongside rows of radishes and beds of strawberries. None of them raised their heads to look at the new arrival but he guessed they were all squinting sideways in his direction.

His guide led him up a central path to a sprawling house

where a large, golden pi-dog lay in the shade. At his approach it jumped up and started baying, rattling its chain. The nun soothed it and gestured to Tommy to follow her up the steps into a shadowy hall hung with religious pictures of Christ and the Virgin Mary. Bunches of flowers from the garden were placed in silver vases beneath the pictures.

'Sit down,' she said, showing him a tall wooden chair. Then she disappeared through another door.

It was cool in the hall for a ceiling fan was creaking slowly round above his head and, even though the chair was hard and uncomfortable, Tommy felt sleep creeping up on him as he sat back into it. His eyelids had begun to droop when he heard the soft slap, slap of sandals and looked up to see a stooped old nun standing quite near and looking straight at him.

'I'm told you are a policeman. I am the prioress here. What is your business with us?' she asked.

He stood up and bowed as he told her, 'I came to ask about a girl child who was born in your convent, a very long time ago, I'm afraid. I don't know if you'll be able to help me, but I thought it was worth trying.'

'When was the child born?' asked the nun. Her voice was strong and definite but her face looked very old.

'In 1934,' he told her.

She shrugged and smiled. 'That was the year I took my final vows,' she said.

A rapid calculation told him that she must be eighty-one or -two, older than he was himself.

'What was the child's name and why do you want to know about her?' was her next question.

'I don't know the name her mother gave her but as a grown woman she was called Sonya Walker. A couple called Walker adopted her from here when she was six weeks old and gave her their name. I am interested in her because twenty years ago she was found dead on a train in Bombay and I was in charge of the case. Recently someone

69

asked me to find out about her background,' he said, thinking his explanation sounded very lame.

The prioress thought so too because she said doubtfully, 'She died twenty years ago?'

He nodded. 'Twenty-one. In 1969 actually. It was a natural death, heart trouble apparently.'

'So why does anyone want to know about her now?'

'I don't know. I received an anonymous letter saying I should make enquiries,' said Tommy.

The prioress nodded. Everyone who lived for any time in India knew about the fondness of informers for anonymous letters.

'We have some records about our babies, but I am not sure if they are complete. Do you want to come and look?' she said, gesturing towards the door from which she'd entered the hall.

She took him into a dim room with cream cotton blinds pulled down over its two windows. When one was raised, cupboards and wooden filing cabinets were revealed standing round three walls. Each cabinet drawer had a label in a raised slot on its face. Tommy walked across to the nearest one and saw that it was dated 1914–1918. The nuns' system of keeping records was much more orderly than that of the police, he reckoned.

He walked along the line of cabinets till he found a drawer marked 1931–35. Watched by the prioress, he pulled open the drawer and felt his heart starting to race a little. Inside the drawer was a pile of cardboard files.

He lifted them out carefully and saw that some of the containers only contained one sheet of paper, but others had several. He laid his burden out on top of a large table in the middle of the floor and the nun came across to help.

'What did you say was the name of the couple who adopted the child?' she asked.

'Walker. I think he was in the British Army.'

She nodded, 'We gave away a lot of babies to Army

people in those years before the war. I often wonder what happened to them,' she said softly.

They both bent over the files and ran their eyes down the pages they contained. Eventually the nun exclaimed, 'Perhaps this is the one. Walker – they're the people you're looking for, aren't they? Here's the name.'

From the way she spoke when excited, Tommy suddenly realised that she was Anglo-Indian like himself and he warmed to her. 'Well done!' he exclaimed, 'What are their names?'

'William and Barbara Walker,' she read from the paper in her hand. 'He was a captain in the Army – a Britisher. It must have been an English or a Eurasian child. They didn't often take Indian babies.'

'Did you get English children?' he asked in surprise. Sonya had that very yellow hair, he remembered.

A look was shot at him from pouched old eyes, 'Often in those days. For all sorts of reasons. Not many now though.'

She was hanging on to the file and though he longed to read it, Tommy could not snatch it out of her hand, so he waited patiently for it to be handed over while she ran her eye down the page.

'Yes, yes,' she was saying as she read. 'Yes, I think I remember something about that baby and its mother. I was just a girl, about the same age as the mother. She cried so much when she gave the baby away. Poor thing! Yes, I do remember, I think.'

'Please let me look,' pleaded Tommy and at last she passed the faded file over. All the facts were on two sheets of paper. The first one was a note of the adoption by Captain and Mrs Walker. They had signed their names and accepted full responsibility for the baby. A donation of five hundred rupees, which was a fair sum of money at that time, had been paid to the convent so the Walkers must have been pleased with their new child.

The other sheet almost stopped Tommy's heart. He felt himself stagger as he read it and had to grip the edge of the table to keep standing up. The facts were stark. A female child was born to a girl called Theresa Morrison, aged 17, who had been delivered into the care of the convent by her father two months before she gave birth. Her father, who was her legal guardian, co-signed the adoption paper, and gave his name as Edward Morrison, Superintendent of Railways at Nagpur. The name of the baby's father was not recorded.

Theresa Morrison was safely delivered of her daughter on November 6th, 1934. Six weeks later it was adopted by the Walkers and the mother left the convent, delivered back into the care of her father.

'Are you all right?' the old prioress asked Tommy, for his face had drained of colour and she could hear his breath rasping in his chest.

'The mother was my sister,' he said slowly, 'her baby, that woman, whose body I found in the railway compartment, was my niece.'

When Raj Singh came back after two hours to collect his old friend, he was shocked to see how grey and old he looked. 'Did they not give you any *khana*?' he asked angrily as he drove away from the convent gate.

'Yes, they gave me soup and bread, more than enough, and a mug of beer,' said Tommy faintly.

'Are you ill? Do you want me to take you to a doctor?'

'No, I'm not ill. I'm only tired. Do you mind if I don't talk?'

'Lie down on the seat, try to sleep. I'll go very slowly and not jolt you about,' said the anxious driver. When Tommy's long frame was stretched as much as possible along the back seat, the boy leaned over and draped a cloth over him. Then Tommy closed his eyes – but he did not sleep. His mind was racing.

Now he knew why the mysterious letter was sent to him – it was because his eldest sister, Theresa, was the mother of Sonya Richards. He'd never suspected such a thing. He knew nothing of his sister having been pregnant.

Theresa was four years his senior. When he was small, he followed her like a little shadow, but in their later years he'd felt remote from her because she turned into a depressive mouse of a woman who scuttled around trying to be as unobtrusive as possible, much beholden to their parents. The family returned to Bombay from Nagpur after Partition in 1947 when Tommy's father lost his job on the railways. By that time Tommy was already working as a policeman and married. Theresa died in a cholera epidemic in the city in 1950.

When she died, she was only thirty-three. A short, sad life, he thought.

Their parents had been very strict and respectable. His father was extremely protective of his status in their Eurasian community, which at that time considered itself to be far superior to that of the ordinary Indians. In Nagpur, where they went from Bombay when Tommy was about nine, he occupied a senior position in the railways. They lived in a large bungalow, near the houses of the English community with whom, however, they had little social contact, but they were leaders among their own kind and copied the ways and manners of the British. After the British left India in 1947, Mr Morrison's job was given to an Indian and he was forcibly retired.

Tommy lay in the moving car trying very hard to remember the young Theresa, fighting to cast his mind back fifty years. He'd been an only son with three sisters and Theresa was the first, two years senior to the next girl, Madeleine. The third, called Alice, was born the year before Tommy, but she died at two years old and he had no memory of her at all.

He'd been a sporty boy, playing cricket in the summer and

rugby during the rainy season. Absorbed in his own interests he took very little notice of what went on at home, which always seemed to be the domain of women. No matter how hard he tried, he had no memory of Theresa disappearing from the family for any great length of time, although both of his sisters used to go down to Bombay occasionally to visit their mother's family. It must have been during one of those 'visits' that she'd gone into the convent to have her baby. For it was definitely hers. He'd recognised his father's bold copper plate handwriting the moment he saw it on the adoption agreement.

He sat up in the seat when the taxi was going through the town of Thana which marked the entrance to Bombay Island, and said to Raj Singh, 'I wonder if you'd drop me at the house of my sister? She lives in Juhu. I've not seen her for years but I think I can still find her house.'

Raj Singh looked over his shoulder, relieved to see that Tommy seemed to have perked up. 'It's nearly seven o'clock. You should go home to supper. Are you sure you're well enough to be visiting?' he asked.

'Yes, I'm sure. She lives in the residential part of Juhu, set back from the beach. If you drive towards the hotel, I'll be able to guide you from there.'

Madeleine's husband, a Goan, had been a clerk in a city office. His father left him the seaside house and the whole family – Madeleine's parents and her sister too – went to live there when they left Nagpur. By that time Tommy was married and Madeleine had never got along with him. She was an irritable woman who was jealous of her beautiful sister-in-law Christine, Tommy's wife, and could never resist making nasty remarks about her. After Theresa and his parents died he felt he could stand no more of her back-biting so he and Madeleine had not been in contact for a long time. However he knew from occasional visits by his oldest nephew, who also suffered from his mother's sharp tongue, that she was still alive, though now widowed.

Although it would soon be dark, her house was not hard to find. It stood in a line of brightly coloured villas, shabby and unloved looking, with unsightly blotches of faded pink paint peeling from the walls. Madeleine's husband had once owned the whole building, but now that everyone else in the household, except her son, was dead, she lived on the ground floor only, having sold off the first floor and terrace.

He could hear her calling out fearfully when he knocked on her door.

'Who is it? What do you want?' she yelled.

'It's your brother, Tom,' he called back, gesturing to Raj Singh to show that he would be all right.

The Sikh stood at the gate and shouted, 'I will wait for you.'

'No, no,' said Tommy, 'that won't be necessary. Take your boy home now. You must both be tired. It was a long journey.'

'I will wait for a little while to make sure you are all right,' said Raj Singh turning on his heel.

Madeleine's voice was closer now, on the other side of the door. 'Who is it so late at night?' she croaked again.

Tommy looked at his wristwatch. It was half-past seven. 'It's your brother,' he said.

The door was opened a crack and she peered out at him, 'What do *you* want? Has someone died?' she asked.

She was hunched over like a question mark; her hair as white as cotton wool, and her hands like gnarled roots folded over the handle of a walking stick.

'Let me in, Madeleine,' said Tommy.

Reluctantly she opened the door wider. 'It's taken you a long time to come to see me. You didn't even come when my husband died,' she said resentfully.

He ignored the comment, although he remembered she had not informed him of his brother-in-law's death and he had only heard about it much later. 'I've not come to fight with you,' he said.

'Really?' she sneered, 'Why have you come then?'

They were facing each other in a nasty little room that smelt fetid and airless. 'You should open a window here,' he said.

'We don't all live officer-style. We don't pretend to be English any longer,' she said.

He remembered how angry she'd always been that, alone of the Morrison children, she looked very Indian. Theresa and Tommy could easily pass for British if they chose but Madeleine could not because her complexion was much darker.

He ignored that jibe, too. 'I've come to ask you about Theresa,' he said.

'Theresa! What about her?' She sat down on a plastic-covered sofa that squeaked under her weight, and he sat on a wooden chair facing her. It reminded him of the many times he'd subjected reluctant witnesses to questioning.

'Do you remember our sister having her baby?' he asked, going straight to the point.

She stared at him and for a moment he thought she was going to laugh, but what she said was, 'I remember all right. There was much trouble about that.'

'Did she want to give it away?'

'I don't know. All I know is she went into the convent with a swelling belly and came back thin. Our father never spoke a civil word to her again. She was made to suffer for her sin, I can tell you that.'

He remembered how frightened Theresa had been of their father and how scornfully he treated her. He was amazed that the egoism of youth allowed him to ignore the tensions that must have throbbed around him while he was growing up.

'Did you think she was a sinner?' he asked.

'Of course I did. She'd let us down as a family. She shamed us. She *sinned*!' Madeleine sounded righteous. In his youth, their family attended the local Anglican church every Sunday and she had always been a regular churchgoer, but she converted to Roman Catholicism when she married Philip and became even more devout.

'Who was the child's father?' asked Tommy.

A spark of malice leaped to life in Madeleine's eyes. 'He was English, a young officer posted in the Nagpur cantonment. They met at a dance and he used to come to collect her in a car, tooting the horn at the gate! He was tall and lordly with yellow hair like somebody in the pictures. She thought she had hooked him but she was wrong, wasn't she? He died in Burma, we heard later, a prisoner of the Japanese. I forget his name but it was something like Arbuthnot or Anstruther. Yes, it was Anstruther. He was a colonel by that time.'

In a sudden flash-back of memory, Tommy was carried back to the past and saw his sisters as they had once been – Madeleine dark skinned and envious, hating her sister who was lovely, willowy, and brown-haired, with a tranquil face and ivory skin. The film star Ava Gardner, who played an Anglo-Indian girl in *Bhowani Junction*, was very like Theresa and when he went to see that film after she died it had made him deeply sad.

'Poor Theresa,' he sighed.

'Poor Theresa nothing. She should have known better. She was a loose woman, a fool. Father thought no one knew anything about that baby, but of course there was gossip and nobody would marry her then. You must have been the only person that was deceived if you didn't know about it!'

So that was why Theresa never married and lived with their parents and this malicious sister until her death. What a dreadful price she paid for her indiscretion, he thought.

'Did the English officer want to marry her?' he asked.

'She said so, but he was told by his commanding officer that he'd have to resign his commission if he did. Because she was chichi, you see. Officers didn't marry chichi girls in those days. He was sent to Singapore and she used to tell me he was coming back for her. She got letters. But the war broke out and of course he didn't come and then she heard he'd died,' said Madeleine without a trace of compassion.

Tommy cringed. 'Poor Theresa,' he said again and looked down at his hands clasped in his lap as he asked, 'Did she see her baby again? Did she ever talk about it?'

'No, of course not. It was a taboo subject. Some couple from Bombay adopted it because it was very white and English looking. It landed lucky.'

'The baby grew up to be a handsome woman,' said Tommy sadly.

'I know that. She came here asking about Theresa in the 1960s. She didn't say who she was at first but I knew because of the way she looked. She was very like Theresa but her hair was yellow,' said Madeleine.

Tommy was genuinely surprised. 'She came here? When?'

'In the mid-sixties, I don't remember the exact year. She'd been making enquiries and someone in Nagpur told her where we'd gone. Apparently the woman who adopted her had died and left her a letter with the details of her birth. Walker was her name. Theresa's daughter was very upset when I told her that my sister was dead too. She went away without asking about anything else and I never saw her again.'

She glared at her brother when he asked, 'What else did you tell her?'

'What do you think? I told her what I've told you and I said my sister was a loose woman who brought shame on the whole family. How come you know about her if you didn't know Theresa had a baby?'

'I saw her body. She was found dead in a train in Victoria Station twenty years ago,' said Tommy, standing up and heading for the door, leaving Madeleine staring after him with an astounded expression on her face.

Raj Singh's taxi was still waiting, parked on the other side of the road. When Tommy stepped through the gate, the headlights were switched on and the engine fired. Gratefully Tommy climbed into the back and put his face in his hands.

Who sent me that message? Why did it say Theresa's child was murdered? he asked himself. Then he gave a shudder as he thought, Sonya Richards knew she was my sister's child. She knew. I wonder if she told anyone and it was that person who contacted me?

'Are you all right?' asked Raj Singh, leaning over anxiously and putting a hand on his shoulder.

Tommy shook his head. 'Not really. Take me home please, old friend,' he said.

ELEVEN

Tommy spent the day after his trip to Poona in bed, anxiously watched over by Prakash, and called upon twice by Raj Singh who tip-toed into the room to look at him. When he heard the footsteps, he closed his eyes and pretended to be asleep, but he was actually awake and thinking.

On the second morning, he woke at six as usual and rang the bell by his bed. Prakash, who had been sleeping on the verandah in front of the bedroom door, came running in and his eyes lit up when he saw that Tommy was looking cheerful, yawning and stretching his arms.

'I will bring your tea,' he cried and dashed away to the kitchen.

When he returned with the steaming cup, his employer was rummaging in his desk drawer looking for the cocktail party invitation.

'Have you a passport?' Tommy suddenly asked.

This would have been a ridiculous question if put to most domestic servants in Bombay but Prakash was far from ordinary.

'Yes. I got one when I went to work in the Gulf after the Carmichaels returned to England. I've always kept it up to date,' was the answer.

'I thought you might. Good. There's a possibility we'll be flying to London soon. I'm not sure yet, but I think it's on the cards,' said Tommy.

Prakash, as usual, took this bombshell in his stride. 'It would be good to see London,' he said calmly.

Tommy laughed. The idea of the pair of them going to England to attend a cocktail party no longer seemed ludicrous, but suddenly possible. He had more than enough money because of his son's cheque and there was nothing else planned for the immediate future anyway. Most important of all, he had a trail to follow up.

During his day in bed he'd decided that whoever tipped him off about Sonya Richards being his murdered niece wanted him to be at that cocktail party, so his informant would probably be there too. He was excited by the challenge and the dormant detective instinct in him was activated by the outrage he felt at the fate of his unknown relative. Poor girl, she'd gone looking for her mother, but was too late. Poor girl, she died alone in a railway compartment. Even if she had not been unlawfully killed, what a miserable end. It was a long time since he'd felt so energised.

Prakash regarded the revived Tommy with affection, thinking that he would go with this man to the ends of the earth, far less to London. He'd begun looking after him twenty-one years ago when he returned to Bombay from his job in the Gulf, full of rage and the burning desire to avenge the death of his friend and relative, Swami.

Swami had been seventy years old and was serving out his last year as a domestic servant, and he planned to return to his village in Kerala a few months later. Instead, he died as a result of police maltreatment after the woman he worked for was found dead on a train travelling from Madras to Bombay.

A letter was sent to Prakash breaking the sad news and he immediately returned to Bombay. What he was told by Swami's friends made him weep. The old man had suffered three broken ribs and a ruptured spleen at the hands of a brutal police sergeant. When released from the police station, he had crawled back to his friend's house in a Byculla chawl where he had died after three days of agony.

Prakash raged but he knew there was no point in someone like him lodging an official complaint about Swami's ill treatment. However, by making enquiries, he found out that the officer in charge of the dead woman's case was Inspector Morrison and, full of anger, he staked out Tommy's Colaba bungalow.

His quarry was enjoying a pre-bedtime whisky soda two nights later, when a fierce-eyed young man in black jumped over the verandah rail from the shadowed garden and threatened him with a knife. 'I am going to kill you but I want you to know the reason why before you die,' he said.

The man in the chair, although his stomach was churning, eyed the gleaming blade with every appearance of calm. In fact, he was calculating his chances of fighting off this assailant, which were practically nil, and cursing himself for being so careless.

Since his wife's death he lived alone, and even if he shouted for help and alerted the local watchman or his neighbours, he would certainly be a dead man before help arrived – and he would die without knowing the reason. His curiosity had to be satisfied, if nothing else, he thought fatalistically.

'Why are you going to kill me?' he asked and sipped his drink with every appearance of nonchalance. He was still fit and tensed his muscles as he calculated when to launch himself at his attacker. At least he'd go out fighting.

'Because of my friend, Swami. He was a kind old man who never hurt anyone, but he was beaten so badly by you and your men that he died. All because the woman whose servant he was died in a train from Madras last month. You were in charge of the case.' Prakash was burning up with fury as he spoke and his hands were visibly shaking.

Tommy put down his glass and shook his head. So that was it! He'd heard about what happened to the dead woman's servant in contradiction of his orders, and had been furious. 'I'm sorry, very sorry about that. I told my constable that the old servant was not to be beaten. Mrs Richards' death was from natural causes and there was no suspicion of a killing. But in the station he was questioned by a Goan sergeant who likes to hurt people. I had that man disciplined and demoted when I heard that my orders were ignored – but it was too late for your friend. I'm very sorry. People like me have little power any more, you see.' He was not pleading for his life, only stating a fact. He had too much pride to plead. 'I'm sorry,' he said sincerely again before asking, 'How did you know that old man?'

Prakash, shaken, slightly lowered his knife. 'He was from my village in Kerala. He brought me to Bombay to work when I was ten and looked after me like a father. He was returning home soon . . . I've been sending him money from the Gulf so that he could go. Then I heard he was dead.'

'I assure you, I wasn't the one who hurt him and I certainly didn't kill him,' said Tommy again and his sincerity communicated itself to his assailant who felt the desire for revenge draining out of him.

Once before Prakash had stabbed someone in a rage and the memory still appalled him. He'd attacked an insolent cook in the kitchen of the Carmichael family when he worked for them as second bearer. He'd gone for the cook with a carving knife, really intending to kill him. Fortunately the thrust was diverted, but the blade went clean through the cook's hand and blood had spurted all over the kitchen floor.

The wounded man had screamed and rushed out into the road looking for a policeman. In the melee that followed, Prakash remembered how Mrs Carmichael had rallied to his support and telephoned a senior police officer who was a friend of her husband. She was determined that Prakash would not be rushed off to jail and a certain beating.

To his surprise, he now realised that the police officer who had arrived to calm things down, and by so doing had saved his skin, was the man he now planned to kill. 'Do you remember Mrs Carmichael who lived in Walkeshwar Road?' he asked as he stared across at his would-be victim on the shadowy verandah.

Tommy nodded, 'Yes. I knew her husband well. He was a good rugby player. He was captain of the Gymkhana team that used to play against my police team.' The police always beat the Gym, he recalled with satisfaction, but Ben Carmichael was a good loser.

'She was a fine woman,' said Prakash fervently, and told Tommy the story about the stabbed cook.

The policeman nodded, 'I remember that, too. She certainly saved you from going to jail – probably saved your life. I hushed up the case because she said she'd get you out of the city. She told me the cook deserved it, and it wasn't a life-threatening wound anyway.'

'He did deserve it. He was a thief and a blasphemer. He jeered at me because I'm a Brahmin, but he said I was working for unclean people. He said I had made myself an outcast, an Untouchable.'

The fierce pride and complicated nuances of Indian castes of society were familiar to Tommy. 'So you stabbed him?' he asked.

'He taunted me into it,' was the proud reply.

'And Mrs Carmichael took your side? She got you away?' Tommy said. The tension in his muscles was slowly relaxing as he saw that the young man's murderous fervour was lessening. There was a chance that he might survive this.

'When you left, the cook's friends were waiting in the lane to kill me but Mrs Carmichael drove me to the station in the boot of her car and gave me the money for a ticket to Kerala. Six months later, when it had all died down, I was able to return and work for her again,' Prakash told him.

'And when the Carmichaels went back to England, you found work in the Gulf?' Tommy asked.

Prakash nodded. 'Yes, nearly three years ago.'

'What will you do now?'

'Go back to the Gulf probably – when I've killed you.' But the tone was no longer fierce, more despairing.

'I did not hurt your old friend. I swear it. I understand your anger though, and I promise I'll make sure the man who did hurt him will pay for it. Why don't you come and work for me? I'm looking for a good servant,' was Tommy's suggestion.

And so it turned out that he and his would-be murderer, Prakash Rao, began their companionable and trusting relationship. And now Tommy was planning for them to go to London together.

'When will we leave?' Prakash asked. By this time he was growing into dignified middle age, and looked a patrician South Indian Brahmin with a finely chiselled face and coffee-coloured skin. His black hair was glossy, his body lean and his intelligence staggering. He was a man of many talents, a skilled sketcher in charcoal and an avid reader with a particular fondness for the work of J.K. Narayan, the novelist from Mysore who wrote in English. Prakash often read extracts from Narayan's books to Tommy whose own taste ran more to reminiscences and memoirs like the books of Elephant Bill.

Tommy looked at the invitation in his hand. 'I have to be there on July the twentieth, but we'll go a couple of days in advance. I'd like to see the sights once more. There's one or two things to do before then, however. I want you to find some people who knew your old friend Swami and ask them about Mrs Richards, the woman he worked for. I want to hear everything they can remember about her,' he said.

There was no better source of inside information in Bombay than the servant circuit. They knew and remembered everyone who had ever maintained a household of servants in Bombay for the last thirty years. Tommy deliberately did not tell Prakash that Sonya Richards was his niece because then any scurrilous pieces of information might have been withheld or censored for fear of upsetting him.

Prakash looked doubtful. 'It's a long time since she died,' he said.

'I know, 1969, but servants have long memories. I relied on them a lot when I was working. I don't care what you turn up, no matter how trivial it is, bring it to me.' He trusted Prakash and knew he'd miss nothing.

Three days later he got a result. Prakash came in from an afternoon off and said, 'I found three men who remember Mrs Richards, and also a woman who was ayah to her little girl before she married Mr Richards.'

Tommy was delighted. 'Well done, very well done! What did they tell you?'

'I think you should come and hear it for yourself. There's quite a lot of information and they all talk at once. I've arranged for them to meet you at the home of the ayah tomorrow afternoon. She lives in Chor Bazaar.'

'She's a Muslim?' asked Tommy surprised. Chor Bazaar was a Muslim district and normally their women did not take servant jobs.

'No, but she lives with a Muslim man. She's taken the name of Yamin but she's really Gujerati, I think.'

'All right. What time have you arranged?'

'Half past two in the afternoon. It's hot then, I know, but they both work and it's the only time the two of them can be there.'

'I don't mind the heat any more. At my age I'm used to it and it soothes my bones,' said Tommy.

On Friday afternoon they rode in a taxi to Chor Bazaar, a stinking warren of twisting narrow lanes lined by tall old wooden houses that leaned confidingly towards each other, so that people in the upper verandahs could shake hands over the street below. It was the haunt of thieves – a *chori wallah* is a thief – and whenever anyone suffered a burglary, the first place they visited was the bazaar to tour the little booths and see if their lost treasures were up for sale. They often were. As soon as the rains began in June, thieves stripped windscreen wipers off parked cars and smart drivers went to Chor Bazaar to buy them back. It was also the place to go to buy back your car's stolen hub caps.

In spite of the squalor of the district, Tommy always enjoyed going there because it was unchanged from the India he'd known as a child and full of barefaced rogues who did not pretend to be anything different. Even though it was ten years since he'd stopped being a policeman, many of the stall holders still remembered him and shouted out greetings as his taxi nosed its way through the smelly lanes.

'*Arrey Morrison-sahib*! Big policeman! Who are you looking for today? Come and buy a bargain from me . . .' Then they waved, burst out in raucous laughter and spat long trajectories of red betel juice on to the roadway.

The old man with whom the ex-ayah lived kept a furniture stall and he squatted, impassively smoking a hookah, in the middle of a jumble of merchandise – bed ends, cupboards, table tops and teapoys – with dozens of chair frames hanging from the low rafters above his head. He looked up questioningly when Prakash and Tommy stepped into his dark cavern from the street.

'Aiiiee?' he questioned with a note of suspicion, for he, too, recognised Tommy.

'Where is your woman?' asked Prakash and was answered by a gesture of the head towards the back of the stall.

They negotiated the piles of goods and found a curtained doorway which led them into a back room where a woman and three men were sitting. They all nodded eagerly as Tommy entered, for they had obviously been waiting for him.

Prakash whispered to his employer, 'I said you would pay for their information.'

Tommy nodded. He had taken the precaution of bringing

a roll of small-denomination notes in his pocket – not too much, not too little.

'Sit down sahib,' said the woman politely, indicating a pile of cushions with pristine white covers which had been set aside for this important guest. She was skinny and angular with dry, leathery looking skin. The three men ranged in age from a man in his thirties to a grey-haired, dignified looking old fellow who was probably as old as Tommy himself. Like the woman, they were all Hindus.

When Tommy settled into the cushions, with Prakash standing at his back like a bodyguard, she asked, 'You will drink a Coca Cola?'

He and Prakash both accepted and a small boy was sent running off to fetch two bottles with a shimmer of cold frosting on them and straws stuck into the open necks.

Once the formalities were over it was down to business. 'I understand that you all knew Swami, the bearer who worked for a woman called Mrs Richards, who was found dead on a train over twenty years ago. Swami was a friend of my servant here. We want to find out about the woman he worked for,' Tommy said, taking a small notebook and pencil out of his shirt pocket. Taking notes would make his questioning more official.

They were eager to talk. 'Swami was a good man,' they affirmed, one after the other, and the oldest man said, 'He died in my *busti*. The police – your police – took him there after they were finished with him.' Although it was so long ago, he still sounded angry.

'Was he able to tell you anything about how Mrs Richards died? Did he have anything to do with it?' Tommy asked.

'He would never have harmed her,' they chorused indignantly.

'What did he say?' Tommy asked.

'He kept saying he'd done nothing wrong, only given her tea and her medicine. He said he gave her the same pills every morning but when he went back to help her off the train, she was dead. He couldn't understand what happened,' said the oldest man.

'But she died,' said Tommy.

'Not because of anything Swami did. Her husband prepared her medicines. He told Swami she was only to get one at a time so there was no chance of her overdosing. She was sometimes careless, but there was only one pill left on the morning they got back to Bombay . . . He was sure she couldn't have taken too many, unless she'd been saving them up.'

Tommy looked surprised. The suggestion of suicide was a new one. 'Did Swami think that was possible?' he asked.

The old man shook his head, 'No. He was sure her bad heart killed her. She often complained of it and he used to keep a little flask of brandy to give to her when they travelled. She liked travelling, though. She often went away when she'd been quarrelling with her husband, or her daughter,' he said.

'Why did she go to Madras?' Tommy asked. Sonya had been travelling alone and there were no reasons given for her trip in the police file.

'She went to visit a woman friend who was having a baby. Swami never said anything about where they stayed or what she did there,' his informant told him.

'Do you remember the name of the friend in Madras?' Tommy could not stop himself sounding eager, for he was getting somewhere at last.

'It was Mrs Cameron-Brown,' said the ayah. 'I remember her. She lived in the same block of flats as Mrs Richards, until her husband was posted to Madras. She was a young, laughing woman, but she had bad fate too, because she died in labour soon after Mrs Richards died in the train.'

'It seems as if they were all cursed,' said Tommy sadly as he looked from one informant to the other. He had won their confidence and they were beginning to relax. With relaxation would come loquacity. 'I've heard rumours that

Mrs Richards might have been murdered . . .' He dropped the suggestion like a stone into a pool and waited to see what would happen.

The youngest man was the first to speak. 'People said that at the time because her husband had insured her life. He was not rich till then because he was never a *burra sahib*. After he got all the money, he married again, then resigned his job and went back to England.'

'Tell me about him,' said Tommy.

'He was a quiet man, not noisy or a drinker, but he had not many friends. Lots of Englishmen scorned him.'

'Why was that?' The servants would have their theories; Tommy was certain and he was right.

'Perhaps because his wives cuckolded him – both of them did – but he was not alone in that. The older men turned away from Richards because of the war.'

'The war?' Tommy was puzzled. Kenneth Richards must have been a young man during the war, he reckoned.

'Yes, he was new to India when it broke out, but he joined the army and went to Singapore. The Japanese caught him and put him in one of their camps building a railway. There were other men from Bombay there at the same time and lots of them died, but the ones who came back hated Richards. When he tried to speak to them, they used to turn away and spit on the ground . . . like this.' The speaker spat noisily on to the floor.

'He must have done something pretty bad to earn that insult,' said Tommy.

'So people said,' agreed the oldest servant, 'and he suffered for it.'

'You say his wives cuckolded him. Both wives?' Tommy asked looking around at the faces turned towards him. Each of them nodded in answer to his question. 'Tell me,' he said and put the notebook away to encourage them.

Swami's old friend was the first to start. 'Mr Richards was a timid man, very scared of his wives. They'd both been married to other men first. The Mrs Richards who died had been married to his friend who lived next door, but she moved on to Mr Richards when her husband took a mistress. He thought himself very lucky because she was a fine looking woman. Big and healthy with much yellow hair.'

'How do you know this?' asked Tommy.

'Because I was the cook in the house of her first husband. His name was Redmond and he had a wicked temper, always shouting and hitting her. He was an Irishman and they are hot people. I don't think she was very sorry when he left her.'

'Mr and Mrs Redmond had a child, didn't they?' asked Tommy. He wanted to know what had happened to this other relation of his. Was the child still alive, he wondered?

'Yes, a little girl called Laura. She went with her mother.'

'Tell me about her,' urged Tommy.

The old man shrugged. 'When her mother changed husbands she was sent to school in England, and when she came to Bombay she was a woman. It was difficult between her and her mother then.'

'What do you mean?'

'Although she was only sixteen she was very beautiful and men liked her. Mrs Redmond – or Mrs Richards as she was then – did not like that because she was used to men liking her best. They quarrelled about it many times, shouting and screaming, because Laura, the daughter, had a temper like her father.'

Remembering the details he had committed to memory, Tommy reckoned with surprise that Laura Redmond would have been about seventeen at the time of her mother's death. 'Where was the girl's real father by this time? Did he not take any interest in the daughter?'

'No. He had gone. He went away soon after Mrs Redmond left him. They say he went to America. Mrs Richards used to tell her daughter that he did not care for her and left all the expense of bringing up the girl to her stepfather.'

'How did Laura get on with the stepfather?' Tommy wanted to know next.

The ayah who had been eagerly leaning forward, trying to speak, took up the story at this point. 'Mr Richards was very good to Laura, better than her mother. He had no children of his own and was glad to be a father to her. When her mother died, he did not send her back to England or to her real father, but tried to keep her with him even after he married again. But the new wife would not have that. She did not rest till Laura was sent away.'

'When did Mr Richards remarry?' Tommy asked.

'About six months after his wife was found dead on the train. Once again, he married a woman whose husband left her. They had a big wedding party in the flat.' The ayah made a face of distaste when she said that.

'You did not like his second wife?' Tommy suggested and the response was unanimous.

They all spoke at once, 'No, none of us did. She was not good to us like the first Mrs Richards. The new one bullied everyone. Within a few months she dismissed us all but even the new servants she hired did not stay with her either. She accused everyone of stealing from her, even Laura. There was a bad atmosphere in the house till the girl was sent back to England.'

'Now tell me more about Sonya Richards, the woman who was found dead,' said Tommy, getting to the real reason for his visit.

He saw them exchange glances with each other and the youngest man was the one who spoke first. 'She was good to work for. I was her kitchen boy and everyone said it was sad what happened to her,' he said.

'You mean her dying?'

'Not just that. She changed in the last few years of her life because she fell in with bad people. They spoiled

her.' The others all nodded, and made clucking, agree-
ing noises.

'Who were they and in what way did they spoil her?'
Tommy was curious.

The ex-kitchen boy sighed and said, 'Her women friends
talked her into bad ways, staying out all night, drinking,
meeting other men. She'd have come to a bad end, no
matter what happened.'

'But I thought she had a bad heart. How could she live a
fast life if she was an invalid?' Tommy asked.

The servants looked at each other and shrugged. It was the
ayah who spoke for them, 'She was only ill when it suited
her. At other times she was perfectly well. We joked about
it. That's why we were surprised at her dying the way she
did . . .'

'So you don't think she was as ill as she pretended?'
Tommy asked and was answered by enigmatic nods and
shrugs.

'She could dance all night and play bridge all day; she
could drink as much gin as she liked, she swam and she
went away for the weekends with her woman friends. She
was never ill then.'

Tommy frowned, 'Who were those friends?'

The ayah made a face. 'Loose women, especially
Whitecross *memsahib* and the one they called Belle. They
changed her, made her immoral, took her to places where
she shouldn't have gone. Some people said they met
Indian men in hotels – for money. It might not have
been true, but she had much more money after she met
Mrs Whitecross. But she was a good person when she
first married Richards. She was shy then, but not later.'
Tommy looked at the faces of the servants who were
talking to him and knew that even if he persisted in
asking for details of the old scandals, he would not get
much further.

Servants were very puritanical and disapproved of the

loose sexual mores and heavy drinking of many of the
expatriates for whom they worked. Affairs that English
people took lightly scandalised them. If they liked their
employers, they knew what went on, but did not gloat over
it or pass it on, especially to the police. And he was still
police as far as they were concerned.

They sat silent for a bit before the ayah shot a significant
look at Tommy and added carefully, 'She was of the country,
you know.'

Tommy nodded. To be 'of the country' was to be half-
caste, like him. No secrets, not even that, could be kept
from servants. Sonya's pale skin, English education and
carefully dyed hair would not deceive them. He wondered
if her change of character dated from the time she went
looking for her mother and found out that, not only was
she Eurasian, but that Theresa was dead.

'Who were her parents?' he asked, wondering if they
knew that too. He looked from one face to another, searching
for the fleeting look that would tell him, but Theresa's trail
had apparently been well concealed for the chief gossip, the
ayah, shrugged as she said, 'She was a foundling, taken in
by Britishers in Poona. The English father died long ago but
the mother died in England just before Laura came back to
Bombay. Mrs Richards was very sad when she heard about
her death.'

The afternoon had crept on and Tommy felt his knees
creak when he stood up from his nest of cushions. 'You
have been very helpful,' he said, reaching into his pocket
and distributing money among his informants. They received
it gravely, making folded hand signs of thanks.

'If Mrs Richards was murdered, I hope you find the
person who killed her. She could be demanding but she
was fair, much better than the next wife. We liked her,'
said the oldest man.

'And I loved her daughter, Laura,' chimed in the ayah.

'I'm not a policeman any more, and I don't think anything

could be done now even if I did find out she was unlawfully killed,' said Tommy sadly.

'Ah well, perhaps someone carries the knowledge in their heart and in time they will want to speak,' said the ayah.

A few phone calls to Madras elicited the information that a family called Cameron-Brown had lived in the city in the late sixties. Mrs Cameron-Brown died there giving birth to a still-born child early in 1970 and her husband was moved by his company to Hong Kong, then to Perth, Australia, where he remarried and remained.

Tommy's son lived in Perth, and like his father, was a senior policeman. A letter to him inquiring about a man called Cameron-Brown brought a reply that a man of that name had been killed in a car accident in the late 1980s. If either of the Cameron-Browns had been implicated in Sonya Richards' death, they were beyond questioning or blaming – and it was certainly not them who sent Tommy the mysterious communication from London SW1.

After much thought, Tommy made up his mind. His blood was up. For Theresa's sake he was now determined to follow this trail to the end. 'We're going to London on July the fifteenth,' he told Prakash in mid-May, 'Before we leave you'd better take your month's holiday. Go home to Kerala and see your wife and children.'

Prakash beamed. He owned a neat, white-washed house with a thatched roof in a tidy compound with coconut palms around it and two bullocks in the stable, by the side of a river near Cochin, all bought with money he'd earned during long years of hard work. His wife, Uma, lived there with his son and daughter, both of whom had gone to school. The boy was clever and hoped to study medicine; the sixteen-year-old girl would have a sizeable dowry and his wife was looking for a good husband for her. When Prakash went home for a month each year he was treated like a lord, and sometimes he was also able to bring his wife or the children to visit him in Bombay. He was a prosperous man.

'I'll find a good servant to look after you in my absence,' he promised Tommy and was as good as his word. Often, when a bearer went off on leave, he took care to hire someone inefficient in his place. That way the employer was relieved when the permanent servant returned, and there was no question of him being supplanted, but Prakash sought out the best he knew. He brought Tommy one of the men who talked to him about Sonya and warned him of dire consequences if he did not treat his employer like precious china while he was away.

The plans were made; the tickets bought, and Tommy wondered if he was about to embark on the biggest wild goose chase of his life.

TWELVE

A printer's van delivered two large bundles of printed invitation cards to the Richards' house near Tunbridge Wells, and Kenneth eagerly ripped off the brown paper coverings, while a sceptical Alice looked on.

He took out the top sheaf of cards and examined them closely before saying, 'Good, there's no mistakes. They're perfect.'

Alice lifted one up and said, pointing at two perforated squares along the bottom of the card, 'What're these funny little boxes for?'

'The free drinks. One is detached each time the card holder has a glass of wine,' he explained.

'My goodness, you don't trust them to keep to their ration, do you? But knowing the alcohol capacity of your friends, I expect you're right,' she sneered.

'They're nice looking cards, aren't they?' he said, ignoring her jibe.

There was a thin gold rim round the edges and she tested the thickness of the cardboard, bending it with her finger before she said, 'Mmm, they're a bit like third-rate wedding invitations actually.' She squinted even more than usual in order to read the words on the cards which were printed in flowing italics.

'Since it's the last party, we thought people might like to keep them as souvenirs, so we made the drink tokens detachable,' Kenneth said seriously.

She threw the card on to the table top. 'My God, to

97

think I'm living among people who'll keep a cocktail party invitation because it reminds them of their measly little pasts when they threw their weight around among the natives! It's pathetic, really it is. You're as bad as them too, because you think it's admirable. Wake up, for God's sake.'

He regarded her coldly. 'And what would you keep among your souvenirs if you had any? Old wedding photographs? Divorce papers? Especially divorce papers?'

She was not used to him fighting back and turned on her way to the door to stare at him in surprise. 'What do you mean?' she asked in a slightly different tone. Her pre-marital nursing training was enough to make her wonder how far she'd have to taunt him before he collapsed from a stroke. His colour had been quite high recently.

He stared back at her, his eyes blazing. A nerve was jumping in his cheek and he put up a hand to hide it.

'Nothing,' he replied.

She recovered her aggression. 'If you're not careful I'll have another set of divorce papers to add to my souvenirs,' she snapped.

'I wish you would, I really wish you would but I don't think you will,' he said.

She laughed but without real mirth. 'You're a joke, you know. You're the typical henpecked husband. The nice man married to the bossy wife, according to the neighbours. But I've got old Bombay contacts too, and I know what they say. I know about the act you put on. Sometimes I wonder how much you'll stand; how far do I have to push you before you try to kill me like you killed Sonya. But I won't be so easy to get rid of.'

He sat down suddenly on to a chair by his desk. 'I didn't kill Sonya,' he quavered. It always undermined him when she started on that tack and he usually bolted before she could go any farther, but today she was between him and the door.

'Didn't you? Didn't you, really? In that case it was very

convenient that she died when she did. I had you eating out of my hand, flattering you and buttering you up, and I haven't forgotten how you got drunk and told me about the big insurance policies you'd taken out on each other. I couldn't believe my luck when she snuffed it on that train and nobody even questioned why she died. How did you do it, Ken? I've always wondered.'

He was obviously shaken. 'I didn't kill her. Her heart gave out. The doctor said so. It was as big a shock to me as it was to everybody else when it happened,' he whispered.

She walked back towards him, hissing, 'I could inform on you but it would be difficult to prove. It would make a huge scandal though, but you're used to scandal, aren't you? I remember watching you at her funeral. You never shed a tear. How convenient for you she was cremated. She can't be exhumed. Did you poison her? Did you pay the servant to smother her? Did you tamper with her heart pills? I've always thought that would have been the best way.'

'You're mad, Alice,' he said staring at her as if he was a mongoose being hypnotised by a snake.

'I'm not mad, I'm fed up with you and *bored, bored, bored*! I hate the sight of you. I hate this poky house. I hate your tedious friends. I hate meeting them and seeing how they disdain you. You've never lived down the Siam Railway, have you? I'm amazed that you're so keen to go to that party where there'll still be people whispering behind their hands about you.' She was almost shouting by this time.

He put his hands up to his face. 'No one remembers that any more,' he moaned, but as he spoke he remembered Perkins' cruel jibe.

'But they do. Last time I was up in London I met someone who asked me if I'm still married to the man who betrayed his companions on the death railway. They knew you sucked up to the Japs and fed them information about escape plans, so's you could get extra rice and no more beatings.

'Your colonel, Anstruther, wasn't it? Executed – cruci-fied! – because you ratted on him. It's a miracle the other prisoners didn't kill you, too. I don't expect they had the strength. But they never forgot, did they? And they won't let *you* forget. The ones who survived spread the word. I remember men turning away from you in the club. My ex-husband taunted me with it when I told him I was leaving him for you.' She poured out her venom in an unstoppable flood while he stared at her, appalled.

'He left you first, and no wonder!' he snapped when she finished.

'That's as may be, but he rammed the gossip about you down my throat before he went. By that time it was too late though. I was committed to marrying you.' Her eyes were flashing with fury.

'You were determined to marry me as soon as you heard about Sonya's insurance,' he retorted.

'Well it wasn't for your looks or your performance in bed, I can tell you that. You're pathetic in every department.'

'Except in providing you with money,' he said bitterly.

'You've made your money work for you, I'll give you that. I'm determined to stick to you now, and when you die, I'll spend your precious capital. That daughter of yours – of hers – won't get her hands on it. She had her cut out of the insurance and because she's not your child, she has no claim on your estate. I'm your widow and I'll get everything.' Her face was a mask of fury.

He gave a bitter grin, 'Don't be too sure. You'd better keep me alive as long as you can if you want to go on living in comfort.'

She ran towards him and poked him in the chest with a varnished fingernail saying, 'I've checked on my rights. I'll go to court if I have to. I'd rather the lawyers got the money than your precious Laura. She and her jockey would only gamble it away anyway.'

He grabbed her hand and said, 'I didn't kill Sonya, but

that doesn't mean I mightn't be driven to killing you if you go too far.'

She laughed, 'Making threats! I'll make sure people hear about that. I'll tell my lawyer. I'm going out now so you'd better get on with sending out your cocktail party cards. And remember, lots of the people who get them will remember you as the yellow coward of the Death Railway.'

'I was just a boy. I didn't know what I was doing. I only wanted to get out alive . . .' he moaned.

'You were a rat and you're still a rat. There's nothing you can do to change that, then or now,' she said and stalked away.

As he often did when he fell out with Alice, he telephoned Laura.

She was cooking Irish stew in her kitchen when the wall phone trilled. She lifted it off its cradle and said hopefully, 'Gomez Racing, here.'

'Is that you, darling? It's Kenneth.'

Laura knew from the tone of his voice what was coming, and leaned her back against a kitchen unit, prepared for a long stand. 'Has Alice been giving you trouble again?' she asked.

'Yes, she has. She's just accused me of killing your mother.'

'Oh Kenneth, don't worry, she's said things like that before. She always does when she gets drunk,' said Laura.

'But it's only eleven o'clock and she's stone cold sober. What if she goes and says it outside.'

Laura knew that Alice did say it outside. She'd been at parties where Kenneth's wife had spilled her venom to anyone who'd listen. 'Don't worry. Nobody pays any attention to her. Nobody takes her seriously. Anyway, mother wasn't murdered. She died of a heart attack. It was all properly investigated and there was never any suggestion of foul play.' Laura was endlessly patient with Kenneth, but sometimes she wished he had other confidants to whom he could complain about his wife.

'She actually suggested I paid the servant to smother her. And that I had her cremated so she could never be exhumed.' He did not tell Laura about the Death Railway taunt. That was something he never wanted her to know.

'Oh my God, she's really been going for you, hasn't she?' Laura's eye fell on the kitchen clock. It was three minutes to twelve. 'It's nearly lunch time. Go and pour yourself a gin and you'll feel better. Even if she says mother was murdered – which everyone knows is untrue anyway – nothing could be done about it now. *Nothing!*' The last word was said with great emphasis.

Kenneth was growing calmer. 'I suppose you're right, but it would be very unpleasant if it had to be investigated again or anything like that. You never know what they might dig up. I'll take your advice and try to calm down. I'm sorry to bother you, my dear. Did your horse win the other day? I forgot to back it, I'm afraid.'

'It's just as well you forgot. It lost and we haven't had a winner for weeks. Not only that, but two of the horses have gone lame and their owners are cutting up rough,' Laura sounded despondent.

'Oh dear! That's bad. Would you like a loan to tide you over?' He thought he'd rather give his money to Laura than watch Alice frittering it away.

'I hate taking your money all the time, but a couple of hundred would be a help,' she said, relieved he'd brought the subject up first.

'I'll send a cheque for a bit more than that today. I'll put it in with the cocktail party cards. They've just arrived and they look rather good,' he told her, sounding more cheerful as he remembered this.

'I'm glad. I told Roly and he's looking forward to the party.' This was true. Roly liked going to parties – any parties.

'I'd be so proud if you turned up. You're like your mother, but even better looking, and that's saying something. You'll make every other woman there – including Alice – look plain. I'll add an extra hundred pounds on my cheque for you to buy a really nice dress so you can do me proud. And come in your Mercedes. That always makes Alice spit blood with envy.'

Roly had won a large white Mercedes in a bet a few years ago. Because it was so heavy on petrol, he and Laura rarely used it, unless they wanted to impress. She laughed, 'OK, that's a deal. We'll niggle Alice for you, and don't worry, no matter what she says, you're not going to get into trouble about mother dying. I'm sure of it.'

When he hung up she stayed leaning against the cupboard, with her lower teeth biting into her upper lip and a worried frown on her face until a smell of burning brought her back to her surroundings. The Irish stew was turning black in its pot on top of the Aga.

THIRTEEN

The printed guest list that accompanied the cocktail party cards was avidly read by the far-flung recipients.

'Goodness, is *he* still alive?' was a frequent comment from men as eyes were run down the column of names. Women's feelings were more complicated and much more competitive. There was not one of them who did not immediately begin to worry about what she ought to wear to the party. No one wanted to be later described as having gone to seed, let herself down, or 'aged terribly, darling'.

Tricia Keen, returned from Portugal and reinstalled in the Virginia Water bungalow, bought for her by Jim her current lover, ticked off old acquaintances on the list and pictured them in her mind as she ran her pencil through the names. Julia, green eyed, scatty and wicked, whose clothes were surprisingly frumpy although bought from the most expensive shops in Bond Street. And there was raunchy Belle with her cap of black hair who always dressed like an American co-ed, and acid Alice, the second Mrs Richards, who was never seen without her immaculate make-up and tight-fitting clothes, chosen to draw attention to her lissom figure. The most surprising name on the list was long-suffering Barbara, whose manners and clothes were always those of the upper-class mother – check cotton blouses, long skirts, and flat sandals. Tricia thought that Barbara would have wanted to avoid such a gathering. Dee Carmichael was on the list, too. Tricia had never quite made up her mind what to make of Dee Carmichael.

She stood up and surveyed herself in the gilt-framed over-mantel mirror of her sitting room. Tiny, Titian-haired, full breasted, and pleasantly tanned from a winter in the sun, she still looked pretty good, especially when she pulled the skin back from her eyes with the tips of her fingers. How many weeks were left before the party? she wondered, and counted them off on her fingers – almost six, not long enough for a full face lift perhaps but she could fit in an eye-job to remove those annoying dark bags that always looked worse when she was tired.

So, an eye tuck was the first thing she had to arrange. Then she'd go out to find a really super outfit, something that would make her look like an American millionairess, but most of all, she must find a man to flaunt. It would have to be as young a man as possible because her current protector would not do at all. Poor Jim was far from flauntable.

An idea struck her. She'd hire a gigolo to play the part of her enamoured lover. Wouldn't that annoy the girls! She laughed aloud at the prospect of how they'd react when she floated into the party with a mouth-watering escort.

She was on the telephone to the receptionist of the Harley Street plastic surgeon who had operated on her before, when her brother Gene came in from the car, all dressed in black leather and with an enormous bunch of keys dangling from his back pocket. He'd been named Gene by a film-mad mother after the cowboy star, Gene Autry, but he could not have looked less like his namesake because he was built like a cube. His shoulders filled the doorway as he came in, although he was barely five feet four inches tall.

'When can Mr Sullivan fit me in for the operation?' Tricia was cooing into the receiver, 'Two weeks on Wednesday? Not earlier? You're sure? Oh, all right, I'll take that appointment.'

When she put down the phone she said sulkily, 'I hope I don't bruise too much this time. I don't want to go to the party looking like Mohammed Ali.'

Gene Flanagan threw himself down in a fragile chair that creaked alarmingly under his weight. 'What're you getting cut off now, sis? There soon won't be nuffin' of you left,' he said.

'I'm only having my eyes done again. I've got to go to the Bombay Cocktail Party with a lot of old friends and I want to look my best,' she told him.

Gene was fond of this little sister who'd done so well for herself and he regarded her fondly, 'You look all right now. There can't be many of them looking better than you.'

Tricia's heart-shaped face brightened under her flowing hair and she said, 'D'you mean it, Gene?' When she spoke to him her careful diction was relaxed and she sounded more like her old self, more the way she'd spoken when they were kids growing up together in East London.

As he looked at her he remembered the stroke of luck that took her – and indirectly him – out of their working-class background into another, more exotic world. It all began in 1946 when she was almost fifteen, though she looked much older, for she was voluptuous even then. She went to help out their mother's sister, Sadie, who ran a bed-and-breakfast establishment in a place called Dunoon, somewhere in Scotland. Aunt Sadie had undergone an operation for a women's complaint and asked if Evie (as she was then known) would go north to help her for the summer.

Evie, who had just left school and taken a job in Woolworths, was bored at home in bomb-site blighted London, so she agreed to go for a few weeks. The next thing the family knew was a letter telling them that one of Aunt Sadie's boarders had taken such a shine to Evie that he wanted to marry her. The trouble was that he was a middle-aged bachelor in fragile health. The poor man, wrote Sadie, was in Dunoon recuperating after being a prisoner of the Japanese in Burma. However, he had a good job in India to go back to when he was better, and, said Aunt Sadie, he had plenty of money. That bit of the letter was underlined.

Evie's family in London discussed the proposition. She was an only girl with two tough brothers and a docker father, all of whom treated her as if she was a precious piece of china – for she was indeed very pretty. Her mother, who worked as a counter assistant in a baker's shop, dreamed of her lovely little girl going on the stage, even appearing in films. The late lamented Carole Lombard was nothing to look at compared to Evie, thought her mother. After much discussion it was decided that the suitor should travel to London to be interviewed by the men of the family. Their meeting took place in the cocktail bar of the Strand Palace Hotel.

Bertram Keen was sallow skinned and very thin. His dark hair was streaked with white and he spoke with the sort of well-bred voice that chilled the Flanagan menfolk, rendering them almost tongue tied. Things got easier when he bought them all beers and leaned towards Evie's father to say, 'I've come to ask your permission to marry your daughter, sir.'

This gentlemanly approach stunned Flanagan senior who said, 'Yeah? What does our Evie think about that?'

'She's in favour of the idea. At least that's what she told me,' said Bertram.

'What have you got to offer her?' asked Mr Flanagan, trying to sound like a *pater familias*.

'I'm well off. My job as an oil company executive is being kept for me in Bombay and my salary there will be three thousand a year with annual increments. Besides that, I have money invested in this country and I've inherited my parents' house in Sussex. My father worked for the same company as I do now but he died about ten years ago. My mother died during the war,' the suitor told them while they fought not to allow feelings of astonishment about the size of his salary show on their faces.

'Evie's sixteen in a month's time. How old are you?' asked Gene.

'Thirty-seven,' was the reply. More then twenty-one years

difference. Evie'll be a rich widow when she's still young enough to marry again, was the thought that struck all of them except Bertram.

But they did not commit themselves. Evie had to be consulted first, said her father. She arrived home a few days later, bursting with good health and high spirits. Indeed she wanted to marry her suitor, she said. His age didn't matter because he promised to take her to India, where she'd live a life of luxury and have as much money to waste as she wanted. Even at fifteen, Evie had a firm grasp on practicalities.

It was only when everything was agreed, that Bertram Keen revealed his master plan. He realised that it was not suitable for him to marry such a young girl, he told the family, so he suggested that the marriage be deferred for two years. The Flanagan men looked at him suspiciously. Was he trying to get out of it? they wondered.

'You're not running out on her, are you?' asked Evie's father.

'Oh no, far from it. I'd like us to be married when she's eighteen. That's a less shocking age for the bride of a man of my age. Next month I must return to Bombay but I have a plan for Evie. I want her to go to school,' said Bertram.

'What for?' asked the brothers. Their sister had already been to school and learned everything she needed to know as far as they were concerned.

'To a *finishing* school,' said Bertram.

They looked at him bemused and he went on, 'To the sort of school that'll teach her how to be a lady, how to speak properly and all that sort of thing.'

They drew themselves up defensively but Bertram rushed on, 'You see, in Bombay the British people are very snobbish. I wouldn't want Evie to be at a disadvantage with them. I've picked out a very good school at Eastbourne where she'll learn all the social graces.'

'What social graces? She's a good cook already,' said
Evie's father.

Bertram smiled. 'She'll never need to set foot in a kitchen
when she's married to me. We'll employ a cook. All she'll
have to do is arrange flowers and make conversation. That's
what the school will teach her.'

He was determined that his pocket Venus should have her
rough edges rubbed off so she could fill her future position
as his consort. Bertram may be a romantic but he was also a
crashing snob. Because Evie was determined to marry him,
even if she had to go back to school to do it, the Flanagan
family swallowed their pride and agreed to his terms.

Her time at the school taught her more than social graces.
It also introduced her to the delights of sex as she discovered
her power to attract men – the fathers and brothers of her
schoolmates in particular. When Bertram returned after two
and a bit years, she had renamed herself and answered only
to Patricia. Although she'd been devastatingly pretty when
he left, he found that a beauty awaited him. She'd learned
how to charm and moved around as smoothly as if she was
on tiny oiled wheels. His aspirations for her had all been
achieved. She ate with extreme delicacy, spent hours in
the bathroom, laughed like chiming bells, and spoke like
an actress in a play on the Home Service. Amazingly, she
was still eager to marry him and to take India by storm.

The wedding was a quiet affair with no representatives
of Bertram's family present, and Evie's side were secretly
relieved when the groom whisked her off the next day on a
P&O steamship heading for Bombay. Her new pretensions,
and the biting tongue that she seemed to have developed
while away at school, overawed them.

'Gawd, you've come a long way, haven't you?' said Gene
looking at her admiringly as she poured drinks for them both
from behind a leather-fronted cocktail bar. Nearly sixty now
– although she said she was fifty-four – she still looked like

a fashion model, but was as formidable as a dreadnought. You had to get up early in the morning to put one over Evie, thought Gene.

She frowned slightly as she splashed soda into their whiskies. 'I've not done badly. Money's no problem and I've Jim to look after me, too. The only thing I've missed out on was having any children.'

'Would you have wanted a kid?' he asked in surprise. Although he himself had none either, his older brother had four, who were also parents now, and at the rare family get-togethers, he'd never seen Tricia showing much interest in the junior members. In fact she seemed to go out of her way to avoid them, especially the babies. If anyone passed her an infant, she quickly passed it on like a parcel in a party game.

'I might have at one time, but it's too late now,' she said slowly.

'I don't suppose that Bertram had any lead in his pencil,' said her brother, remembering the gaunt appearance of her late husband. She shrugged. It wouldn't hurt Bertram now to be thought of as sterile, although in fact she'd been the one to blame because, while in the Eastbourne school, she'd fallen pregnant with the child of one of her suitors. Supplied as she was by Bertram with more than enough money, she found an abortionist who often 'helped out' pupils at the school, but the operation was bungled and she was lucky to survive. The terrified headmistress was only too glad to hush up the whole matter, especially since the man concerned was the father of another pupil. Although Tricia subsequently risked pregnancy many times with many different men, she never conceived again.

She turned her sweetest smile on her brother as she changed the subject. 'Talking of that reminds me there's something else I need for the party as well as a new dress and an eye job. I need a man to take me there.'

'What about Jim?' asked her brother, but she shook her

head, 'Jim hasn't enough class for the crowd at this party. He will insist on wearing that gold necklace and all his diamond rings. I don't want to hurt his feelings by telling him they're common.'

Gene, who was wearing a gold necklace himself, bristled, 'They may be common, but they're pricey. Twenty-two carat gold; the best!'

'I know, but they make him look like a bookie.'

'He *is* a bookie. And a bloody big one.'

'I know that, and I'm really fond of him, but I need a young man for this party. I need a toy boy.'

There was no way that bookmaker Jim, a friend and contemporary of Gene's, could ever pass as a toy boy, although his devotion to the fragile Tricia was guaranteed and obvious to all who met them.

'Jim won't like it,' said Gene cautiously.

'He needn't know. I'll just say I'm meeting old friends from my India days. It's only a cocktail party – two and a half hours at the most. I want you to find me a really eye-catching boy to take with me,' said Tricia.

'Why don't you hire one of those agency studs?' asked her brother but she shook her head doubtfully, 'I might have to, but they're usually pretty obvious and often they're gay. I want someone special, a real eye catcher. A young actor or something.'

'I could ask around,' said her brother, but she did not look very optimistic about this offer. Gene had recently come out of prison after serving a short sentence for GBH, and fighting in a Lambeth public house. Since his release he'd worked as a driver for Jim and most of the young men he knew looked as if they were in training to be old lags as well.

'I think it'll be better if I put my name down with an agency. There's one in Shepherd's Market,' she told him, 'but if you do come across somebody that fits the bill, bring him along so's I can have a look at him. A foreigner would be best so there wouldn't be trouble with accents, but nobody coloured.'

'I thought you said it was the Bombay Cocktail Party? Surely they won't mind a coloured chap?' asked Gene.

'They'd not approve at all! They'd be shocked. South African apartheid is mild compared to how most of them feel. Whoever I take with me has to be white,' Tricia told him.

'Can't say I blame them,' agreed Gene, whose own political affiliations tended towards the National Front.

Their conversation was interrupted by the arrival of Jim, slightly tanned from a shorter sojourn in Portugal than Tricia's, but dapper in a pinstripe suit, a grey fedora hat and much jewellery. He embraced her fondly, patting her taut bottom with a proprietorial hand, and glowered at Gene. 'What're you doing hanging round here? You should be working. I thought I told you to drive the boys to Chepstow,' he said.

'I'm off sick. I've got a doctor's note,' said Gene.

Jim despised scroungers. 'What's meant to be wrong with you?' he asked.

'Me stomach's acting up,' Gene told him.

'Oh yeah. In that case you won't be wanting to come with your sister and me for a bite of supper, will you?'

Gene never refused a free meal, as Jim well knew. 'I could maybe manage something,' he said, 'Where are you going?'

Jim turned to Tricia, 'One of my boys was telling me about a good Indian place up town in Mortimer Street. Your brother here can drive us. I thought you'd enjoy a good curry. It'll make you remember your days in India.'

He couldn't understand why both Tricia and Gene burst out laughing.

FOURTEEN

B elle Bolitho was a woman who often said one thing and did another. Her image of herself frequently clashed with her true personality, but although she could be surprised at her own mild reactions to situations, that did not stop her making extreme pronouncements and taking up definite attitudes when talking to other people.

'Of course I simply do not believe in any of those feminist ideas,' she was fond of saying, 'I like a man to hold a door open for me and give me his seat in a bus. I want to be a feminine woman.'

However, when faced with a challenge, or threatened with any defeat or set-back on grounds of her sex, Belle could be more militant than the most violent bra-burner. 'Men! Who needs them? Women are the only people with an ounce of sense,' she often said to her bridge-playing friends.

Yet when her son Hector's marriage broke up, Belle never for a moment considered that his wife might have reason for complaining about his macho behaviour. The ex-daughter-in-law was immediately cast in the role of Cruella Deville.

Throughout her married life, in public Belle sustained a semi-amused attitude towards her husband, talking about him and treating him as if he was a slightly retarded child. When recounting any of his exploits, she would say with a tolerant little laugh, 'He's useless really. But he can't help himself, bless his cotton socks!'

His cotton socks were blessed whenever he reeled home

from a drinking bout, crashed the car or fell foul of a traffic warden, before he was finally warned off. Privately, however, socks, cotton or of any other material, played no part in their relationship and she berated him mercilessly. She never let him forget his misdemeanours. When he died of cirrhosis of the liver, the misery she felt surprised even her. 'I do miss him,' she whimpered, 'I never thought I would but I do, so much.' In fact she'd loved him, with a love that she'd packed away in the back of her mind years ago. It was a surprise even to her when she was faced with it.

Her ability to say one thing and do another guided Belle through life. Inside, she disapproved of hanging and flogging, really quite liked the French and was not appalled by the thought of being part of the Common Market, but she stubbornly admired, and backed up, the most rabidly right-wing representatives of the Tory party. She went to church every Sunday, solemnly nodding during the vicar's tedious sermons that were full of exhortations to his parishioners to lead pure lives, and never gave a thought to her past and the abandoned sowing of her own wild oats. What was past was past, she thought. She'd forgotten most of her younger frolics anyway.

Then Julia phoned up and her voice over the line revived dormant memories. Belle could not decide whether she was pleased to look back or not. 'Yes, we enjoyed ourselves in those days,' she'd agreed cautiously with Julia, but her inner self was saying, We were only young. It was just a phase. The heat, and having nothing else to do, was to blame.

Her inability to take up a position and stick to it, made her swither about going to the cocktail party, but curiosity, always a strong element in her nature, made her avid to see Julia again and to witness her friend's present situation.

In Bombay Julia had led the most lavish life of anyone the Bolithos knew or heard about – even some princely families hardly matched her. Much kudos was cast on Belle when she was appointed to the position of Julia's best friend, although she was always aware that she was there on sufferance. One false step and she'd be cast into the wilderness.

'But if I go to the party with her, I hope she behaves herself. I don't want to get into one of the great Julia rows,' thought Belle. Then she considered ringing up and calling off attending the party as she knew from the past that Julia was capable of causing a great deal of trouble. With a chill, she remembered one Bombay dinner party when Julia went upstairs to the lavatory, stripped entirely naked and came swanning back downstairs with her arms spread out and her eyes closed, pretending she'd had some sort of blackout. The trouble was that it was Julia's own party, thrown in the honour of one of her husband James's company directors, out from London to oversee the Indian company. He was a very important 'visiting fireman' who expected to be impressed and flattered and what he got was his employee's wife stark naked, showing off in front of everyone.

That exploit could have got James fired. As it was, the director swallowed the story that Julia was on tranquillisers after the tragic death of her son and had suffered a nervous breakdown. In a way James's stock went up when the London board heard what a great success he was making of the Indian end of the business, while also coping with a demented wife. Belle knew that Julia was not demented by grief or anything else. She was only out to get at James.

Yet twenty-odd years later they were still together. How unfair that couples like that, who hated each other really, went on in double harness for years when people like Belle and Tom were separated by death. Julia said James might even go to the party and Belle could not resist turning up to see what would happen. Something must. Julia must have a plan, or else why invite the old crowd – and Andy Parnell? Can't bear to miss it, said Belle to herself.

On the morning that her ticket and the guest list arrived, Belle sat at her breakfast bar and perused the names intently. Julia was there, as was James. Tricia was not there but Andy

Parnell was. Belle's own name was near the top of the alphabetic list, so Julia had been as good as her word and bought her a ticket.

She leaned over and picked up the phone, dialling Julia's number which she'd noted down on a pad on the wall. A foreign voice answered, and when Belle asked for Mrs Whitecross, it lisped, 'Wait pleath.' A few minutes later Belle was on the line.

'Darling!' she trilled, 'Have you got your ticket yet?'

'It came this morning. I rang up to thank you for it,' said Belle.

'You *are* coming?' said Julia sharply.

Until that moment Belle had not been *entirely* sure, but Julia was so forceful that she said, 'Of course. I'm looking forward to it. When will I arrive and how do I find you?'

'Will you be driving?'

'I thought I'd use the train,' said Belle. She didn't want to tell Julia that she no longer kept a car.

'Then take a taxi to our address. Come about two and we'll all go up to London together.'

Belle's mind swung into action. A taxi from the station to Wimbledon would cost a fortune. 'Why don't we meet at the party? I could leave my overnight bag in the ladies' cloakroom. That would suit me better because I have things to do in the morning here.'

'Really?' Julia sounded disappointed. She was looking forward to showing off her house to Belle, but that would have to wait till after the party. 'Can't you come earlier?' she asked.

'Sorry darling. I'm committed to my voluntary work. I help out at the local hospital two days a week, pushing a trolley of books round the wards, and I don't get back till after lunch. I don't want to let the other women down because they all work so *hard* – for nothing, you know.' Belle had never done any voluntary work in her life but Julia was not to know that.

Julia silently grimaced at the very idea, but said, 'Oh well, if you have to . . .'

'I'll see you at the party,' said Belle firmly, thinking she'd scored the first victory and wondering if there were more to come.

'Andy's accepted. Did you see his name on the list?' asked Julia.

'Yes,' Belle replied.

'I wonder what he's like now?' Julia's voice was eager and Belle said shortly, 'He sounded all right when I spoke to him, but he'll be older, like the rest of us.'

When she hung up, she sat back remembering the young doctor who'd been pursued by her friend during their last year in India. He was gorgeous – tall and muscular with golden skin and strong legs that looked wonderful when he wore his shorts. His curly black hair glittered in the sun, and his brown eyes were merry because he'd been good natured and kind – too kind to send Julia packing.

He'd also, like Belle herself, been impressed by Julia's largesse and grandiose attitude to life. Everything she did was larger than life and more extreme than normal. She bought her friends, tying them to her by their obligations. She took them up to the hills and paid for everything; she pressed bottles of imported gin and wine on them; she even plied the hard-up with money. When they'd accepted, she called in her dues.

Belle remembered how Julia had pleaded with her husband to build a Hollywood-style swimming pool beside the Whitecrosses' bungalow on Malabar Hill. The progress of this project was overseen by James – who probably saw it as a means of keeping his wife quiet – and watched eagerly by Julia's friends who were promised unlimited access to the pool when it was finished. When inauguration day came, a party was arranged, but Julia refused to swim and would not allow anyone else to do so either. During a frustrating day of sweltering heat, they all sat on Julia's terrace and looked at the silken sheet of aquamarine water lapping at their feet while their hostess railed at her husband, accusing him of every base reason for trying to mollify her with the gift of a pool. Throughout the months that Belle spent in India after that no one ever so much as dipped a toe in Julia's pool except the neighbour's dog that was allowed to swim in it because it suffered from prickly heat. It was Belle's theory that Julia relished not only infuriating James, but tantalising everybody else. Why nobody called her bluff and dived straight into the pool fully clothed was beyond her now.

Another way that Julia demonstrated her power over other people was by her alms-giving. Every Friday morning, precisely at ten o'clock, she appeared immaculately dressed at the gate of her bungalow, accompanied by a servant. There she stood and dished out money to a queue of beggars. Word of this ceremony got around among the indigents of the city and soon there was a mob of desperate people – old men and women on the point of death, frantic women with babies at their meagre breasts, legless men on trolleys, noseless lepers – lined up at Julia's gate every Friday. She employed a Pathan watchman with a long bamboo stave to keep them under control and firmly refused to hand out any money except at the appointed time and to the appointed number of people – always a hundred. The others were turned away and told to come back on the following week. Belle was once inveigled by Julia into helping with this ceremony but it filled her with deep disquiet and she never agreed to do so again.

There was every reason, then, for a niggling little worry in the back of her mind to warn her against Julia's reappearance in her life. There had to be a reason for Julia wanting Belle around to witness whatever she had planned to do at the cocktail party. Once more Belle put up her hand to take down the phone but something stopped her. 'What can she do to me now? Nothing. I'll go and watch,' she told herself.

FIFTEEN

Algy was sulking. He did that sometimes, sitting at the patio table with his head propped up in his hands, giving vent to low groans every now and again. Normally those attacks only lasted for a few hours, but this one went on all day.

Dee stood it until the evening when she was forced to say, 'What on earth is wrong with you? Are you ill?'

He looked up and asked, 'Do I look ill?'

She studied his face. The whites of his eyes were clear, his colour good. 'No,' she said, but he went on brooding.

She tried to read the newspaper but his misery seemed to hang over them like a cloud, obscuring the setting sun, taking the brilliance out of a glorious sunset. At last she yielded, put down the paper and asked, 'Have you hit a block with the book? Is that what's wrong?'

'No, it's going all right. I did two thousand words before you got up this morning.'

'Then for goodness' sake, what's the matter?' she asked.

'I was thinking about us,' he said.

She stared at him. 'Us? What's wrong with us?'

'I don't know,' he replied.

'Is there something wrong with us?' she persisted. They had been living together for almost a year and she had never felt so happy or secure in her life. A chill spread through her when she thought that it was perhaps different for him.

'I was thinking that you're very eager to get away from here,' he said, 'It's pretty quiet after all, nothing happens.

It's not like being in Bombay among all those interesting people.'

'So that's it. You don't want me to go to the cocktail party,' she said. The invitation card and guest list had arrived a few days ago and she had read the names out to him adding potted biographies to many of them. He'd laughed at the time, but he wasn't laughing now.

He sat back in his chair and spread out his hands, 'Of course I want you to go to the party. I don't expect you to share my exile. These people amuse you, so go and see them again. It was a big part of your past, after all.'

She studied his face. The drooping cheeks and long upper lip sometimes made him look like a melancholy bloodhound, as he did now. '*You* amuse me,' she told him.

'Hum,' he said as if in disbelief.

'Do you want me to call off going to the party?' she asked.

'Certainly not. I've been thinking it's probably a good thing for us to have a break from each other,' he replied.

'Yes, you're right,' she snapped back for she was stung, 'perhaps a break is what we need. It seems we might have been getting on each other's nerves.'

'Do you think so?' he asked.

She didn't, but she said, 'Perhaps.' Like children forced into confrontation, they glared at each other.

'When do you leave?' he asked.

She studied the date on the newspaper. It was two days old and had been issued on July the third. 'I'll ring up and book a seat on a plane now,' she said.

She could sense a row blowing up on their horizon like a tropical storm, or one of the spectacular deluges that they occasionally watched sweeping towards them across the Strait of Gibraltar that divided them from Africa. It was important to avoid being swept away by it so she had to stay cool.

'Please yourself,' he said.

120

Made furious by his apparent indifference, she jumped to her feet and ran inside to call Malaga airport. When she returned, with her cheeks flushed, she said, 'I've booked a seat for tomorrow. I'll go to visit my children and take a trip to Scotland before the cocktail party, I think. I haven't been back to see my house since Christmas.'

He was looking deceptively milder by now as he said, 'It's not good to leave property untended for too long, is it?'

She looked hard at him, trying to work out whether he was relieved she was leaving or not. 'I'll have to go to pack,' she said.

'What time's the plane?' he called after her.

'Ten past twelve from Malaga,' she replied as she disappeared through the terrace door.

'I'll drive you there,' he shouted.

In their big bedroom, she pulled out a drawer and tumbled clothes on to the floor. 'He's pleased I'm going. He can't hide it,' she thought.

With her toe she ruffled up her underwear, wondering what to take. Should she pack it all? Was that what he wanted?

For a moment she considered storming back outside and shouting at him. 'Tell me the truth. Is this it? Are we finished?' He'd been married three times after all, and, as far as she was able to ascertain, he'd simply walked out on all the wives. This time he couldn't go anywhere, so she would have to be the one to walk. Was that how he wanted it? The best thing to do, she decided, was to be dignified. Quietly and methodically she packed essential clothes – one bag only. After all she had plenty of others at home. When she came to live with him, she'd only brought thin, summer things. What do clothes matter anyway? she asked herself. She was on the verge of tears.

That night they lay silent, side by side in bed, both staring out of the uncurtained window at a brilliant moon, but pretending to be asleep. They didn't want to speak because they didn't know what to say.

She's keen to go. She's had enough, thought Algy, I'm not going to do anything to stop her if that's how she feels.

He wants me to go. If he didn't, he'd say something, she was thinking at the same time.

Morning found them behaving well, politely passing each other the toast or the coffee pot. Words would pop into her mind, but she bit them back before she said them.

'What would you like me to bring you back from London?' she almost asked before she considered that perhaps he didn't want her to return.

He looked up at her eventually and said casually, 'Did you get one of the bargain fares?'

'I don't think so. I just booked the first available flight,' she said.

'Return?'

'I don't think so. It wasn't a return price. It's always easy to get a seat if you're prepared to take a cancellation,' she said. He nodded. She hadn't said she was coming back, but on the other hand, she hadn't said she wasn't. They retreated again into stubborn silence, both feeling stupidly tongue-tied and insecure, both thinking, why should I be the one to break down?

The two hour drive to Malaga was undertaken in artificial bonhomie. Dee tried to make conversation, pointing out things on the way. 'Look there's a new antique store,' she exclaimed unthinkingly at one point, 'We'll have to visit that!'

He glanced sideways at her, noticing the 'we'. 'Yeah, maybe,' he said, and immediately felt like kicking himself for missing the opportunity to ask her if she *was* coming back.

She registered his tone and felt snubbed. How ridiculous to be acting like children at their age, but they were both stubborn and neither of them was going to be the first to break and admit their insecurity.

He carried her bag into the marble-floored reception area of the airport and stood with her while she queued at the London check-in. They were only just in time and she had to go into Departures at once, so she turned to him, stood on tiptoe and kissed his cheek.

'Goodbye darling, take care of yourself,' she whispered.

His arms tightened round her and he wanted to say, 'Don't go. Stay here.' But he couldn't.

'You, too,' was all he did manage before she disappeared.

In her plane seat she stared out of the tiny window while they lifted up into the sky. There were no clouds and as the plane turned for the north, she saw beneath her the road leading back to the west. One car was driving alone in the middle of an empty stretch and she wondered if it was his.

Stricken, she leaned back and closed her eyes. 'Is this it? Is this the end of my last and best love affair?' she wondered. How foolish to allow the situation to build up between them as it had done. Why did she not swallow her pride and fear of rejection and tell him how much she loved him? Come to think of it, she realised that neither he nor she had ever actually said, 'I love you' to each other. They had come together and stayed together, buoyed up by a mutual feeling of amusement, sexual attraction and comradeship. Their love making was intense, but light hearted at the same time. They were past the stage of hearts and flowers, past the swearing of eternal devotion, past the weeping. The best they had to hope for, she thought, was to spend their last years together in mutual enjoyment and appreciation.

But it's more than that. I do love him, said her anguished inner mind. That was no help if he didn't love her though. If he did, surely he wouldn't let her go so casually. He would have tried to stop her leaving if the reason for his bad temper had only been pique and jealousy. She'd told him that her old friend, who was accompanying her to the party, was gay, so he couldn't feel threatened by him. Did he imagine she was going back to London in search of someone else who might turn up? Was she really going to the party because of nostalgia? Was it still connected with her late husband, Ben? She'd thought long ago that he was out of her system, but now she was not so certain. Could Algy feel unsure of her because of that? Could he possibly be so childish? Or was he relieved to see her go?

As he drove back towards his hill-top home, Adam Byron saw the shadow of her plane cross the road in front of him like an enormous bat of ill-omen.

'Take care of yourself,' she'd said. That was as good as goodbye, wasn't it? Well, OK, if that was what she wanted. It was great while it lasted. He'd lived most of his adult life out of a suitcase and it was only in Spain that he'd put down any roots. When Dee, whom he'd secretly loved for years, came looking for him last September, he had hardly been able to believe his luck.

But perhaps it was only meant to be an interlude. Perhaps he was destined, even programmed, to live in solitude after all. When he reached the house, it was empty because Maria the maid had gone off for her afternoon siesta. He lay down on a sun lounger beside the pool and closed his eyes. There wasn't a sound. Thoughts ran through his head at random. Would she have gone if he'd said to her, 'I'll miss you. I'm scared if you go away you won't come back.'

But he had no claim on her. It wasn't fair to make demands. It wasn't part of their deal. Did they even have a deal? She moved in with him but she knew she was free to go at any time. She'd been back home once without him and it hadn't caused him any concern – so why was he so worried now? Why had he allowed his resentment to blow up into a major rift? Was it because he wanted it to happen? Was it because *she* wanted it to happen?

He was still lying in the lounger when Maria came back

in the evening. He opened his eyes to see her standing over him with her arms crossed. 'So the lady has gone away, has she?' she asked.

'Yes.'

'When does she come back?'

'I don't know. Maybe she isn't coming back.'

Maria snorted. 'Did you ask her to come back?'

'Do I have to?'

She snorted even more loudly. 'You are a fool. I am very fond of you but you are a great fool.'

He sat up and said, 'Why should I be the one to ask? She's off to meet her old friends. She probably prefers them to me.'

Maria was walking away and she said over her shoulder, 'Well you'll know soon enough, won't you? Either she'll come back or she won't.'

'That's what I think,' he agreed.

That night, in their house by the villa's gate, Maria said to her husband Ramon, 'If she doesn't come back, what's going to happen to him? He's miserable already.'

Ramon, eating supper, raised his shoulders, 'There's nothing we can do. They're not children.'

'What worries me is that I don't think they have any idea what they mean to each other,' said his wife.

'Well I don't suppose *you* can tell them,' said Ramon.

SIXTEEN

James Whitecross was a very tall, angular man with neatly cropped black hair that was greying at the temples. Indifferent to fashion, he always wore heavy horn-rimmed spectacles with thick lenses that made his brown eyes look as if they were swimming in water. He was still wearing his glasses when, on a Sunday morning, he posed in front of a full-length mirror in his bedroom and looked at himself, turning slowly to get the full effect of the gorgeous scarlet and gold sari with which he was bedecked.

Langorously he stretched out one bare arm and shook it slightly, making the line of multi-coloured bangles around his wrist jangle. The very white top half of his body was tightly encased in a scarlet silk bodice and round his neck he wore several strings of pearl necklaces. His large feet were stuck into leather slip-on sandals.

On the CD player behind him, Ravi Shankar was playing a morning raga. In rapture James closed his eyes and very slowly performed a few dance steps, swaying like a tree and waving his arms to and fro. On and on he danced, bending seductively in front of the mirror. The silk rustled sensuously round his legs and he imagined himself to be a beautiful temple dancer, performing in front of a rapacious rajah who, without warning, would leap up and ravish him.

His dressing room was at the back of the first floor of his sumptuous house in Wimbledon, and the door was locked, but even then, when he heard his wife's voice shrieking up the stairs, he swiftly unwound the sari from around his waist, bundled it unceremoniously up and thrust it into the back of his wardrobe. He was struggling out of the bodice when the door handle was rattled and Julia's voice called, 'What are you doing? Come out at once.'

Looking vulnerable in striped boxer shorts and nothing else, he opened the door and glared at her. 'Can't I even get dressed in peace?' he demanded.

She was on the landing, leaning on her walking stick, her eyes sharp. 'Dressing up you mean? Pretending to be a beautiful woman? Who were you this time? The Rani of Jhansi or Marie Antoinette?'

The last notes of Ravi's sitar died away on the CD player and she smiled, 'An Indian temple girl, obviously. You've forgotten to take off your bangles, darling.'

With one hand over his wrist he watched her limping back downstairs and felt an enormous surge of hatred fill his heart. Would he ever be rid of her, he wondered? It would be so unfair if he was the first to die because only death, he knew, would break the contract between them.

All pleasure gone he turned back into the room, pulling the bangles over his hand. He bought his Indian clothes from little shops in Walworth and greatly enjoyed searching about among the fabulous swathes of fabrics for the saris he wanted. He had them all carefully folded up on a top shelf in his wardrobe, glittering greens shot with silver, purples threaded through with gold, creams and yellows, blues like the sky and scarlets like blood. No one but himself was ever allowed into that particular part of his private sanctum and he imagined it was his secret. But not from Julia, of course. She had a genius for nosing out his innermost thoughts and desires.

As he put on his everyday clothes he remembered the first time he ever saw the group of Indian dancers who sparked off his most cherished secret fantasy. It was a long time ago, two weeks after his son Max was born in Breach Candy Hospital, Bombay. When he and Julia brought the child home, the servants were ecstatic, for the birth of a son was highly auspicious, and that night, when James was settling down to his sundowner whisky, he'd heard the sound of drums. He'd walked on to the terrace and was confronted with seven or eight Indian women dancing most elegantly in his garden. Their thick black hair was wreathed with flowers, bangles jangled round their wrists and their saris made a whirlpool of colour that entranced him as they circled round, bowing, bending and clapping their hands. Surprised, he'd called to Julia who came out too, carrying the baby wrapped in a blue blanket.

'What's happening, darling?' she'd asked.

They had been in Bombay for a few months and married for only two years. The discordances between them were not yet manifest. James put an arm around his wife as they watched and their bearer appeared saying, 'They've come to dance for the baby boy. It will bring him good fortune,' he told them.

'Who are they? How did they know about the baby?' James asked, realising for the first time that there was something odd about several of the dancing women. They were raw boned and rangy, not feminine at all in spite of their ogling eyes.

'We sent for them,' said the bearer, 'It is always done. They are eunuchs who dance so that your son will not become like them. So he will be a real man – not a lady-man.'

James looked at the dancers again. Their kohl-rimmed eyes flashed challengingly at him and he realised with a shock that they were all men dressed as women, 'God, they're men!' he exclaimed to Julia.

She recoiled. 'Send them away. Send them away at once! I don't want them in my garden!' she exclaimed and ran back inside.

Yet when James was handing over a few rupee notes to pacify the dancers for not being allowed to perform their routine, he felt a peculiar thrill. He longed to know what it felt like to swathe yourself in silk, to smile and flirt, to pretend to be a woman. A few months later, he yielded to the impulse and began dressing up. The first time he did it was a week after Max was found dead in his cot. He'd been perfectly well when put to bed by the ayah who slept on the floor beside the child all night. Early in the morning, when she woke, the woman found that the baby was cold and not breathing. He had died during the night without as much as a whimper.

It was the bearer who had the thankless task of breaking the news to the parents. James was stunned into silence but Julia went completely berserk, screaming and howling, tearing out her hair with both hands, banging her head against the wall. He was seriously afraid she was about to kill herself.

The terrified ayah, hearing the din, took to her heels and was never seen again, but in spite of Julia's conviction that her child had been deliberately smothered, the English doctor who turned up from Breach Candy said that Max had simply died in his sleep.

'There's no explanation for it. Perfectly healthy babies can die unexpectedly like this. It's a mystery. I'm so sorry,' he said cradling the pathetic little burden in his arms and looking almost as devastated as the parents. He took Max's body away for forensic tests, but, as he warned them, nothing significant was found. Max had simply died, breathed out for the last time and never breathed in again.

Julia was inconsolable and had to be tranquillised for a long time. It was then that her character changed. The doctor came to see them frequently, and after one of his visits, he took James aside and said, 'I think the best thing you can do is try to get her pregnant again.'

So they took a trip to Ceylon but she refused to sleep with him and spent the nights prowling their hotel bedroom, keening like a wounded animal. He was considering sending her home for recuperation and mental treatment, when she woke up one morning in a very different mood. Now she was brittle and febrile, set on making her mark in Bombay society.

'We're going to throw a party,' she told him, 'We're going to invite everybody we know, all the people in your tennis club, all the young mothers I met in the maternity clinic, all the neighbours . . . It'll be the best party they've ever had in this terrible place.'

'Do you think that's a good idea? Are you ready for giving parties yet?' he asked cautiously.

'Of course I am,' she told him, and she was. The party was a huge success because most of the guests knew nothing about the baby's death. James endured the din, music and drunken revelling, reflecting that, although it cost a fortune in bootleg liquor, it achieved its objective by launching his wife into society.

Never again did she utter Max's name in her husband's hearing. She seemed to put the child out of her mind completely and embarked on a series of wild affairs which he tolerated. He even paid for her weekends away and lent her his company car and driver so that she could take one of her lovers, a young ship's doctor, up to the hills. From then on her behaviour became more and more bizarre and their marriage degenerated into a token affair. Everyone knew she slept with anyone who asked her – anyone except James for she refused to share a bed with him.

He knew he could have divorced her – there were plenty of grounds – but somehow it did not matter too much. Everyone assumed he must have native mistresses because he was a good-looking, virile and successful man, but he took his comfort in dressing up, play acting for himself in front of the wardrobe mirror. Sex with Julia had never meant very much to him anyway, and he was better satisfied by bringing himself to orgasm by the soft caress of his saris and the rhythmic Oriental music that he played as a background to his fantasies.

He knew that the people were intrigued by his peculiar

marital situation and often he sat alone in his study wondering how it happened. The son of a low-ranking policeman and a quiet woman from the Western Isles, James was a clever boy who went to Glasgow University to study engineering. He was not a sociable animal but one night, in his third year, he went with some friends to a university 'hop' where he saw Julia across the dance floor and was stricken as if by a thunderbolt. He knew he had to have her. To him she was a flickering flame, darting around from group to group, giggling, talking, inclining her head like a dancing daffodil. He couldn't take his eyes off her. When they eventually met, he was tongue-tied but she took his silence for indifference and was stung by it. He was a tall, dark and imposing young man who never showed his feelings on his face. She was in her first year of English – her first and only year – and she dropped out after a round of disastrous exam results. She never did any work and had no ambition to end up with a degree. They went to the cinema and she talked while he listened silently, drinking her in. She went out of her way to enrapture him and he had no idea what a prize he'd captured till one of his friends said, nodding after Julia who was walking away after stopping to tease him, 'You're a crafty bugger, aren't you? You'll never need to work if you marry her.'

'What do you mean?' asked James.

'Don't pretend you don't know who she is,' was the reply. He shook his head, 'I know who she is. Her name's Julia Stevenson.'

'Yes, Stevenson of Stevenson and Lambert,' said his friend and James gasped for Stevenson and Lambert was a huge shipbuilding company that dominated the industry of the Clyde. 'Stick in there,' advised James's friend, 'and it'll be a seat on the board for you.'

'I don't want a seat on the board,' said James truthfully. All he wanted was Julia. To him, used to his parents' gloomy, linoleum-floored flat in a Clydebank tenement and their grim and humourless lives, she was like a creature from another planet. She dressed in expensive clothes, smoked through a long ivory cigarette holder, and drank many gins and orange which she ordered without a thought to whether or not he could afford to pay for them. He'd have starved rather than refuse her anything and was kept in a continual fever of suspense and sexual desire by her capriciousness. He was a high-calibre student and eventually graduated with a first-class degree and several job offers. He accepted the one with the largest salary and on the same day proposed to Julia, who, to his surprise, accepted him. Her family were not so ready to accept the policeman's son however. He was summoned to their red Art Deco mansion in Milngavie to be interviewed by her father and their lawyer.

His patent honesty and steadfast insistence that he would want to marry Julia even if she was penniless, convinced them he was not a fortune hunter. However, she was an only child with immense expectations and it was agreed that her money would be hers alone and he would have no expectations at all from her father's estate. The final stipulation was that Julia should be paid a monthly allowance of 'only two hundred and fifty pounds'. The sum was to be reviewed every two years. Two hundred and fifty pounds was roughly what James's father earned for six months' work and he was astounded, especially because the men facing him in Mr Stevenson's library seemed to think it niggardly.

'You realise that you will be responsible for everything else she requires and for maintaining her in the style to which she is accustomed,' he was warned and he nodded. Permission for the marriage was thereupon granted.

The lawyer saw him out into the marble-floored hall and on the front doorstep put a hand on his arm as he said, 'Good luck, young man. I hope you realise what you're taking on. What her father didn't tell you is that he's putting a limit on her allowance, not to keep it from you, but for her own protection. She's not *unstable* exactly but she has no money sense at all and is liable to spend thousands if given her head. They've had a lot of trouble with her in the past . . .'

James didn't care. He'd have married her if the lawyer had told him she was a homicidal maniac.

In the beginning he thought it was his fault that their sex life was disappointing because he'd been a virgin on his wedding day, as she was, too. In actual fact, they were both out of love after only a few months but Julia soon became pregnant and overcoming a sense of disillusion, they settled down to married life. When high-flying James was offered the chance to apply for a big job in India, they were both enthusiastic. Going east would change everything, they thought. But it didn't. Things between them only became worse.

The situation drifted from the unsatisfactory to the disastrous, and after Max's death, Julia seemed to lose her mind. Torn between pity and indifference, James stayed with her, employing every means to mollify her and keep her quiet. He never lusted after other women, for his basic drive was to succeed in business, and his sexual urges were sublimated in his dream existence as a seductive siren. Julia raved away on the edge of his life, trying to touch him, but he was blandly indifferent to anything she did or said. It could go on like that until one or other of them died, as far as he was concerned.

When he went downstairs after she'd interrupted his moment of privacy, she was sitting in her wing chair staring bleakly out of the window.

'I wish Max had lived,' she said.

He stared at her. It was the first time the boy's name had been uttered between them for more than twenty years.

'So do I,' he whispered.

'I want you to come to the cocktail party with me,' she said.

'All right, I'll come,' he told her.

SEVENTEEN

hings just happened to Kenneth Richards. From childhood it seemed to him that he floated through life like
a twig floating in the middle of a river, pushed to and fro by
the current, diverted by rocks and eddies, always controlled
by other arbitrary forces and not making any major decisions
for himself.

His parents chose his school; his father found him a job
through friends; his wives spotted, tracked him down and
married him. He made none of his own decisions and went
along meekly with whatever he was asked to do, taking the
easiest way out.

By and large it worked quite well, he thought. His first
wife Sonya had been good looking, sweet natured, amusing
and faithful – at least at first. She brought a bonus into
the marriage in the shape of her daughter, Laura, whom he
loved dearly.

Alice was different. She moved in with him after Sonya
died and he was flattered because she was handsome, a
good housekeeper, amorous (also at first), and an excellent
hostess. They drifted on together for a while but recently
their life together was conducted in an atmosphere of
sustained irritation, which was degenerating into outright
warfare. If only she would calm down and not expect so
much of him!

His presently fraught domestic arrangements however
were idyllic compared to the part of his life when he'd
felt most powerless and prone to outside forces. That was

during the war when he found himself a prisoner of the Japanese who marched into Singapore, where he was part of the garrison, and swept him up in their relentless military machine.

Forever afterwards he tried very hard not to think about the Siam Railway, not to remember his misery, his belly-aching hunger, the wretchedness of continual diarrhoea, the cruelty of the guards and the sight of men continually dying around him. The only way to survive, he'd decided was to let things happen, to drift along, and not stand on his principles. When one of the guards started to give him an extra handful of rice every now and again, he accepted it gratefully and gulped it down. When another spoke to him in broken English, he answered politely, not swearing or spitting as so many of the other prisoners, especially the Australians, did.

A sore on his leg broke out into a fearful purple wound and oozed puss. Terrified of gangrene, he tried wrapping green leaves round it and was caught doing this by the friendly guard who slipped him a medicated dressing. The wound healed. It was difficult to remember how or why he began informing on his comrades. The questions were quite innocuous at first. One day the English-speaking guard asked him if he prayed to his God. 'Of course,' said Kenneth without thinking.

'Do the other prisoners pray to their God?' he was asked.

'I suppose so. The padre prays with them,' Kenneth told him.

'Where do they meet?' He pondered that and said that the prayer meetings were held in different places, usually out of the hearing of the guards.

'What do they pray for?'

'For their families at home. For safe deliverance. For an end to the war . . .' He didn't add that he'd heard prisoners praying for death, both for themselves and for their captors.

Little by little the questions became more specific. Who was the most important man in the camp, who was most respected? There were four or five senior officers among the prisoners but Kenneth told the guard that the man everyone looked up to was Colonel Anstruther, a fair-minded, staunch type who kept up the morale of everyone.

It did not take very long before the other prisoners noticed that Kenneth was receiving favours from the guard – the occasional half-smoked cigarette, a bit of smoked fish. They disapproved of him for accepting.

'Jap lover!' they jeered, and so he began trying to cover up his friendly conversations with the guard. One day, on a stinking hot morning, the commandant asked to see him. He was marched away by two guards he did not know and he was so scared that he could hardly see. He stumbled and almost fell as he crossed the baked earth in front of the huts. Faces of other prisoners watched from the shadows, obviously thinking that was the end of him. The commandant began by hectoring him, shouting that he was a British oppressor, a hound dog, an object of hatred, a coward and a man to be scorned for allowing himself to be a prisoner of a superior race. He stood with his head bowed waiting for a sword to descend on him and separate his head from his shoulders. He felt pee soaking his tattered shorts and trickling down his stick-like legs and knew the guards saw it too.

Instead of being murdered however, a proposition was put to him. If he eavesdropped on his fellow prisoners and reported any suspicious conversations to his guard friend, his life would be spared and not only that, but he would occasionally be thrown into solitary confinement, without being beaten and starved, as was usual. Instead, away from the others, he would be given extra rations and allowed to rest. It was the only way to survive this hell, he thought, and so he accepted.

How many times was he to regret passing on the news

that Colonel Anstruther was encouraging an escape attempt by three desperate men – a Scot, a Yorkshireman and an Australian. Their friends were to create a diversion so they could get away in the confusion. They probably knew there was little chance of surviving in the jungle but they were prepared to take the chance.

The day after Kenneth passed on his information, he was marched off to solitary again with guards beating his back with staves to make his arrest look plausible, and while he was away the attempted breakout was staged and thwarted. The Colonel was taken into custody, summarily sentenced and crucified in the blazing sun in front of his lined-up men. All day long they had to stand and watch him dying slowly and silently with his blond head hanging down on to his chest. When the sun set one of them sneaked up to the terrible cross and stabbed Anstruther with a specially sharpened table knife so that his agony would cease. For that act of deliverance, the man was beheaded, as were the three would-be escapers.

Before he died, one of them had the opportunity to pass on the news that he had seen Kenneth in the prison block being feted and given sake by the guards. The obvious conclusion was reached and when he returned to normal conditions, he was set upon by furious men.

'You bastard. We're going to kill you. You told, didn't you?' said one man who was sitting on Kenneth's chest and thrusting his face down, but before he had time to carry out his threat, the guards burst in and Kenneth was taken away again. He spent the rest of his time in the camp alone, segregated for his own safety. By the time the prisoners were freed the few who survived were too ill and emaciated to kill a fly. He was very ill himself, suffering from malaria and hepatitis, but the only surviving prison doctor refused to treat him, so he was taken to hospital in Calcutta. Fortunately for him, none of his fellow prisoners went with him, but, in time, gossip of his inglorious war got out and even men who had not been on the Railway scorned him. He was never able to live it down.

The rest of his life was spent trying to atone for the terrible thing he'd done. He never gossiped with malice, he never cheated or indulged in double dealing, he tried to think well of everyone, he gave to beggars and went regularly to church, shouldering any voluntary work there without complaint. When newcomers arrived in Bombay where he spent his working life, he went out of his way to speak to them, to invite them out, to ease their way into society. He was a willing workhorse for his employers and for people like Marian and Peter, who made use of his eagerness to help with anything they asked.

Yet he was only tolerated. Even people who did not know the Death Railway story, thought that he was 'a queer fish'. Recipients of his kind attentions wondered suspiciously when he was going to show himself in his true colours. He could never find out if Sonya knew about his past or not, but to do her justice, if she did, she never referred to it or threw it in his face as Alice did.

When Sonya died, he was not surprised that he was an object of gossip and malice, but drifted on, apparently unaware, for after all he was inured to people whispering about him behind their hands. He'd long ago become used to fulfilling the role of the man in the background, the support force. He was 'good old Kenneth'.

Unusually for him, he was allowing himself to feel dispirited on a bright morning, ten days before the cocktail party, when he carefully put the party's bank statement and a list of the people who had paid their ticket money into his brown leather briefcase and took himself off to London.

The thought of what he was carrying raised his spirits a little because he had received the staggering sum of £2,570 from would-be party-goers, which represented several voluntary donations as well as payment for two hundred tickets. Marian and Peter would be over the moon when they heard, he reckoned. There had never been so many acceptances for one of the cocktail parties before, not even when it was first launched.

Before he went to St George's Square, however, he had an appointment with his lawyer who had an office off Fleet Street. The lawyer greeted him warmly because Kenneth was a man of substance who had always been very careful with his money, increasing his capital bit by bit year after year; a quality that lawyers admire.

'I've come about my will,' said Kenneth when he was seated.

The lawyer had Mr Richards' file on the desk awaiting his arrival, so he nodded, and lifted the will off the top of his papers. 'Ah yes,' he said in a noncommittal tone, as if he'd expected that.

For a moment Kenneth wondered if he looked or sounded feeble enough to be on the verge of death, but then reckoned that at his age a concern about his will was most probable.

'It was made fifteen years ago. They all need updating from time to time,' the lawyer added encouragingly, sensing his client's discomfiture.

'Yes. I'd like to leave my entire estate to my stepdaughter, Laura, and after her, everything is to go to her son, Lance,' Kenneth told him.

The lawyer ran his eyes down some other papers before him. 'It's a considerable estate, Mr Richards. Well over £800,000.'

'It's more than that,' said Kenneth who had a sharp mind for money, 'My house is worth more now than it was when the will was made and I've increased my capital, too.'

'Well done. But if this is all to go to Mrs Laura Gomez, what about your wife?'

Kenneth had anticipated the question. 'Well there's a certain problem about that. I want you to advise me about what I should leave to her,' he said.

The lawyer put his finger tips together and looked over the top of his glasses at his client. 'You and your wife are on bad terms?' he asked.

He had met Alice once fifteen years ago when she came into the office with Kenneth and only remembered her as a leggy, attractive blonde who looked much more sophisticated than her husband.

'We are not on very good terms these days,' said Kenneth cautiously.

'Does she know you are changing your will?'

'Well, not exactly. In my previous will I left her the house and a considerable sum of money as I recall.'

'You did,' said the lawyer leafing through the papers before him, 'and if you predecease her, she will of course have a claim on your estate. You can't leave *everything* to your stepdaughter.'

'What if Alice and I were not legally married?' asked Kenneth.

The lawyer's face expressed surprise, 'But you refer to her as your wife?' he said.

'Yes and she refers to me as her husband, but in fact she has never divorced her first husband. She's a bigamist but she doesn't realise I know that. You see her husband Mike Field simply vanished one day. Got on a plane and flew away, leaving her high and dry. There was also a little unpleasantness with his company – he worked in insurance. Apparently he went off with the contents of the office safe. They never caught up with him – and neither has she.' There was a note of satisfaction in Kenneth's voice as he spoke and the lawyer sat back with a surprised expression on his face. This man whom he always thought of as a nonentity was showing an unexpected side.

'Is she aware that you know the marriage is bigamous?' was his next question.

Kenneth shook his head. 'It was easier to go along with

her. We married in a civil ceremony and she produced documents – I've no idea where she got them. I've never challenged her about the matter.'

'But are you sure? If she had documents she might have obtained a divorce.'

'No she hasn't, because a couple of years ago I had a letter from him, an attempt at blackmail. I ignored it.'

The lawyer groaned and put his head in his hands. 'Mr Richards, this is very confusing. In what way was it a blackmail attempt?'

'He wanted £10,000 or he'd go to the police and accuse Alice of bigamy.'

'How were you to pay him?'

'It was to be paid into a numbered bank account – Swiss I think.'

'What did you do?'

'Nothing.'

'Have you kept the letter?'

'No.'

'Did you show it to your wife?'

'No. I thought it was best to see what would happen next and nothing has done.'

'A policy of creative inaction,' mused the lawyer, thinking for a moment before he said, 'The husband might have died since then.'

'He might,' agreed Kenneth, 'but even if he has, Alice and I have not married legally. She can't suggest it now really, can she, or then I'd know it was bigamous from the beginning? I go on from day to day as usual, biding my time. She'll be furious when she finds out that I've known all along. My only regret is that I won't be there to enjoy the scene, so I would be obliged if you don't write to me about this because she reads all my mail. I want it to be a surprise for her – when the time comes.'

'Isn't that rather cruel?' asked the lawyer, but Kenneth said nothing.

Instead he asked again, 'What exactly do you think I should leave her?'

'Under the circumstances, you could make it nothing but I assume that over the years you've been together you've introduced her to people as your wife. You've given her your name, you've co-habited, and claimed the married man's tax allowance?'

'Of course, because I wasn't meant to know that our marriage is bigamous. I was duped by her,' Kenneth sounded put upon and peevish.

The lawyer groaned as if he wished his client hadn't told him so much. 'I presume your relationship has deteriorated. If it hadn't, would you have persevered in pretending you didn't know? Would you have treated her in the will like a legal wife?'

'Yes, I would and I want to put a bit into the will saying so.'

The lawyer got up and walked over to stare out of his office window, standing with his back to Ken and his hands in his trouser pockets. 'My advice is that it would be best to be moderate and flexible, not too revengeful. You don't want your – er – wife rushing into a lawsuit against your stepdaughter. I suggest that you be more generous than is absolutely necessary, but put in a clause saying that if she disputes the will she will receive nothing. That usually works in difficult cases.'

Kenneth nodded, 'All right. How much do you suggest?'

'You could leave her a life rent of your house and the income from a specific sum of money – say £100,000. That's fairly generous under the circumstances. I assume she has not contributed any capital to your establishment during your marriage, and since you've not run a business, she hasn't contributed to your earning capacity either?'

Kenneth nodded again. 'Most of my money originally came from an insurance policy in the life of my first wife who died from a heart attack, and the rest I've made myself by investing in the stock market. It's been a long-standing hobby and I want the profits to go to Laura. After all, the insurance money came to me because her mother died,' he said.

And so it was decided. Alice would have the house to live in but not to own, and her income would be only just enough to run it. She would not be able to bequeath anything to anybody else on her death – everything would eventually end up with Laura or Lance. An appointment was made for Kenneth to visit the lawyer again in a week's time so he could sign the redrafted will because it could not be sent to his house in case Alice saw it.

Ha ha, he thought as he left his lawyer's office.

He was euphoric when he reached his second stopping-off place of the day. Marian's house was looking lovely with burgeoning window boxes at the two big ground floor windows and neatly clipped bay trees standing like sentries on each side of the front door.

She greeted him warmly, 'Come in, dear Kenneth. It's so hot we're in the garden and drinking Pimms. I'm sure you'd like one, too.'

He accepted with a smile and followed her down a flight of stone steps into a pretty, sunken garden where a fountain splashed away gently, surrounded by russet-coloured Japanese maple trees. His bonhomie was not even dispelled by the sight of Perkins sitting in a deck-chair with a glass in his hand. This time he was dressed in a cream seersucker suit and – horror of horrors, thought Kenneth – pink shoes.

There was no sign of Alex, who was presumably working, but Peter was dispensing drinks with his usual generous hand. As his fingers closed round a chilled, moist glass Kenneth raised it towards his hosts and said, 'Well, here's to our party. I'm glad to say it's been a sell-out!'

Marian squealed girlishly, 'Darling! Do tell. How many are coming?'

Kenneth grinned, 'Including ourselves, two hundred, and there will probably be more wanting to pay at the door. There have been several donations, too, so we have the grand sum of £2,570 in the bank.'

Even Perkins looked impressed and Marian was positively skipping over the grass. 'Wonderful, wonderful,' she carolled, 'Our expenses and overheads won't be more than £1,500. That leaves us with more than a thousand! What will we do with it?'

'Perhaps we should give it to a charity,' suggested Kenneth.

Perkins sneered, 'Exactly which charity would you suggest – Alcoholics Anonymous? An association for fallen women?'

Kenneth looked at him with loathing, 'No, I was actually thinking about something like Mother Theresa's organisation or the Salvation Army. They used to do a lot of good work in Bombay.'

'Oh yes,' agreed Perkins, 'I remember they looked after all the old chi-chi drug addicts in Colaba Causeway and all the broken-down tarts. But then your first wife was chi-chi, wasn't she? Their welfare must be close to your heart.'

Kenneth gasped. How the hell did Perkins know that about Sonya, he wondered? She never told anyone about her background and he himself only found out by accident when he saw her birth certificate after they married.

Marian was not prepared to put up with such calculated cruelty in her house, however. 'Let's get back to the matter in hand,' she said firmly, 'What are we going to do with the surplus money? We can't keep it in hand till next year because there isn't going to be another party. I think we should have a raffle, give everybody a free ticket when they come into the party and use the money to buy a really good prize. It'll have to be something worthwhile.'

This problem was debated for a while and in the end they decided that instead of raffling several smaller prizes, they should aim for one mammoth prize that was really worth winning.

'What about two air tickets or a travel package to a destination of the winner's choice – perhaps Bombay?' suggested Peter and everyone looked at him with admiration.

'That's clever of you, darling. There are a couple of people on the list with business links to travel companies and airlines. We could ask them to get us a good deal for a package, couldn't we? Yes, that's what we'll do. I'll organise it,' said Marian, glancing at the clock. It was nearly half past four, time to see her guests off the premises.

EIGHTEEN

A frantic round of visiting her children kept Dee busy on her return to Britain, but did nothing for her peace of mind. Eventually she hired a car and after a while, found herself back in her Scottish cottage where she sat by the fire – it was unexpectedly chilly for July, especially for someone used to Andalusia – with her chin in her fists staring into the flames.

'What am I going to do?' she wondered, 'Do I act in a sophisticated way and just let it go with him? Do I pretend it was only an interlude? Will I be able to act with dignity if we ever come across each other again?'

But she knew it wasn't a casual interlude. Already she missed him so badly that she felt there was a huge, black aching void inside her. She rose from her chair and went over to look out of the sitting room window into her garden. The man she'd paid to keep it tidy had done a good job but it looked like a well-brought-up but unloved child, tidy but unspontaneous. It needed a loving owner to wander through it every morning, speaking to the flowers, deadheading the roses, yanking out the bindweed, staking top heavy lupins.

'I'll move back in after the cocktail party,' she told herself. On the window shelf the old-fashioned phone squatted like a black frog, staring at her. Unable to resist, she lifted the receiver and dialled his number in Spain.

It rang and rang. Where was he? It was nearly dinnertime. He couldn't be far away. She put the phone down and walked across the room, wringing her hands, unconsciously adopting a mannerism of her mother's that used to irritate her almost beyond endurance. On impulse she dashed across the room again and redialled the number. This time it was answered after the fifth ring.

'Hello!' he barked.

'Hi!' she chirped, artificially cheerful, 'It's me.'

'Oh yeah, where are you?' His voice was not giving anything away.

'In my cottage in Scotland. It's looking lovely. The weather's perfect,' she gabbled.

'Good. It's nice here as well. I was swimming just now . . .'

So he wasn't languishing in a darkened room anyway. She closed her eyes and saw the azure blue pool that he'd had built right on the edge of the hill so that when you swam in it you felt as if you would be able to strike out into the ocean. An infinity pool, he called it. They'd swum in it naked and made love in the water when they were alone in the house. She felt her skin prickle at the arousing memory and mentally chided herself, At your age!

'How's everything?' she asked, hoping he'd say, 'Awful. Come back. I love you.'

'OK,' was the reply, however.

'How's the book?' she persisted.

'Nearly finished, but I've got an idea for the next one.' He had the most fertile brain of anyone she'd ever met.

'Great,' she said weakly, and then added, 'Well, it's nearly supper time. I'm going to grill a kipper.'

That interested him. 'Kippers! I haven't had a kipper for years.'

She nearly said, 'I'll bring some back for you,' but then she remembered he hadn't asked her to return so she bit the words back.

'I'll ring again soon,' she said.

147

'When's your cocktail party?' he asked.

'In four days. I've hired a car and I'll drive down to London the day after tomorrow.'

'Have a good time,' he said, and after a slight pause, rang off.

She was left standing with the receiver in her hand and chucked it across the floor. It flew through the air for the length of its wire and bounced on to the carpet. 'Why can't I say it?' she shouted aloud, 'Why can't I tell him? I'm behaving like a stupid teenager.'

But then, so was he.

After the call finished he stood barefoot on the marble floor and stared across the open patio to the shimmering pool. Shit! he thought, because he knew he should have said more to her, opened up a bit. But she sounded so cocky, so pleased to be back in her home. Maybe she was telling him that it was over. His pride made him think, If that's how she wants it, that's how she can have it. He'd never run after women, or fallen over himself to please them like some men did.

That night he drove down to Tarifa and sat morosely in the café, indifferently watching pretty girls parading past him. Heavily disgruntled, he returned home and sat out until after midnight, finishing the latest John Grisham and wondering why his agent didn't demand the same high advances as Grisham was paid. When he reached the last page, he sent the book skittering across the paving stones into the shrubbery. He was in a very bad mood indeed.

I need a change, he thought, Everything's gone stale on me. I need to get away. Where will I go?

The house was empty and seemed to be full of a silence that hung in the air like a curtain. He padded through to the kitchen and poured a generous slug of whisky into a glass and sipped it, standing with his back against the purring fridge which seemed to be about the only living thing for miles around. He spoke to it.

'She was pretty keen to go, wasn't she? Not as much as a backward glance.' The fridge hummed agreement.

When the whisky was finished, he poured another and carried it into the sitting room. Maybe he should have tried to stop her, but what if she'd said she was going anyway? Squatting on his heels he let his eye run along the books in a shelf that lined the back wall, for he felt it was essential to find some other escapist fiction to take his mind off his unaccountable dissatisfaction.

Dee had added some of her favourite books to his own, and he looked at the titles. Books by Trollope, Graham Greene, Evelyn Waugh and Nancy Mitford. Dee'd laughed a lot when she reread *Love in a Cold Climate*, and *The Pursuit of Love*.

'You should try them,' she'd said when he poured scorn on her preferred reading, saying it was snobbish and elitist, 'They're actually very funny.'

He pulled out *The Pursuit of Love* and carried it off to bed. The Pursuit of Love, he was thinking, was it worth all the trouble?

Dawn woke him and when he opened his eyes he was surprised to realise that his mind seemed to have cleared and he knew what to do next. Whisky was a marvellous medicine, he thought, as he showered, sorted out some clothes and packed them into a canvas holdall. He also put in the Mitford book, which, to his surprise, he *was* finding funny. When Maria arrived to give him breakfast, he was loading the Land Rover with camping gear.

'You are going away?' she asked in surprise.

He grinned, 'I thought I'd take a trip to Portugal. I've never really explored there.'

She frowned, 'What if the lady comes back? Where will you be?'

'I don't think she's coming back,' he said, chucking his holdall into the front passenger seat.

'I've already told you that you are a fool,' said Maria in disgust and stalked back into the house.

He had disappeared down the rutted track several hours ago, and Maria was busy putting dust sheets over the furniture, when the telephone rang. It was Dee.

'He has gone away,' said Maria in reply to the request to speak to Algy.

'Where to?' asked Dee in a voice of apprehension. Her first hopeful thought was that he was following her, but surely he would not be so rash as to travel to England? No, he wouldn't risk that because he was very careful about where he went. Her heart sank again.

'Portugal. He took his camping things,' said Maria.

'Did he say when he was coming back?'

'No.'

Later that morning Dee tidied up the cottage, switching off the electricals and closing all the windows. Then she took the keys to the caretaker and said, 'I'll be back next week but don't worry about me. I've a duplicate set of keys. And don't forward the mail, I'll collect it when I come back.' Problem over! she thought. Algy was not the only one to make decisions.

On the long drive down the M6, she talked herself into the 'independent woman' frame of mind. You don't need anyone, she told herself, after all you did very well for all the years you were on your own. Sharing your life with someone only holds you back. If this break is managed tactfully, you can stay friends and meet from time to time . . .

'Until he finds another woman and you won't like that much,' said a nasty little voice at the back of her mind, but she ignored it.

She was tired when she reached her daughter Kate's house in London and went to bed early, but next morning was up by nine, intent on storming Bond Street and Harvey Nichols in search of something to wear at the party. It was important not to let Colin down for she was mindful that he expected her to look like a French film star and to live up to his cream suit – a considerable, if not impossible, achievement.

In a way she was flattered he'd cast her as French because she knew she fell into the category of the *jolies laides*, women who made the best of what they'd got. For that she had to find eye-catching, daring clothes. Exhausted, she staggered home on the tube at half past five, burdened down with carrier bags. She laid her trophies out on Kate's spare room bed and pored over them, with her granddaughters exclaiming at the pretty colours.

'Gosh, that's lovely,' said Kate, lifting a length of gauze-like fabric striped in iridescent colours like a butterfly.

'I couldn't resist it. It's a turban and a sort of floating coat, and you wear it over a long, tight black skirt and this chemise top – look . . .' Dee held the clothes out in front of herself, adding, 'And there's long earrings. What do you think?'

'I think it's beautiful,' said the eldest granddaughter.

Kate looked doubtful, 'Maybe a little theatrical, Mum.'

'Theatrical's exactly what I want. I've been restrained for far too long,' said Dee.

That night when the children were in bed, Dee asked if she could make some phone calls. First she rang Colin and confirmed their meeting arrangements, and then rang Spain again, hoping that he might have returned home and given up the Portugal idea.

The phone rang and rang with the strange echoing sound that always tells the caller it is ringing in an empty house. After a long time she hung up feeling sick, although she took great care to hide her disquiet. 'No reply,' she said lightly, throwing herself on to the sofa to watch television with her son-in-law.

That night she dreamt Algy had been assassinated by the CIA and was floating face down in the swimming pool. She woke up weeping.

NINETEEN

The escort agency was a dead loss. Tricia had explained very carefully what she wanted when she signed on to their books, but the three possible escorts they arranged for her to see were totally unsuitable.

The first one was a coarse-looking, loose-lipped lad who seemed to think that he was to be rated only on his sexual potency.

'What's your room number? I can go for hours, me,' he boasted straight off when they met for a drink and a chat in the Hyde Park Hotel.

She glared at him. 'I won't be needing anything like that. I merely require a gentlemanly escort to attend a social function with me,' she said icily.

'You a dyke, then? You should've asked for a gel,' he sneered, seeing by the way she was gathering up her handbag that his interview was at an end.

The second candidate was scheduled to turn up an hour later in the same place. He was on time, but she quailed at the sight of him because he was dressed in black leather with an assortment of keys hanging out from every available pocket. He reminded her of Gene but was worse because he also sported two enormous gold earrings that looked as if they were welded to his ears. When he sat down facing her, closer examination revealed that the backs of his hands were tattooed with hearts and flowers.

She sighed. The earrings *might* be removable but the tattoos certainly were not.

'Thank you for coming and goodbye,' she said, passing him a ten pound note, which was the agreed 'survey' fee.

At four p.m., a man she took to be the final candidate walked into the hotel and started staring at the people waiting in the hall. Her heart rose a little for he was young – probably late twenties – presentable and dressed in a passable lightweight brown suit with a crisp white shirt and a discreet tie. She waved lightly in his direction and he walked over, smiling. 'Mrs Keen?' he asked.

'I think he'll do,' she exulted to herself, for at least he looked like a gentleman.

She offered him tea and he accepted, sitting down facing her and pulling at the legs of his trousers so as not to spoil the crease.

She made the conversational running, determined to try him out. 'Dreadfully sticky today, isn't it? London's often insufferable in July,' she said.

'Yes,' he agreed.

She couldn't tell much about his voice from just that, so she tried again. 'Do you work in town?' she asked.

He looked doubtful. 'Actually, I'm an actor. I've been touring in rep, as assistant stage manager. We went to Bognor this time but right now I'm resting.'

She stared at him in horror, wondering if he was teasing her because he had the most camp voice she had ever heard, except for the actors who used to play two gay men in a radio programme called 'Round The Horn' that she and her brother had enjoyed as children. It was high pitched, fluting and very affected.

After a moment, she collected herself and asked, 'You're an actor? Can you act someone slightly more – masculine, do you think?'

He drew himself up. 'What do you mean, Mrs Keen?'

'I mean I want a *stud*,' she said frankly.

'Oooh, the agency didn't say anything about *that!* I don't think I can help you there.' he protested.

'No, I don't think you can,' she agreed, opening her bag to produce another ten pound note.

She was fuming as she walked down Sloane Street to the underground car park where she'd parked the Jag. Escort agencies are like estate agencies, she thought, you ask them for a bungalow and they send you the details of a moated castle; you ask for a presentable man and they send you a selection of total misfits who wouldn't deceive the sharp-eyed cocktail party lot for one moment. Even Gene or Jim would be more likely to pass muster than any of the three she'd spent this afternoon surveying.

And the party was in three days' time. She'd had her eyes fixed, she'd bought a beautiful trouser suit and she knew she looked stunning because she'd topped up her Portugal tan at the local sunbed parlour. However, she had no man to wear on her arm like a Gucci handbag. Damn, damn, damn.

From the car phone she rang Gene. 'You said you might be able to find me someone to take to the cocktail party, didn't you?' she snapped.

'Didn't your fancy agency come up with the goods then?' he asked.

'No they did not. Let's see what you can do. For the right man I'm prepared to pay a hundred quid. Not bad for two and a half hours' work, booze and small eats thrown in and no hidden demands. But I don't want any of your muscle-bound bruisers. I want a gent . . . I don't suppose you can come up with one, but you're my last hope.'

Gene laughed. 'It's funny you should ask, but I've been looking around and in the boozer the other night I saw a guy that might fit the bill. I'll go in tonight and see if he's there.'

'Which boozer? In Stepney?'

'No, your local boozer. In Virginia Water. Leave it to me, sis.'

She and Jim were finishing supper when the phone rang and she rushed to answer it. Gene sounded as if he'd been drinking but was also cheerful.

'He's up for it, girl,' he croaked.

She looked across at Jim who was sitting on the patio with his sleeves rolled up and all his jewellery glittering. 'When can he come around?' she asked.

'Right now if you like.'

'Oh that's not very suitable. What about tomorrow morning, say about eleven?' she trilled.

When she went back into the big drawing room she said, 'Gene's bringing one of his builder friends over tomorrow to look at that en suite bathroom off the blue room. I fancy one of those showers with jets coming out in all directions. We could have some fun in that, Jim, couldn't we?'

He grinned indulgently at her. If Tricia wanted a shower with water spouting through the ceiling or up through the floor, that was all right with him. 'Just make sure you get a quote. Gene's your brother but he's not above taking a cut for himself, you know,' he said.

'I know that,' she agreed.

Exactly on the appointed time, Gene's white van drew up into the drive and crunched to a halt on the deep red gravel. Tricia, watching from a window, saw a slim young man jump athletically down from the passenger seat, and if she had not had such a disappointing previous day, she would have allowed herself to feel optimistic.

When the bell rang, she walked downstairs and opened the wide front door. Gene was grinning as he thrust out a hand towards his companion and said, 'Meet Fraser!'

'Farquhar,' corrected the man on the step beside him. His voice was pure cut glass and he looked like an officer cadet from Sandhurst. His checked shirt was open at the neck and rolled back from the wrists, his duck trousers elegantly crumpled and he was wearing yachting shoes – perfect! He was unmistakably a gent.

Gene came bouncing in, tremendously pleased with himself, and told Tricia, 'I've explained things to Far – what's your name again? – and he thinks it's a great joke so he'll do it for you. You're into it, aren't you Far?'

'Farquhar. Yes, I'll do it,' said the vision of manliness. He was eyeing Tricia with unconcealed appreciation, 'although I can't understand why you've got to pay someone to go to a party with you. I'd go with you for nothing.'

This did not suit Gene, who, as Jim had unconsciously warned, was treating this commission as a personal money-raising venture. He'd already negotiated his terms – sixty quid to Farquhar and forty for himself as broker of the deal.

'Come on Farquhar,' he said elbowing his new friend in the ribs, 'Don't spoil things. Tricia wants to pay. It's a business proposition, isn't it, Trish?'

She smiled and said, 'Yes, strictly business I'm afraid.'

'Pity,' said Farquhar.

They all went inside and Tricia made them coffee in the kitchen for she'd taken the precaution of sending her maid off in the house car to do a massive shop at Sainsbury's. She'd be gone for at least an hour and a half.

As they sipped the rather anaemic brew, she explained what she wanted. Farquhar, dressed like a gentleman, was to be her escort to the cocktail party. He was to pretend to be her lover, to behave very affectionately towards her and respond to any leads she gave him.

'What sort of leads?' he asked looking puzzled.

'Things that come up in conversation. You know, if I say we've just come back from Portugal, you say something about how wonderful it was . . .'

'How about saying we've been to Italy? I've an Italian friend with a wonderful castle near Portofino that I know well. We could have been staying there,' he suggested and she looked pleased. He'd obviously got the idea.

'We'll say we're going there next,' she told him, 'You see, there's a few women who are going to be at the party that I want to make sick with envy.'

His eyes were dancing, 'We'll do it! We'll be as convincing as any film stars in a Hollywood romance,' he crowed.

She told him where and when the party was to be held and he said he knew the place. 'Where will we meet?' he asked.

She frowned. 'Do you live nearby?' she asked.

'Down there, a couple of miles away,' he said and gestured vaguely southwards.

'Mmm. We could go up to town together but I think it would be safer if we meet near the club. Jim, who I live with, can be quite jealous. What about meeting you at the entrance to the Sloane Street underground car park at six o'clock?'

That was agreed, so when Gene and Farquhar left, Tricia switched on the radio and danced joyously around the kitchen, doing her exercises to the music playing on the Jimmy Young show.

The next day – party day – Jim and his boys were working at Newmarket, which gave Tricia plenty of opportunity to prepare herself without exciting his curiosity. She warned him that she might not be at home when he returned, because she was going to London to meet some old friends, but that she would not be very late because her friends were all women who were older than her, and did not like staying up late. 'We'll have an early supper someplace and then I'll drive myself home,' she told him.

Painted, tanned, buffed and magnificent, with her hair artfully curled round her face, she drove carefully into town and parked the car. While she was walking up the ramp from the parking bays, she suddenly felt a grip of panic. What if Farquhar didn't turn up? Without knowing anything about him, she'd given him half of his fee in advance and now she regretted her generosity.

As she stepped into the open air, she looked like some nymph emerging from the underworld, staring around anxiously. Then she heard his voice.

'Hi, Tricia – can I call you Tricia?' came his voice and she was flooded with relief.

'Of course, you *must* call me Tricia, when you're not calling me *darling*,' she joked as she turned and saw him. In delight she took his arm. Oh bliss, he looked wonderful – charcoal grey suit, pale pink shirt, a striped, official looking tie.

She laid a red-tipped finger on it and asked, 'What's the tie?'

'Wellington,' he said.

'The Duke?' she asked playfully.

'The school,' he told her.

She stopped on the pavement. 'Good. You're a public schoolboy? I'd better know some more than that about you in case anyone asks.'

He grinned down at her. 'I should have given you my CV, shouldn't I? All right, I'm the youngest of two sons. My father was in the Army, a colonel by the time he retired. He died last year. I joined the Army, too, but I didn't like military life and I've just quit. I'm trying to make up my mind what to do next. That's why I've been hanging around at my mother's place near you.'

Made suspicious by this apparently ideal background, she said, 'You're not thinking of going on the stage are you?'

He laughed, 'No, I'm not. I'd rather like to go abroad somewhere. I actually want to paint. I was quite good at art in school.'

She gripped his arm again tighter. 'We'll say you're a painter. That's perfect. Look we're a bit early. Let's go into that hotel over there and have a drink to give us courage. I don't want to arrive too early at this do. It's always best to make an entrance when the house is full, isn't it?'

TWENTY

A ir travel was not a novelty for Prakash, for after all, he'd been to the Gulf three times, but he was secretly highly excited at the prospect of seeing London. His innate dignity meant that he kept this excitement to himself and looked totally cool and self-possessed as he pushed Tommy through Heathrow in a creaking wheelchair. He would not allow anyone except himself to push it.

As they traversed corridor after corridor and trundled along on travelling pedestrian belt after pedestrian belt, he was glad that the Bombay travel agent had advised booking a wheelchair for the old man. Tommy had protested of course, but he too was relieved when he saw how far they had to go after leaving their plane.

Emerging into the crowded baggage retrieval hall at last, he looked around and sighed, 'If there really is a hell, it'll be like this place.' Prakash hid his own dismayed amazement and nodded in agreement.

Their agent had booked them into a modest hotel in South Kensington to which they travelled in a taxi. Prakash was in charge of their money and peeled off the number of notes the driver wanted with a rising sense of disbelief and indignation. He resolved to make it a personal crusade to prevent his employer from being ripped off too badly by these white-faced rogues, who he thought were worse than the most blatant Bombay *goondas*.

For the next three days they went sightseeing, riding on the top of red tourist buses and admiring the sights of the city. Both of them were awed by what they saw, especially by Buckingham Palace. When they reached it they got out of their bus to stand and stare, deeply impressed by the enormous fountain standing outside the railings. Their awe was focused on the huge statue of Queen Victoria sitting high above the water jets.

Both of them were very familiar with the Queen Empress because images of her were dotted all over India in the old days. Even in the most remote places, she brooded over her Indian subjects like a goddess, but the majority of those old statues were removed after Partition and were now stored in monumental graveyards, along with Viceroys and various generals who had trounced the natives, in various Indian cities.

As Tommy stared up at the effigy of the old queen outside her palace he remembered the effect she used to have on him when he was a young man. Like so many people of his kind, he had revered her and all she stood for; he had given up his whole life to serving the regime that had been created in her name. Yet here she was, a dumpy old woman with an unpleasant face. The Rani of Jhansi, who was the heroine of the other part of his ancestry, was a far more glamorous figure.

Both he and Prakash were sobered as they walked down the Mall from the palace. On the way they passed a stall selling ice cream. Prakash, worried in case Tommy was overdoing things, suggested they stop to buy an ice which they could sit and eat in the shade of the trees in the park. When he went up to the stall to do this, he was appalled at the sum asked for two cones and gave the standard Indian response to any hawker, '*Arrey*, that is too much. I will give you half.'

'Half? You mad?' yelled the stallholder leaning over his wooden counter, 'You Pakis are all the same!'

Prakash drew himself up and his high-caste sensibilities rose, 'No, I am not mad but you are a *badmash* who is asking for too much money.'

Tommy, watching this, came over swiftly, remembering that his bearer had a flashpoint temper and a fierce pride that once made him stab an insolent cook and almost kill Tommy himself in a fit of revenge. 'Just pay him, or let me pay him,' he said, grabbing Prakash's shoulder before he could throw himself at the stall.

Prakash turned away and Tommy laid down the money, before taking up the two dripping cones. Prakash refused to eat his and ostentatiously threw it into the dirt beneath the roadside trees, in full sight of the glaring vendor.

'This is a strange country,' was all he said when they rode back to Kensington on another bus.

That night, sitting in the hotel lounge before a blaring television set, Tommy decided to take Prakash into his confidence and tell him the real reason he was making his pilgrimage to London. 'Swami's *memsahib*, the woman who died in the train from Madras, was my niece,' he said suddenly.

Prakash looked solemn and said, 'I thought there was more to it than you were saying.'

'She was my sister's illegitimate child who had to be given up to the nuns when she was a baby. I had no idea she even existed until I started looking into the case again earlier this year. I'd received an anonymous letter about it, you see. Remember I went to Poona with Sergeant Raj Singh? That was when I found out about my sister being the dead woman's mother.'

Prakash nodded, 'You were ill afterwards.'

'It was a shock to me, especially because the letter said that she'd been murdered. I felt I had to find out about her, to put my mind at rest. I was very fond of my sister, you see, and Mrs Richards was my niece, although I never knew her.' Another understanding nod urged him on. 'I asked around about the people your servant friends talked about, and it is pretty certain that she was not leading a good life when she died, but she started out as a good woman and something happened. Perhaps she was weak. My sister was weak – but gentle, too. I want to find out her story before I die, and if someone *did* kill her, I want to know who did it and why.'

'Will you find the answer at this party tomorrow?' asked Prakash.

'It's the only place left for me to find out anything. Her husband is still alive and he will be there because he is one of the people running the party. I will speak to him, and to her friends. Some of the names of women mentioned by the people in Chor Bazaar are on the guest list. They're bound to remember Sonya. I can't force them to talk, and I won't be able to do anything if I find out who killed her – if anyone did. I just want to know . . .'

The old man's voice trailed off and he sighed. Prakash got up, went to Tommy's room and fetched a bottle of whisky, which he'd taken the precaution of buying from a nearby supermarket because he considered the hotel bar charges too expensive. He poured a generous measure into a tooth mug, and carried it back downstairs to the bar where he said to the bartender, 'Put ice and soda into that.'

The man considered protesting but when his eyes met Prakash's something told him to say nothing and he meekly did as he was told. The whisky was a good idea because it drove away some of the demons that haunted Tommy and they sat watching television till he dozed off in his chair and agreed to be led upstairs by his servant. Prakash closed Tommy's bedroom door with a melancholy look on his face. This journey had tired the old man more than he was prepared to admit, and away from Bombay he seemed to be out of his element and unsure of himself. It was only to be hoped that his strength would hold out long enough to allow him to seek out the information that he so much wanted to find.

TWENTY-ONE

The day began very early at Gomez Racing and people were bustling about the yard when it was still dark. Laura was standing in the office in a pool of lamplight, nervously biting at her fingernails, when Roly came in after giving Lance and the staff their instructions. He looked at her and grinned, saying, 'Cheer up Lor, you look as if you were going away to be hung instead of going to a party.'

She snorted, 'Some party! I hate those ex-Bombay people, Roly. They're so artificial, so out-of-date. Most of them are stuck in the 1950s. They talk as if Winston Churchill's still Prime Minister or as if we have an empire to rule.'

He laughed. 'We'll survive them. Kenneth told me he'll take us out to dinner afterwards and he's always a generous host, I'll grant him that.'

Laura walked across to the desk and pointed at the phone. 'For two pins I'd ring him up and say that we can't make it. I could say you've broken your arm or something.'

Roly, who'd never allowed broken bones to prevent him from attending parties in the past, said, 'He wouldn't believe you. Remember the time I went to his Christmas party with a broken leg and a broken collarbone. You know we've got to go. He's so set on it for some reason. I suppose he wants to show you off, and he's a good old stick – remember he's lent us that money. We can't let him down.'

The wire basket, now brimming with receipts, stood on the office table, testimony to Kenneth's generosity. They were out of the red again – at least for the meantime. Laura

164

said, 'I know he is and I know he's eager for us to be there. I think he needs somebody on his side against Alice, she's such a bitch to him and she's getting worse. Nowadays it seems impossible for her to address a polite word in his direction.'

Her husband agreed, 'She'd be a lot worse too, if she knew he's just given us two thousand quid.'

Laura shivered, 'For God's sake, Roly, don't breathe a word of that. Try to stay sober so's you won't be tempted to talk about it.'

He guffawed, 'Stay sober! Don't be crazy. I'm looking forward to the chance of a blow-out. Come on, let's get on the road. We've got to pick up Kenneth and Alice first, haven't we?'

'Is everything all right out here?' she asked, nodding at the line of loose boxes around the cobbled yard as if she was looking for an excuse to delay.

He nodded, 'Most of the horses are out at grass right now, and Lance and the girls know what to do with the others. We'll be back tomorrow night after Newmarket and they can get us on the phone if there's an emergency – which there won't be. Don't worry.'

'I think that we put too much on Lance; he's still a child,' she said.

Roly, who left school at fourteen, scoffed, 'You coddle him. He's a lot tougher than you think. He's not so young. He's as much of a man now as he'll ever be.'

'Sixteen's a funny age. He shouldn't be forced into things. I remember when I was a teenager. I was so green! I've changed so much that even I find it difficult to realise that I'm still the same *me* . . . I wouldn't like to be held responsible for what I did at that age,' she said and the intensity of her tone surprised him.

'Aw, come on, what did you do? Lost your cherry to some guy probably. I hope Lance's lost his by this time. I suspect that new stable girl Kitty's had it off him. Don't torture yourself. You didn't knock anybody off or rob a bank. Keep things in perspective, Lor,' her husband said indulgently.

Surprisingly tears sprang into her eyes and she gave a terrible sob. 'I was awful, Roly!' Her anguish was so genuine that he clutched her to him and patted her head as if she was a troubled child or a nervous horse. Roly was a man of few words and little learning, but he had an enormously tender heart.

'You're still awful,' he joked, 'Come on, get your act together. Lance's polished the Merc and it's looking pretty good except for the rust. Where's your suitcase? I'll put it in the boot for you.'

She pointed at a case standing in the corner and he lifted it up.

'Your suit's in there. And a new shirt,' she said.

'I hope you put in my Injured Jockeys' Fund tie. I have to hold my own with all those regimental and old school tie chaps,' he said.

She laughed at last as she said, 'Yes, I did. At least it's better than your yellow one with the fox masks on it.'

Before they left the office, Roly opened the top drawer of the desk and took out a battered hunting flask, which he dropped into her open handbag. 'It's full of brandy. If Alice gets too much for you, just take a swig,' he told her.

She turned, bent her head and kissed him on the cheek. 'I do love you, toy man,' she said.

Their son Lance shoved his head round the door and asked, 'Are you going or not then?'

He was tall and slim, like his mother, but he had his father's amused looking, Irish face and a mop of dark curly hair that flopped down over his brow and curled at the back of his neck. She regarded him with frank adoration and asked, 'Are you sure you'll be all right for two days, Lance?'

'Aw Mom, I'm not going to die of starvation. The place is

not going to fall down. The horses aren't going to succumb to strangles or anything like that. I'm looking forward to being left in charge. After all I'm going to leave school and take this place over. You'd better watch out or I'll fire you both,' he said cheerfully.

'You are *not* leaving school!' she protested as Roly grabbed her arm and pulled her towards the door, but she was wasting her time for both Roly and Lance were against her on the question of the boy's future. Loudly protesting, and shouting instructions from the car window, she was driven away.

'Oh God Roly, don't encourage him to leave school. I can't bear to think of him spending his entire life worrying about money the way we've done,' she said in anguish as the car turned on to the motorway heading for the south.

Roly shrugged, 'Money's not everything. He's got horses in his blood, like me and my father and his father before him. There's not much we can do about that. He might be lucky and train a National winner. It's hope that keeps people like us going, Lor.'

She said nothing because she knew that what he said was true.

Although they were early, Kenneth had his wooden garden gate already standing wide open to give room for the Mercedes to draw up beside his Vauxhall, and was watching from the kitchen window to see them arrive. Roly didn't even have time to switch off the engine before he came bursting through the front door with his arms spread wide to embrace Laura. There was no sign of Alice.

'Darling! In time for lunch. I've mixed some really good Martinis. Don't you look well. Are you looking forward to the party?'

Laura seemed to bend like a slender tree before his onslaught, and after he'd hugged her he stood back to take another look. 'Oh my dear, you're so like your mother, except you're thinner and the colour of your hair's different,

167

of course, but then Sonya did have a bit of artificial help with that. Come in, come in. You can have a lie down if you like because we don't have to leave for London until about five o'clock. We'll be driving against the traffic, you see.'

Alice was in the sitting room, perched on the arm of a deep chair with a glass in her hand. 'Hi,' she said casually as they entered, 'There's sandwiches and stuff in the kitchen. Smoked salmon, no less. Ken made them especially for you.' She obviously wanted them to know that she'd not put herself out on their behalf. As she spoke she allowed her eyes to run up and down Laura's slim figure, itemising her clothes, as if noting any plus and minus points. Roly, she ignored.

They were with Kenneth in the kitchen, eating his carefully prepared lunch, when Alice called through, 'I'm off to have my bath. Let me know when it's time to leave.'

'She always makes fun of your cocktail party. Why does she want to go?' Laura asked, chewing on her sandwich.

'She can't bear to miss anything. She'll go through the crowd like a clipper ship, finding out who's dead, divorced or dying and it'll give her tremendous pleasure. If she reckons that she's better looking than all the other women, she'll be in a good mood for days,' said Kenneth wearily.

'Poor you,' said Laura with feeling and he smiled back at her.

'It doesn't worry me actually. I keep thinking that I've got a surprise waiting for her one day and that cheers me up no end.'

Roly laughed, 'What are you going to do? Slip some arsenic into her tea?' Instead of causing amusement, this crack seemed to explode among them like a hand grenade. Laura and Kenneth stared at him stony faced and he shook his head as he remembered their sensitivity about Sonya. In confused apology he said, 'Sorry! Only joking.'

After eating, Laura went to lie down on the spare room bed while Roly and Kenneth watched racing on television and drank beer. At four o'clock she called down to her husband, 'Time to change, Roly.' And he went upstairs to find her sitting before the dressing table with a distraught look on her face.

'I don't know if I can stand this party,' she said staring at him through the looking glass.

He went up and put his hands on her bare shoulders, and said lovingly at her, 'Of course you can. You're through the worst anyway. You've met Alice again. She didn't like what she saw either because you make her look like an aged tart and she knows it.'

Laura shook her head, 'It's not just Alice. This party's going to be full of people talking about my mother and telling me that I look like her. I don't want to look like her – and anyway I don't really. She was a blonde and bold with it. They seem to think I've forgotten what she was like. She was awful, Roly, she hated me for much the same reasons as Alice does. Kenneth's got awful taste in women.'

Roly was surprised. Laura had never really spoken about her mother except to tell him about the day she was found dead on a train. She had a terrible hang-up about that. He thought the traumatic memory must be what was now making her pale skin shiver beneath his hands and her teeth chatter as if she was frozen. Perhaps because of the party, the memory of her mother's sudden death seemed to have come back and was deeply upsetting her.

He stroked her hair and made soothing noises, 'Come on Laura. You're going to be all right. I'll be with you all the time. You can hold my hand if you like. They'll think you're leading me around!'

She turned and sunk her face into his side. 'Oh God Roly, what would I do without you? You're the best thing that ever happened to me, you know. If I hadn't met you, I don't know what I'd have done. Something awful, I'm sure.'

He knelt down and said, 'No, you wouldn't. You'd probably have married a millionaire – or an accountant –

and been a comfortable housewife. You wouldn't have had to ride out in all weathers, muck out loose boxes and fight off debt collectors.'

'But I like mucking out loose boxes,' came her muffled voice.

He coaxed her into getting dressed and soon she was ready, standing like a fashion model in a pale green dress of a soft material that was swathed round her elegant hips and over her surprisingly full breasts. She'd bought it with the money Kenneth sent for the purpose. In high-heeled shoes, she towered over Roly, but he stood back and regarded her with outright admiration.

'You look like a film star, the one that married Frank Sinatra,' he told her.

'Mia Farrow? Don't be daft,' she said as she fixed the clasp of her necklace.

'Not her, the other one, the one that broke his heart,' said Roly, 'You're her spitting image.'

'Ava Gardner? Am I really?' That compliment seemed to lift her spirits and she sailed down the stairs like a queen. Alice, standing in the hall, looked up and was unable to conceal the outright jealousy that showed on her face.

'You're so thin, Laura, you're not anorexic are you?' she asked spitefully.

Kenneth clapped his hands together and said cheerfully, 'Right then, let's be off. Next stop St James's.'

TWENTY-TWO

The flat in St John's Wood was, as always, immaculate. Recently Colin had begun collecting Chinese art, influenced by a dealer with whom he'd had a short affair. Although his heart was once again broken, during their time together he'd managed to assimilate a certain amount of valuable information that enabled him to go to sales and pick up some attractive bargains. He had several lovely scroll paintings, three bowls of celadon china that he filled with pot-pourri, ewers and teapots salvaged from the Nanking cargo, carpets woven in pale colours, and a green glazed Ming horse with a saddle on its back and its head down in the grazing position.

It was when he had attended previews with his dealer friend that he'd come across again the man called Perkins whom he remembered from Bombay. He was surprised that Perkins seemed to want to be friendly towards him in London, perhaps because he had not been aware of Colin's homosexuality during their days in India, but his advances were rebuffed. Colin was repelled by the other man's bitchiness. It seemed impossible for Perkins to say anything pleasant about anyone, especially their mutual acquaintances from the past.

'You were friendly with that muscle-bound rugby player – Carmichael – weren't you, and his peculiar wife,' said Perkins one evening when they met at an art gallery viewing in Dover Street, sipping sour white wine.

'I don't think Dee's a *bit* peculiar,' said Colin loyally.

171

'But all those books! She played at being a bluestocking and had shelves of books in their flat. I don't think she ever read any of them. Do tell me, were they there just for show?' hissed Perkins.

'She read them,' said Colin.

'So odd if she did! She wasn't from that sort of a background. Her father was a gangster, you know,' Perkins sneered.

Colin laughed. He'd never given any serious consideration to Dee's background. 'I thought he owned bars and public houses,' he said.

'Of course, he did. Exactly. And he was a gangster! I have it on reliable authority from people in Edinburgh who knew of him, but weren't friendly with him of course.'

'Good for him! I've always thought Dee has a whiff of Chicago about her,' said Colin lightly.

He was remembering this conversation as he prepared for the last Bombay Cocktail Party which he and the gangster's daughter would attend together. He was looking forward to it because Dee was good company. As he sorted out his clothes for the evening, he wondered, Why hasn't she found herself another man after Ben? She was probably too fussy, or too scared, like himself. There was this strange association she had with someone in Spain but that didn't seem very promising because she was very cagey on the subject. He'd have to ask her more about that.

Standing beneath the shower, he lathered his hair, relieved that he wasn't going bald and his blondness had silvered to a pleasant shade not very different to what it had been when he was young. Towelling himself dry, he dusted on Dior talcum powder and pulled on new silk boxer shorts. They were very smart but there wasn't much chance of anyone but him seeing them tonight. Perkins would be at the party, of course, but Colin was not so desperate as to consider taking up with *him*. During his time in Bombay there had been one or two of the married men with whom he'd had mild flirtations – Tom Bolitho among them, but he'd seen his death in the *Times* not too long ago, so that possibility was also closed. He sighed.

'Might as well sign up for a monastery,' he said aloud to his reflection in the mirror. In fact he was seriously considering leaving St John's Wood. He'd lived there since he returned from Bombay in 1969 but city life was palling and he had recently been fantasising about moving to the country, or even going abroad. Perhaps Dee would be able to give him advice about living in Spain. Constant sunshine would ease his rheumatics which were growing more painful, especially in the winter. He was sixty-five after all, although he certainly didn't look it. After he pulled on his shirt, he stared into the full-length mirror and reckoned that he could pass for ten years younger.

When he left the flat in a taxi, he was looking magnificently smart in an immaculate cream suit, with a tightly furled red rose in his buttonhole. In his hand he carried a pale cream orchid which he intended to present to Dee.

She was waiting in the ground floor hall of the Ritz, sitting on a fragile chair in a corner, with an *Evening Standard* spread out on the table in front of her. Dee never went anywhere without arming herself with something to read, and she was so absorbed in it, that he was able to walk up without her seeing him.

'Darling,' he said, leaning down to kiss her cheek, 'You're simply magnificent. Like the Queen of Sheba.'

She looked up and he saw that she'd outlined her eyes in kohl and highlighted the upper lids with pale brown powder that accentuated the pale blue of her irises. Her maquillage was a magnificent ivory and her lips painted in the same scarlet as the stripes on her coat and dashing turban.

She glittered at him, 'You look pretty good yourself. A very dapper dude.' She giggled nervously as she spoke.

He sat down opposite her, put the orchid box on the table

and asked, 'Giving you an orchid is like taking coals to Newcastle. What are you going to do with this?'

She looked at it through its cellophane lid and said, 'It's beautiful. No one's given me an orchid since my wedding day. I had one instead of a bouquet and I pressed it between the pages of my copy of *Pickwick Papers* but it went brown and crumbled away to nothing. Like the marriage I suppose.'

She sounded sad so he said, 'Pin it on to your shoulder. It won't clash. Now we're going to drink champagne. I've a feeling that we're about to have a splendid evening and we better get into the mood before we hit the party. Don't be nervous. You're going to be a sensation. I've never seen you looking so – dangerous!'

That brightened her and she laughed, 'I am a bit nervous actually. I think I've overdone the dressing up.'

He protested strongly, 'Nonsense, if that's overdoing it, you should have started long ago. You look like Jeanne Moreau.'

'Really?' The French actress Jeanne Moreau was a woman Dee particularly admired and the thought that she might resemble her even slightly, made her draw herself up and spread her finery out around her on the chair.

Colin clasped his hands, 'I'm proud to be seen with you,' he told her and his kindness brought tears to her eyes. How she wished she could tell him about Algy but knew that if she launched into the tale she'd probably weep and ruin her make-up which the girl in Harvey Nichols had applied with such care, so she said nothing.

Why was it that an old friend like Colin was the man to tell her those lovely things, when Algy said nothing flattering? He'd never even said he loved her. I'm not going to think about him for the next three hours, she silently swore, looking discreetly at her wristwatch. Its hands stood at five thirty-five.

Colin looked at his, too. 'Time for several glasses of

champagne each before we hit the party at quarter to seven. It's only a short walk away, but we mustn't be there first. You've got to make an entrance,' he said.

'You, too,' she told him, 'Because you're a knock-out. I love your suit and you haven't aged a day since the first time I met you.'

'Dearest, not only do you look like an angel but you talk like one too,' he told her and toasted her with his first glass of champagne.

TWENTY-THREE

Bustling and business-like in a full-skirted dark blue dress with a wide white collar that framed her face and showed off the gleaming olive skin of her fine shoulders, Marian Salisbury hurried into the Royal Overseas League building at five forty-five. Peter followed in her wake, carrying a grey top hat under his arm, although his clothes were casual – a navy blazer with a gilt crest on the pocket and sharply pressed grey trousers.

The club staff were used to Marian by this time and hurried forward to show her the layout of the party room and she walked to and fro, checking on everything, missing nothing. People always said that Peter could not have achieved his heights of success without marrying her, and it was true. He took all his dilemmas home because, faced with a logistical problem, Marian was like the Duke of Wellington on a battlefield, sweeping all before her.

Delicately she lifted one of the canapés off a silver tray and tasted it before nodding her head to show that it met her exacting standards. She patrolled the length of the long tables that formed the bar, lifted up glasses to check for finger marks, cast a critical eye on the flowers that stood in tall vases at each end of the bar. She was examining the carpet to make sure it had been properly hoovered, when a voice hailed her from the entrance to the room.

'Checking up, Marian? In half an hour nobody'll even notice if there's a carpet on the floor at all.'

Arthur Perkins stood there, garbed in a pale fawn suit,

and a shirt patterned all over with flowers. Her face showed surprise at the sight of him because she was wondering why he always took so much trouble to dress up, especially considering his physical unattractiveness. He must be hiding behind his clothes all the time, she decided.

'Aren't you wearing a tie, Arthur?' she asked, 'It's club regulations, you know.'

'So they told me. I have one in my pocket., Don't worry, Marian, I'll put it on.' He fished out a tie that looked as if it was made of brown silk and knotted it round his neck. The effect was even more bizarre than before, but the regulations were met.

Peter hurried over, still carrying the hat, to greet Arthur and was met with a sardonic gaze, 'Going to a wedding tonight, are you? Or planning on doing some conjuring tricks and producing a bunny rabbit from that hat?'

Marian laughed, 'Of course not. We brought along Peter's topper – the one he wore when he got his gong – so we can use it for the raffle draw,' she told him.

Perkins sneered, 'I suppose the tickets could be pulled out of a pudding bowl or a chamber pot, but you'll be able to rub it in that he had it on his head in Buckingham Palace when you make the draw. Don't forget to say so, darling, but you won't will you?'

She looked hard at him and a steeliness came into her gaze, 'I won't forget,' she said stonily.

Their exchange was interrupted by the arrival of Alex, all eager and beaming, bearing two file boxes. 'I've brought the guest list, some extra tickets and a cash box because there might be some people wanting to pay at the door. Isn't this fun? It's a lovely night, too. I was afraid it would rain,' he said cheerfully.

'Why? Because you might melt?' asked Perkins casting his eye down Alex's plump figure, but his sarcasm went to waste because Alex never picked up on anything except what was patently obvious.

'Of course not. Because people won't have to walk through rain to get here. Parking's difficult, you know. Rain would really put a damper on the party, ha ha ha!'

'Ha ha ha,' said Perkins mirthlessly and turned away. After a bit he turned back to Peter and asked, 'Where's Richards? Isn't he here yet? He's late.'

'He's got quite a distance to come. He's not as close as us. He lives in Tunbridge Wells,' said Marian.

'Perfect place for him,' said Perkins and their conversation was then interrupted by a babble of voices in the vestibule. The guests were beginning to arrive . . .

TWENTY-FOUR

At half past six Tricia and Farquhar emerged giggling
from the hotel where they had been drinking dry
Martinis and she said to her companion, 'I'm ready for it
now. Whistle up a taxi and let's go.'

They were alighting from their cab at the gateway which
gave entry to the forecourt of the club, when Dee and Colin,
both laughing happily because their champagne had made
them euphoric too, came up the slight slope of Park Place.

Dee gripped Colin's sleeve and said, 'Look, there's
Tricia Keen. She's exactly the same as she was twenty
years ago.'

'Probably pickled in formaldehyde,' joked Colin, but he
wasn't looking at Tricia. He was more interested in her companion and a faint expression of envy crossed his face.

'That's a lovely chap she's got with her, too,' he sighed.

In a long black Daimler facing up St James's Street
towards Piccadilly, James and Julia Whitecross sat behind
the chauffeur and made stilted conversation.

'Don't you think we should go in?' he asked, watching
groups of smartly dressed people, who must be on their way
to the party, walking along the pavement.

She shook her carefully crimped head. 'I said we'd wait
for Belle. I want to see her arrive.'

'Why?' he asked.

'Because I'm pretty sure she'll be coming by bus.' The
malice in her eyes made him shrink, big and imposing
though he was.

Suddenly she sat forward and gave a little cry. 'Oh, he came after all!' His eyes followed her pointing finger to a man on his own hurrying down from Piccadilly with a bulging briefcase in his hand. The casual suit he was wearing was crumpled as if he'd sat in a hunched and uncomfortable position all day. He looked like a tired commuter who should have been on the train going home.

'Who is it?' James asked.

'Andy Parnell,' she told him, sitting back with a pleased smile on her lips.

'The doctor? Not the dashing lover any more, is he? That suit's seen better days,' said James.

She glared at him. 'I'm sure he doesn't wrap himself up in a sari in the evening, though,' was her reply. Her husband said nothing because he guessed that she had been drinking steadily all afternoon and, by this time, was probably spoiling for a fight. He wondered who was to be her unlucky protagonist. Not him, if he could help it.

Silence claimed them again for another five minutes until once more Julia leaned forward in her seat, 'Here she is now. I'm right. She's just got off a bus. Probably can't even afford a taxi!'

A tall, slim woman with a close-cut cap of dark hair was hurrying along the road towards them, leaning to one side because she was weighted down by a bulging striped canvas bag. Julia threw open the car door in front of her, almost knocking her off her feet.

'Belle! You haven't changed a bit,' she carolled leaning out with her hands extended.

Belle peered into the interior of the limousine and said, 'Hello Julia. Hello James. Have you been waiting for me? The train was late I'm afraid. Sorry.'

Julia looked at her watch. It was six thirty so Belle was dead on time. 'Just a little bit late. Was there a long queue for the taxis? There usually is at this time of night,' she said.

'Quite long,' said Belle, flushing.

'Let's go in. I've just seen Andy go past,' said Julia, who was obviously straining at the bit to start whatever it was she had in mind.

James said to the chauffeur, 'We're going up there to the Royal Overseas League. Come back for us at half past eight.'

Belle looked in at him and asked, 'Do you think I could leave this bag in your car. It saves putting it in the cloakroom. I brought you a bottle of champagne as a present for putting me up tonight and it's quite heavy.'

Julia smiled, 'Champagne darling, how sweet of you! Is it Krug?'

Belle flushed again. 'No, I'm afraid it's Tesco's.'

James felt he had to rescue her. 'They have a very good reputation for their wines,' he said.

Belle stood back and they could see that she was wearing a scarlet dress that was tightly belted with black patent for she'd always had a beautiful figure and knew how to accentuate it. The dress's neckline was very low cut, revealing that she still sported an eye-catching cleavage. Her earrings were big golden hoops like a gypsy's. The only discordant element was a thick white cardigan that she wore slung across her shoulders. She had taken it off when alighting from the bus but wore it buttoned up to the neck to hide her cleavage while travelling.

'Why don't you leave your cardie in the car, too,' suggested Julia as she got out of the car. The way she said 'cardie' showed that she was being very nasty. Belle said nothing but took the garment off and laid it on the seat beside her bag.

They walked in a line up the short cul de sac to the club with Julia in the middle, limping along on her silver-topped cane. She was wearing a tight dress of silver lamé that made her look like the fairy from the top of a Christmas tree. She always overdressed, thought Belle, and that was followed by the thought that Julia would make good pickings for a mugger because round her neck hung a necklace of emeralds set in gold, and emerald earrings flashed in her ears. A grey gauze scarf as fine as a spider's web encircled her shoulders.

They disappeared inside the club as Barbara and John Carlton-Grey turned the corner from St James's Street. They had come on foot from their house in Hans Place to the party because they enjoyed walking and neither of them was in a hurry to get there. Barbara, in an understated long black skirt and a pale blue silk blouse, was regretting her decision to attend what she feared would be a noisy, drunken revel among people with whom she had nothing in common. She glanced sideways at her husband, still magnificently handsome in his dark suit, and her complex feelings for him almost overwhelmed her. She loved him passionately and always had done, but he'd wounded her pride so often that her love went hand in hand with a deep and passionate anger. Even now that she had to all appearances tamed him, she feared that he might be capable of wounding her again.

'Perhaps I'm some sort of a masochist, who deliberately puts herself in the way of pain. Perhaps that's why I married him in the first place,' she thought. When they returned from India, and she was weighing up whether she should divorce him or not, she went to see a psychiatrist but found the experience too searing to repeat. It was best for her to go on acting, to present her serene face to the world, to act out the play in which she had cast herself. But all the time, she knew that within her fires were raging and she was afraid of what might happen if she ever opened the furnace door.

Marian had joined Alex at the desk when the Carlton-Greys walked into the side hall that led to the party room, and her face lit up when she saw them. 'I'm so glad you could come,' she carolled, and rushed up to take Barbara's arm as if they were intimate friends.

'It's really filling up,' she said in a confiding tone, 'but head for the window at the far end. That's where they've laid out the bar. Peter's over there with Arthur Perkins taking the drink tickets. You remember Arthur, don't you?' She didn't ask if they remembered her husband because she was sure they would – Peter was important, after all, and his name was often quoted in the *Financial Times*.

'Arthur Perkins?' drawled John as if he was parodying Edith Evans as Lady Bracknell saying 'a *handbag*?'

Marian was slightly taken aback, 'Yes, ex-dramatic club. He produced that superb show we put on in 1966, *Half a Sixpence*. And he did *My Fair Lady* the next year. Did you see it? Absolutely West End standard everyone said.'

'Really. Perkins . . . ?' mused John in the Evans role again and Barbara felt a laugh bubbling up inside her. That was another reason why she'd never leave him, he could be so very funny.

Escorted by Marian they entered the melee. She pushed her way through, towing them behind her like a tug towing a pair of ocean liners, and presented them at a long table covered with a white cloth and lines of wine glasses. Behind it, marshalling stony-faced waitresses in black dresses, stood Peter and Arthur.

'Darling,' said Marian to her husband, 'Barbara and John have arrived. Do give them a glass of wine.' She produced her trophy people like a magician producing a festoon of coloured streamers. Peter knew how important she felt the Carlton-Greys to be because of their superior social connections, and hurried round to shake John's hand.

Behind him Arthur was pouring the wine, 'White or red?' he asked.

They opted for white and when it was handed over Peter said, 'You remember Arthur from the old days, don't you? He was our theatrical genius.'

John remembered acid-tongued Perkins very well and his eyes crinkled as he smiled. 'Ah yes, *My Fair Lady*. Which part did you play again? Was it Eliza?' he asked.

Arthur gave a gasp as if he'd been punched in the stomach. For the first time in years he'd met his match.

TWENTY-FIVE

It took longer to come up from Tunbridge Wells than Kenneth had calculated, and as the Mercedes crossed the Thames, heading for St James's, Alice said irritably, 'We're late. Where are you going to park this thing?'

'Outside the club, or at least as near to it as possible,' said Roly, who always displayed supreme indifference to parking regulations and amazingly got away with it most of the time. When he did get a parking ticket, he usually tore it up, but Laura wearily knew that he would eventually be forced to pay.

'They might tow it away,' said Alice.

Roly laughed, 'If they do they're welcome to it. It's on its last legs, I'm afraid. If it gets us home after Newmarket without breaking down, I'll be very surprised.'

Alice laughed, pleased to know that the grand old car was not as good as it looked for she'd not been able to date it since it carried a personalised number plate – GMZ 100. The few parking spaces inside the courtyard were already full and people were walking in through the gates while Roly carelessly parked with two wheels on the Park Place pavement.

Alice leaned forward in her seat to scrutinise the other party-goers, 'There's that Ellington woman. Just look at her legs! So swollen! Heart trouble, I bet. She always ate too much. And look at the Thomsons, hasn't she aged! There's Belle Bolitho with the frightful Julia. Julia's walking with a stick and Belle looks about a hundred!' Her satisfaction was obvious. She was about to have a very good time indeed.

They went into the club and, on the way, Roly passed the car keys to Laura saying, 'I'll let you drive back because I'm planning to get stuck into the booze here.'

She slipped them into her handbag while Kenneth handed their tickets over to Alex who was manning the desk at the door on his own.

'You're late, Kenneth,' he said reprovingly.

'I know,' Kenneth snapped back and ushered his family into the crowd.

Roly felt Laura squaring her shoulders as she faced the ordeal, and his grip on her hand tightened when a woman in front of them turned round, spotted her and cried out, 'It can't be Laura Redmond! It *is*, isn't it? My goodness, don't you look like your mother! Exactly the same face, the same eyes. It's uncanny. If you had blonde hair, you'd be her double.'

The excited woman was Julia. 'Where's your father? I mean where's Kenneth?' she asked looking eagerly around.

Laura gestured behind herself and said, 'He's here, just coming. This is my husband, Roly Gomez.'

She remembered Julia very well from the long afternoons she spent with her mother in the house with the unused swimming pool. As far as she could recall Julia and Sonya always seemed to have their heads together as they giggled, whispered and drank gin and limes. In those days her mother's friends never bothered about her, certainly not as much as they were doing now – at least they hadn't until the last big row, and that she did not want to think about.

It was unsettling how enraptured Julia seemed to be at seeing her. She clasped Laura's arm, and said, 'Of course, Gomez. So that's your name now. I saw it on the guest list but I didn't know who it was. When I saw you though, I recognised you straight away. You've not changed at all really. And what does Mr Gomez do for a living?'

'He's a racehorse trainer,' said Laura shortly.

Julia gave a little scream, 'Fancy that. How unusual. There

are so many friends of your mother's at this party who'll want to see you again. You must meet up with them. Belle Bolitho's over there, and so's a very special friend, Andy Parnell. Come and I'll reintroduce you to them.'

She took a firm hold on Laura's arm and dragged her into the middle of a crowd of people. Laura cast an anguished look at Roly, who shrugged, indifferent to the fact that Julia had completely ignored him. He had his eye on the bar and made his purposeful way towards it. Belle stood in the middle of a group of eager-eyed women, towering over them, for she was tall, almost as tall as Laura. Julia elbowed her way into their circle and said, 'Look who I've found. It's Sonya's daughter!'

Belle turned slowly with an inscrutable expression on her face and stared at Laura. 'You've grown up, but of course you were only a kid the last time I saw you. What have you done with yourself?' she asked.

Laura saw Roly suddenly popping up beside her with a glass of chilled wine in his hand. He pushed it towards her and when she took it, her hand was shaking so badly that some of it splashed over the skirt of her dress, but she gulped down a big mouthful of what was left, grateful for the pause it gave her, before she said, 'This is my husband, Roly Gomez, he's a racehorse trainer and we've got a son called Lance.' She half turned to Roly for support, but he'd disappeared again.

One of the women exclaimed, 'Gomez? Isn't that a Spanish name?'

'It's an Irish name, too. Roly thinks one of his ancestors must have been washed up when the Spanish Armada was wrecked off the Irish coast,' said Laura. She'd always thought Roly's Spanish connection was the reason Lance had such beautiful black hair.

'How exciting – an Irish racehorse trainer!' drawled another woman. She wouldn't think it very exciting if she had to get up at five o'clock in the morning to ride out at exercise and spend hours mucking out boxes every night, Laura thought. But in spite of the hardships of her life, she wished she could be transported back to the yard at that very moment.

Belle was still staring silently at her as if weighing her up. Unspoken words hung between them. Laura remembered that Belle was always on the edge of her mother's circle, dragging along her small son who was sometimes left in Laura's care for hours at a time while the older women disappeared on some mysterious ploy – at least it was mysterious then.

'How's your son?' she asked Belle.

'Hector? He's fine. He's twenty-seven now and divorced so he's back at home with me. I quite enjoy his company.'

'What does he do?' asked Laura.

'He's a rep for a pharmaceutical company, selling drugs to doctors,' said Belle, with a funny little smile.

Julia was almost hopping with excitement, tapping her walking stick on the carpet as she spoke, 'Doctors! Andy Parnell's here too. We must get hold of him. Go and fetch him, Belle. I think I saw him over there by the bar. Bring him over to meet Laura.'

Belle swanned off. Her height gave her a great advantage when it came to seeking people out in the growing throng. She bore down on Andy as he was striking up a conversation with Roly, and laid a hand on his arm as she said, 'Hello Doctor Parnell. Come and meet your past.'

He recognised her at once and his face broke out in a smile, 'Hey Belle, I'd have known you anywhere. It's good to see you. Where's your husband?'

'Good to see you, too, and Tom's dead,' she said. She had always liked Andy though he'd acted rather stupidly at times. He'd grown up a lot since then though, she reflected, for now he looked tired and rather careworn, not the dashing young lad of their Bombay days.

'Come on. Julia's waiting,' said Belle and Andy gave

a rueful smile. 'I've got to get it over with, I expect,' he said.

He was awkward when he saw Julia, probably finding it difficult to know what to say for she had indeed changed a lot and was almost unrecognisable. She was jubilant however and threw out her arms as if delighted to see him, 'Dear Andy! Such a long time! Let me look at you. Oh, didn't we have some wonderful times. I often think of them . . .' and she gave a wicked chuckle which made him step back a bit as if he was afraid she was going to throw herself at him with intent to ravish there and then.

Belle looked around for James, but he was nowhere to be seen and the other people outside their own little group were all talking with their faces turned away in other directions, oblivious to what was being said beside them.

'Are you married, Andy?' Julia asked, and he said he was.

'And we've two children, teenagers now. Great kids,' he added.

'Teenagers!' she exclaimed, 'You were little more than a teenager when we first met – and yet you were very worldly even then, weren't you? Do you remember Laura, Sonya's daughter? She was a teenager then, too.'

Andy looked at Laura and a shadow that was impossible to read crossed his face but he smiled and said gently, 'Hello Laura. You are looking very well.'

She stared back at him, wondering what he was thinking. Her lips were twitching and to prevent that weakness from being seen she raised the glass of wine to her mouth and gulped its remaining contents down. When Andy saw the glass was empty he held out his hand for it and said, 'Let me buy you another.'

'I've still one free token left,' she stammered but he shook his head, 'Don't worry about that. Let me get you one, or would you prefer something stronger?'

She was feeling so upset that she heard herself saying, 'Actually I'd like a brandy.'

'Good idea,' he said, as if in agreement, and went off with her glass in his hand.

TWENTY-SIX

T ommy and Prakash had enjoyed a quiet day, sitting in Hyde Park watching the world go by. They'd lunched in a park café facing the Serpentine, and at four o'clock, made their way back to the hotel to prepare for the party.

Prakash borrowed an iron from the hotel housekeeper with which to press his boss's clothes. She had offered to have the pressing done for him, but he had refused because he did not trust anyone else to do it properly. There was not a wrinkle or an unseemly crease to be seen when he finished. Before they left Bombay, he'd picked out a Bombay Rugby Club tie as being the most suitable neckwear for the party. Tommy told him that, long ago, it had been swapped for a Police Rugby Club tie with Ben Carmichael after a close-fought match.

When Tommy was dressed he looked proud and patrician, a worthy descendant of the great Hodge, but he'd lost weight recently and his jacket hung loosely on him, a fact that his servant noted with some disquiet.

'What are you going to wear?' he asked Prakash as he sat down in the armchair of his room and looked at his watch. He was lingering because he wanted to arrive at the party when most of the guests were already there.

'Do you want me to go with you?' was the surprised reply.

'Of course. How am I going to manage making my way around London without you?' Tommy joked.

'Will I wear my bearer's uniform?'

'Certainly not. Wear your grey suit, the one that Moosa

my tailor made for you. You're very smart in it, and you're not going to the party as my servant, you're going as my friend and assistant.'

Despite money-minded Prakash's protest, Tommy refused to travel to Piccadilly on a bus and insisted on going to the party in a taxi, which swept them past the glittering front of the Ritz, down to St James's and back up again till they reached the Park Place cul-de-sac. At the end of the lane, they saw people thronging through the wide front entrance gate into an enclosed courtyard that faced an imposing old house.

Prakash stood on the pavement holding Tommy's walking stick as the old man lowered his head to get out of the cab, as he was still very tall in spite of shrinking in old age. The fare was paid without protest by Prakash and they walked solemnly into the club.

Peter was alone on the entrance desk and, because he had never been one of the rugby club set, he did not recognise Tommy.

'Remind me of your name again,' he said politely, and, when told it, found it on the list, looked up, slightly surprised, and asked, 'Detective Inspector Morrison? Not on official business, I hope.'

Tommy smiled. 'Retired now, I'm afraid, and just passing through London.'

Peter's gaze shifted questioningly to Prakash and Tommy supplied his name, 'This is Mr Prakash Rao. You'll find him on the list beside me because we bought our tickets at the same time.'

'This list is alphabetical, I'm afraid,' said Peter looking down. His mind was racing. It would never do to allow this man to take a servant into the party because he was pretty sure that was the function Prakash filled in Tommy's life – servant, or something even more personal which would be much worse.

Tommy was leaning down looking at the list, too, and

sharp-eyed still, he pointed out Prakash's name with a knobbly finger. 'There it is,' he said.

'Ah yes,' said Peter looking up, desperately wondering what to do, but at that moment Perkins came limping out of the main room mopping his brow after the unsettling exchange with John. He smiled – actually smiled – when his eye fell on the men at the table.

'Inspector Morrison!' he exclaimed, 'I'm so glad you've come to the party. I saw your name on the list. My name's Arthur Perkins and you won't remember me but we met a few years ago when one of my friends was involved in a rather unfortunate case when someone tried to blackmail him.'

Tommy regarded the foppishly dressed man with a jaundiced eye. He remembered both him and the case, which involved a decadent young man who'd been involved with a young male prostitute who tried to blackmail him. Unwisely he had retaliated by hiring someone to kill the prostitute, but the intended assassin had told the police and everything became rather nasty. The Englishman's employer, a large bank, saved his bacon by shipping him back home within twenty-four hours and all charges were dropped.

'I remember that business,' said Tommy slowly. It had left a bad taste in his mouth.

'Inspector Morrison and his friend Mr Rao have just arrived,' said Peter to Perkins, trying to mentally transfer his anxieties about the servant to his fellow committee member, but Perkins stared back at him, blandly. He obviously had no objection to Prakash's presence at the party.

'That's very nice. Have you kept your drink tokens and received your raffle tickets?' he said, throwing out an arm so they could go into the big hall. It seemed to Peter that there was unusual animation and friendliness in his bearing.

When the newcomers disappeared into the throng, Peter said to him, 'That man with Morrison is a servant, I think. I wonder if it was all right to let him in. There might be some people who object, you know.'

'Why? Things have changed, Peter. Morrison's an Anglo-Indian anyway. At one time we wouldn't have let him in either,' said Perkins, hurrying back into the hall as if he was eager to see what was going on in there.

TWENTY-SEVEN

P rakash and Tommy stepped into a huge room that was packed full of people, all shouting at each other. The din was terrific and disembodied scraps of conversation hung in the air like torn flags:

'Good heavens, fancy seeing *you* again!'

'Darling, how wonderful!'

'Hello, great to see you after all this time!'

'You haven't changed a bit!'

'I'd have known you anywhere.'

Lies were mixed with genuine compliments; false bonhomie with real delight. Only one or two individuals seemed to be forcing themselves into party mood but most of the guests were genuinely enjoying themselves, turning back time, forgetting the present, forgetting overdrafts, divorces, illnesses, and disappointing children. They straightened their shoulders and became their old selves, became the people they were years ago when the future was full of possibilities.

Sometimes a reveller on the far side of the room would spot an old friend in the throng and give a yell or a whistle, crying out, 'Stay right there I'm coming over!' Then, with wine glasses held high, and arms waving, they elbowed their way through the crowd, intent on picking up old ties, meeting again after many years, hugging and kissing, some of them almost weeping. Memories of youth and happy days seemed to fill the room in clouds of euphoria as the volume of noise rose and billowed. To anyone standing at the door, the din sounded almost like music, theme running above theme, undermotif and crescendo. The top noises were the greetings, squeals, sometimes shrill screams, laughter and shouting. Beneath that ran the sound of people attempting conversation, question and answer. 'Where are you living? Are you still working? How's your wife? Who are you married to now?' Heads had to be bent close together to hear the replies.

The deepest notes, the throbbing undercurrent, came from the mutters, the whispers, and confidences poured into ears. That was when the scandal, gossip, and things that really mattered were exchanged. There had not been any time of awkwardness, or any period during which people carefully circled each other wondering how to break the ice. No, this crowd had plunged straight in, speaking to people they did not immediately recognise, asking things like, 'When were you out? Where did you live? Who did you work for?' Bombay was the common factor that united them all, the background of their lives, the place that formed them and gave them an identity.

The two free glasses of wine per ticket were soon downed and people queued eagerly at the bar with bank notes held out, clamouring to be served. 'Let me buy you a drink,' old friends told each other, and the offers were accepted, even by people whose regime was usually restricted by doctors or bank managers. Tomorrow would be the time for regret, they thought. Tonight they were young again. As the alcohol intake rose, people shed years and actually began to look more like their old selves. Not only did they feel younger but their friends stopped noticing the walking sticks, the grey hair and the wrinkles. Again, through the bottom of a glass, they became as they used to be, tight-muscled, young, with everything in their bodies functioning so perfectly that they were not even aware they had livers or kidneys or beating hearts that might one day come to dominate their thoughts and actions.

Marian and Peter stood side by side like hosts on a receiving line, listening to the noise level rising and beaming, even at people they had never liked. The party – *their* party – was a huge success.

Marian, watching, took her husband's hand and squeezed it. He looked at her and said proudly, 'This is all due to you, darling.'

'I'm so glad it's going well,' she replied, 'It *is* the best party ever.'

Dee and Colin both quailed slightly when they heard the din that reverberated around the club's hall as they stepped inside the main door. She looked at him and asked, 'Oh God, can I face it?' Although he thought at first that she was joking, he quickly realised she was actually being quite serious. He could see that crowds of people terrified her. She was fighting with her fear because she knew it would be unfair to cling to him like a limpet. The first thing she had to do when she stepped into that throng was seek out someone else she knew. But as far as she could see from where she stood the people in the big room were all strangers and totally absorbed with each other, standing chattering in tight circles like so many rugby scrums. How could she ever break in among them?

The backs of her hands prickled and her heart gave one of its funny little jumps. It hadn't done that for ages, not since she went to live with Algy in Spain. I miss you, how I miss you, she silently told him. He'd made her feel safe and without him she was defenceless again. Tears pricked her eyes and she felt her head swim.

'God, what if I faint amongst all those people? How shaming,' she thought in panic and Colin looked at her in surprise for unknowingly she'd spoken the words aloud.

'Of course you won't faint. You're all right,' he said reassuringly and she saw the genuine concern on his face.

Gathering herself together she grinned back and said, 'Only joking! Let's go.'

'Yes, let's go Jeanne Moreau,' he joked and patted her shoulder as they stepped purposefully into the crowd.

He knew she was apprehensive, although she said she wasn't and he didn't want her to know that he felt that way, too. The sight of men with broad shoulders and spreading waistlines, men he remembered thundering like Ganymedes up and down the rugby field in the days when he had to pretend to be one of the boys like them, made him deeply depressed. He still had nothing in common with them; he'd only come to the party to keep Dee company. He escorted her because he knew she liked remembering the happy days of her marriage to Ben, and he was always grateful for their friendship during his early months in India. In those days they were living in a lovely house by the sea on Walkeshwar Road and seemed to know everybody, but they welcomed him uncritically and soon became about the only straight couple in the city with whom he was able to relax.

When Ben died, Dee's misery and loneliness had wakened Colin's sympathy and, because she could not face the Bombay Cocktail Party on her own, but still wanted to attend it, they started going to it together – not every year, but every second or third year. She went because it revived her memories and kept them green but, left to himself Colin would never have shown his face at one of these gatherings. He only attended because he was kind and felt sorry for Dee. Afterwards he always took her out to dinner and listened as she talked about Ben.

She did not only talk about herself though, because she was a sympathetic listener and from time to time he'd let slip hints about his own forlorn love life, always making jokes about it, and had never, he thought, revealed the sad truth. His loneliness, his longing for a lifetime companion was always sharpened when he went into such heterosexual gatherings as the cocktail party and he emerged from them wondering why he couldn't find a companion who would stay with him for ever? Why was he always to be the one who got his heart broken?

When he went home tonight he knew that, as usual, he would brood about his situation, wondering why he had not abandoned his true sexuality long ago and settled for living a lie. He loved children and home making. If he'd married – if he'd been able to pretend to be something he wasn't – he wouldn't be so lonely now. There were men like himself, he knew, who lived that lie, but he was also aware of the complexities and heartbreaks that such deception could lead to. By now he had reconciled himself to never finding a lasting love. The substitute for it had to be fleeting relationships and friendships. He sighed and squared his shoulders as he smiled at Dee and they plunged into the party.

She smiled back, full of misgivings and wondering why she had been so keen to come to this nostalgic occasion. Was it just because Algy didn't want her to go? Was it because of him that she'd been so bloody-minded and awkward? No. Deep inside herself she knew that, once more, she was at the party because of Ben. She was intent on clearing the last vestiges of him out of her system.

When she thought about her husband, she always remembered him in India, although they had lived in England for the last five years of his life. Those five years, however, had been unhappy, for they were years of growing disillusion and a gradual falling out of love. When he died, she chose to forget the bad times, and remembered only their happy days. She kept those good memories topped up every few years by going to the Bombay Cocktail Party where she met their old friends, talked about old times, and reactivated her good image of him. She did not want to admit to disillusion.

At the cocktail party she was not Dee Carmichael, the journalist and independent woman she had become after his death, but was Ben Carmichael's wife. People talked to her about *him,* and were not interested or aware of anything that had happened to her since they last saw the Carmichaels as a couple. She never talked about her own successful career because no one ever asked. It was as if she was going about in disguise, in dark glasses and a headscarf like Garbo.

Strangely she never minded this sublimation of herself, in fact for the short time of the party, she gloried in it, as if she was remembering an enjoyable play she had once watched from the stalls. This year, however, she realised with sudden clarity, it was different. This year, if she had not persuaded Colin to accompany her, it would have been easy to turn on her heel without stepping into the party room and walk away. Her relish for it, she realised, had gone. It was not that she was scared of mixing with the crowd; it was not as if she dreaded talking about Ben, but she had no need of him any more.

She was cured. Her life was going forward in another direction – or at least it had been until she threw her chance of happiness with Algy away. Oh God, what have I done? Where is he? Will I ever see him again? she wondered in anguish. All around her now were familiar faces from the past, but she was not thinking about them, but about Algy. You fool, you damned fool! she castigated herself. Her heart ached with a terrible dull pain, made all the worse because she knew she was now being called to put on one of her acts. For the next two hours she was to be Ben Carmichael's brave, but grieving widow.

As she and Colin pushed their way into the crowd together she put her lips to his ear and whispered, 'Off you go and meet people. We'll bump into each other every now and again, I'm sure. Don't worry about me. I'm perfectly all right. I've just seen some people I know,' she said pointing across to a group of gossiping women.

'I'll get us some more drinks first,' he said, 'We can't face this sober.'

*   *   *

Tricia Keen went straight to the cloakroom when she arrived at the club and spent a long time crimping her hair and repairing her make-up. Then she went into a cubicle and shook some white powder out of a small plastic pouch in her handbag on to a five pound note which she flattened out on the top of the lavatory cistern. Holding back her hair with one hand, she leaned forward, rolled another note, and snorted deeply before shaking her head and then giggling.

When she emerged into the main cloakroom again it was still empty. Laughing, she bounced on the tips of her toes, pirouetted round in the empty cloakroom, pointed like a pop singer at her own reflection in the mirror above the washbasins. Then she pouted seductively as she repaired her lipstick and went out to take on the world.

Farquhar was waiting, lingering at the door, looking in at the throng. He's really gorgeous, she thought; although I said it was to be strictly business, it would be rather nice to slip away with him to a hotel for a couple of hours. In the old days, she wouldn't have thought twice about it – just jumped right in, but Jim was a formidable man and she was rather frightened of him. He'll never know, said the daring side of her personality, so why not? She went up to her young man and laid a hand on his back, stroking the muscles beneath his jacket. He feels lovely, why not?

Alex on the desk watched her with deep suspicion, for she had always terrified him. Her blatant sexuality was too much for him to take. She glittered at him, thinking, That poor slob looks exactly the same as he did twenty years ago. I'm damned sure he hasn't had a facelift so he must have looked forty when he was only twenty.

'I've forgotten to buy any tickets,' she said, 'Can I pay for them now?'

Blushing scarlet, he said that she could. 'How much?' she asked airily. When Alex said 'Twenty pounds', Farquhar, bless him, seized his cue.

'I'll pay, darling,' he said and fished out a crocodile-skin wallet. He was playing his part well. She decided to pay him back with interest.

When he took the money Alex handed them each a yellow raffle ticket with black numbers printed on it. 'What's this?' asked Tricia.

'We're having a raffle. The prize is a pair of business class air tickets to Bombay or any other destination in the same price range – and two nights in a top-class hotel when you get there as well,' said Alex proudly.

Tricia's laugh was loud and pealing as if he'd said something hysterically funny, 'What a brilliant idea,' she said, clutching Farquhar's arm, 'You simply must win it, sweet. I order you to win it so we can go on a trip and enjoy ourselves.'

'Your wish is my command,' said Farquhar, and arm in arm they swept into the party, the last people to arrive.

'Well, my next command is that you go to the bar and bring me my first glass of free wine,' she said, rising on tip-toe and kissing his cheek so that everyone near them could see.

Catching her mood, he played along and kissed her back, full on the lips and when he did so, he noticed how enormously enlarged were the pupils of her eyes. Oh my God, I hope she isn't high, he was thinking as he pushed his way towards the bar. He was making his way back to her with a glass of wine in each hand, when a large lady stepped back from one of the groups barring his way and almost knocked him off his feet. He staggered, and was only saved from falling by the press of people, but his side-step sent a man beside him ricocheting. Wine splashed up from the glasses he had in his hand on to the stranger's cream silk sleeve.

'I'm *so* sorry,' apologised Farquhar.

'Not your fault. It's this huge crowd to blame,' said Colin, looking ruefully at a splash of wine running down his jacket and thinking, 'Thank God it isn't red.' The glasses he was carrying had also been emptied in the collision.

Farquhar apologised again. 'Let me get you another two glasses. I insist. It's my fault yours are spilt. And over such a magnificent suit!'

Colin thawed when he saw that a handsome young man with concerned brown eyes and the longest, thickest lashes he had ever seen was rubbing at his arm with a large handkerchief. Those eyes would have won him round even if the spilt wine had been red.

'It won't mark. White wine washes out,' he said, reassuringly. When he smiled his genuine kindness and good nature showed, making the lines round his eyes wrinkle up and the eyes themselves begin to twinkle.

'It's a great suit. Where did you get it?' asked Farquhar, passing Colin two full glasses and firmly taking the empty ones. Their hands met and so did their eyes.

'In Hong Kong,' said Colin slightly distractedly, wondering if he was imagining more into the exchanged look than was intended.

'Marvellous tailors in Hong Kong,' said Farquhar, 'Do you work there?'

'No, I'm retired. I worked for a while in Bombay, though. That's why I'm here. I come every few years with a friend who I met there.'

Farquhar's face fell slightly. 'I'm with a friend, too,' he said, 'But I've never been to Bombay so I suppose you could say I'm here on false pretences. Is your friend waiting for the wine?'

Colin recovered himself, 'Oh yes, of course, so she is. Come over and meet her, bring your friend. She's in that group by that big vase of flowers beside the window.'

She, noted Farquhar, perhaps I'm wrong after all. 'I'll fetch my friend and come over. I must apologise again for being so clumsy,' he said politely, and they smiled at each other, both very much liking what they saw.

TWENTY-EIGHT

T he crowd was immense and the noise deafening. Although she felt oddly disembodied, the fumes of brandy from her glass seemed to curl round Laura's tongue and rise into her head, clearing it slightly. She took a big sip, then smiled at Andy Parnell to show her gratitude. He was watching her carefully, she noticed, and she was surprised how different – how much more sympathetic, in the French sense – he looked compared to the way she remembered him.

Julia was talking loudly, dominating their group, ebullient to the point of hysteria.

Excitedly she gripped Laura's forearm and asked, 'Where's Kenneth? Where's your mother's husband?'

Laura looked behind her and surveyed the sea of people without really seeing them. 'He's over there somewhere, we came in together. Oh yes, I see him. He's talking to that man wearing an amazing shirt.'

'You came in together? You're still friendly with him?' Julia was clearly surprised to hear this.

Laura stared levelly at her, 'Why not? I love him.'

'Of course, I never believed it when people said he'd killed your mother. He was really very fond of her even though he married again so quickly,' said Julia.

'He did not kill my mother. She died of a heart attack. I love Kenneth and think of him as my father. I don't really remember the real one, you see, and Kenneth has always been very kind to me,' said Laura vehemently.

Julia laughed, 'Your own father, Redmond, was an Irish rogue. Maybe that's why you've married an Irishman, too, darling.'

Belle let out her pent-up breath in a little gasp, because she was thinking, This is why Julia was so keen to come to this party and have an audience. She's out to hurt as many people as possible. I wonder when she's going to drag us all in?

Laura flinched. 'I don't think that has anything to do with it. I didn't even know my father was Irish. My mother never told me that.'

Julia was beaming, pleased at getting a reaction, 'Didn't she? Well maybe she wanted to put him out of her mind. Still, it's interesting that you married another Irishman. Perhaps racial memory or something attracts you to them. On the other hand it might equally have attracted you to Indians . . . through your mother of course.'

Surprised, Laura asked, 'What do you mean?' although something told her she should not ask that question.

'Because of your Indian blood of course. Didn't you know your mother was Eurasian? Her mother was an Anglo-Indian girl. God knows who her father was. Just think how many different nationalities your son has in his veins – Indian, English, Irish and Spanish too. Is he good at languages? How old did you say he was?'

Gritting her teeth and determined not to give Julia the satisfaction of seeing that she'd scored a hit, Laura took another encouraging sip of brandy. 'He speaks French quite well and he's sixteen. What makes you think my mother was Eurasian? She didn't look it,' she said, sounding cool but feeling foolish because of her inability to return Julia's venom with equally hurtful words.

'I know because she told me. When her mother died she was sent a lot of papers that told her she'd been adopted, and was actually the child of a half-caste girl who lived in Nagpur of all places. It upset her a lot, I can tell you. She went to Poona, where she'd been born, and to some awful suburb of Bombay to try to find her mother but discovered she'd died some time before. She met a sister – your aunt – though, and said she was as black as your hat. She confided in me because I was her friend. Probably her only friend.' Julia was delighted to be able to spring this surprise on Sonya's daughter.

Andy Parnell decided to put an end to her tirade of cruelty and acted as if he was unaware of the portent of what was being said, by interrupting Julia to say, 'I haven't seen James yet. Where is he?'

She grimaced. 'God knows. Probably sitting in a corner surveying the crowd and fantasising about being a dancing girl. He dresses up in a sari almost every night now and cavorts around upstairs to Indian music. He doesn't think I know, of course, but the music's so loud! I can't imagine what our maidservant thinks. Perhaps he should see a psychiatrist. You're a doctor, you don't know anyone to recommend, do you? My husband definitely needs counselling about his sexuality.'

She raised her voice when delivering this speech, and several people standing near them turned around to stare. Tricia, who was just then bearing down on their group with Farquhar in tow, gave a shrill laugh and cried out, 'Here's Julia, not a bit changed. As vicious and malicious as ever. Hello darling!' And she rushed forward to kiss Julia on the cheek.

Julia recoiled from her embrace. 'I thought you weren't coming. Your name wasn't on the guest list,' she said.

'I like to surprise people. I like to pop up like a Jack in the Box. Aren't you pleased to see me?' Tricia replied.

'*Delighted* darling. I've always wondered what happened to you. There were so many possibilities,' said Julia sweetly. It was obvious however that Tricia's state of continued pulchritude, her Dior trouser suit and her attendant young man did not please her much.

She fixed her eyes on Farquhar and asked sweetly, 'Is this your son?'

Tricia was expecting something like that so she laughed brightly. 'Of course not. He's my lover.' Then she turned to Farquhar and said, 'Aren't you darling?'

Again he responded gallantly. 'I'm a very lucky man,' he said and stroked her hair lovingly.

Julia rallied, forgetting about Laura and went off after this new target. 'Of course, I should have remembered that you couldn't have a son. You were barren, weren't you? So convenient.'

Tricia laughed, 'It saved me a lot of money anyway, didn't it? And I never had to worry about how to explain presenting a husband with a baby when he hadn't done his duty by me for years.'

Julia laughed at that and looked at Belle, 'Have you anything to say to that, darling?' she asked sweetly.

Belle went white. Her time for Julia's barbs had come.

While the women were engaged in these exchanges, Andy put his hand on Laura's arm and said, 'Let's leave them to it. Take me to meet your husband.'

She stared over the crowd and saw Roly standing by Kenneth. There was no sign of Alice who was busily 'working the room', dashing from group to group, gathering gossip like a bee collects pollen.

'He's over there,' she said and he followed her through the press of people. Over her shoulder he said softly, 'Don't let Julia get at you. From listening to her I'm pretty sure she's mad. She never was really sane but now she's the one that needs a psychiatrist and not poor old James.'

Laura said nothing, only shook her head. When Roly and Kenneth saw her approaching them, they knew straight away that something was wrong. She looked years older than she had when they arrived at the party half an hour ago. Her sparkling beauty was dimmed.

Kenneth moved first and put an arm round her shoulders.

'Are you feeling ill, darling? Is the heat too much for you?'

She nodded, 'I think I'll go into the hall for a bit to get a breath of fresh air. It's so airless and noisy in here. I can't hear myself think.'

'I'll come with you,' said Roly, but she shook her head, 'No, you stay and talk to my friend Andy Parnell. He used to know my mother and me in Bombay. Kenneth can take me into the hall. I want to speak to him anyway.'

The hall was empty and cool as Kenneth led Laura to a long leather-covered bench beside a marble pillar. They sat side by side saying nothing for a little before she suddenly burst out with, 'I was speaking to Julia Whitecross in there. She really is a poisonous woman.'

He nodded, 'She always was. I blame her for what happened to your mother.'

She stared at him, 'You mean for her dying?'

'No, not that. I mean for her character change. Before she became friends with Julia, Sonya was a nice person, a good woman, but she was a little weak willed and Julia led her astray, just like she leads Belle Bolitho astray.'

'And Mrs Keen?' asked Laura.

He shook his head, 'Tricia was well astray before she and Julia met up. But at least she went astray on her own, she didn't feel she had to drag other people in with her. Julia on the other hand likes to corrupt.'

'She said you killed my mother, but I told her you certainly did not,' said Laura vehemently.

He sighed. 'I'm used to people saying that. It's because of the insurance policy. We insured each other for a lot of money when we married and the Bombay gossips thought I killed her because of it. Our marriage was going through a bad time – but I didn't kill her, Laura. I swear to you I didn't.'

She took his hand and said with great earnestness, 'I know you didn't. I know it. I won't let them accuse you because it's so unfair. I couldn't bear it if you were accused of something like that.'

'Don't worry. The death was registered as natural. Nothing could be done now even if there were suspicions,' he told her.

She stared at him, eyes wide. 'You're sure?'

'Pretty sure. I've never asked about it, but it would be impossible to prove, wouldn't it? Anyway it wasn't murder. Don't let's talk about it.' His voice was firm and she nodded but she did not get up from the seat to go back into the party.

'There was something else that Julia said . . .' she told him hesitantly.

He looked surprised. 'What?'

'She said my mother was Anglo-Indian.'

His voice was careful as he said, 'Even if she was, what would it matter?'

Laura frowned. 'It wouldn't, would it? I was just surprised by the way she chucked it at me. I had no idea. When I was growing up it was a terrible thing to be called "chi-chi". Mother didn't look a bit Eurasian, though. Is it true?'

'How did Julia Whitecross get her hands on that?' mused Kenneth.

'She said mother told her. If she did, why didn't she tell you or me?'

'She told me,' said Kenneth sadly, 'I saw the papers her mother's executors sent her and she told me then. She'd been born in Poona to an unmarried Anglo-Indian girl but I don't know the full circumstances. She tried to find out as much as she could but that wasn't a lot, although her mother's sister told her that her father was an Englishman in the Indian Army. I'd no idea she would be so ill advised as to talk about it to that Whitecross woman.'

'Well she did,' said Laura sadly.

'And Julia Whitecross will have spread it far and wide by this time. I'm surprised you didn't find out long ago.'

'Why didn't you tell me?' she persisted.

'I thought it would never affect your life. I didn't think it was important. Your father was Irish, your mother was at the most one quarter Indian, if that. What did it matter? I like Indians, you like Indians, there's nothing to be ashamed of.' He took her hand and went on, 'Put it out of your mind. If you let it upset you, that'd be exactly what Julia Whitecross wants.'

'I'm not ashamed. It's just that there's a lot of mysteries about my life and my family that I don't know. I'm afraid of which skeleton will be dragged from the cupboard next.'

'Stop worrying. There'll be no more mysteries. Do you feel well enough to go back into the party now?' said Kenneth gently.

She felt that she was keeping him away from his party, so she stood up and nodded, 'Yes, of course. But do we have to stay much longer?'

He looked at his watch. It was five minutes to eight. 'Not much, half an hour anyway, but Alice won't leave until the raffle is drawn. She's always lucky at raffles and she's sure she's going to win this one,' he said wearily, knowing how impossible it would be to drag his wife away until the bitter end.

Laura nodded. 'All right, it doesn't matter. I'll last the course. Let's go back in.' She took his arm as they went inside.

Standing near the door was a tall old man in a grey suit with a solemn looking Indian beside him. The man turned his head as she passed, and gave an involuntary exclamation of surprise. She paused, looked at him and met his eyes.

'Theresa, oh Theresa,' he said.

'No, I'm Laura,' she said with a smile, thinking he had mistaken her for someone else. Then she saw that there were tears in the old man's eyes.

'You are exactly like my sister, Theresa,' he said softly.

Kenneth, too, had stopped and was listening intently.

210

'I know you, don't I? You used to be in the Bombay police?'

'Yes, Mr Richards, I was. I am – or I was – Detective Inspector Morrison who was in charge of your wife's case when she died on the train,' said Tommy. He'd recognised Kenneth at once because time had not changed him all that much. Sonya's husband had always been tall and thin with sticking-out ears, a high forehead and deeply sunken eyes that made his face seem slightly skeletal.

Tommy looked again at Laura and said, 'Is this your stepdaughter? Is this Sonya's child?'

Kenneth and Laura nodded together and said, 'Yes', as if with one voice.

'Then you are my great-niece,' said Tommy solemnly to Laura, 'Your mother was my niece, your grandmother was my sister, Theresa, and she looked exactly like the film star Ava Gardner. Has no one ever told you that you do, too?'

Laura nodded without speaking, remembering how Roly had so recently pointed out her resemblance to the star. 'I've been told,' she whispered.

Kenneth, standing beside her, seemed dumbstruck with astonishment. 'Sonya was your niece? You're sure?'

'I'm positive. I'm Anglo-Indian and her mother, my sister, gave up a baby for adoption to the nuns in Poona. Then the baby was given to an English couple called Walker. I found this all out only recently myself,' said Tommy.

Kenneth nodded, 'That's true. When Mrs Walker died she left Sonya all the papers about her adoption. She hadn't known anything of it until then. It was a great shock to her.'

'And when she went to try to find her mother, Theresa was long dead,' said Tommy sadly.

'This is so tragic,' whispered Laura and her face looked ashen.

Kenneth put his arm round her and led her to a spindly gilt chair that stood against the wall. 'Sit down. This is all a terrible shock for you, darling. Let me get you another drink.' He dashed off and Tommy said to Laura, 'Yes, sit down and talk to me. We ought to get to know each other, but I find it difficult standing up for too long.'

She shivered but sat down saying nothing, only staring at him with the startled brown eyes that so resembled his sister's that he was filled with a rush of conflicting emotions and sadness.

'I'm sorry if I've surprised you by all this,' he apologised.

She shook her head, 'No, no, already this evening someone else told me about my mother being Anglo-Indian. It's just that I'm amazed you're here, too. Not because we're related to each other but because you're the policeman who investigated her death as well.'

Tommy nodded, 'Yes. There's so many coincidences. Who told you about Sonya just now?'

He was wondering if this loose-mouthed person might be the one who sent him the anonymous letter. Laura pointed into the throng, 'Julia Whitecross over there, that woman in the silver dress. She was my mother's friend and she told me my mother was Eurasian.'

Tommy stared to where she was pointing and saw a hyper-active looking woman in silver, waving her arms about and talking very fast. She looked drunk. He nodded silently. She was the type who might send malicious letters. He also remembered that none of his Bombay informants had a good word to say about her.

'I know her name,' he said slowly.

Kenneth was back bearing two glasses of wine in his hand, one of which he handed to Laura and the other to Tommy.

'Drink that,' he said, pulling up another chair and sitting facing them, 'Now let's talk about this.'

'There's nothing much to say,' Tommy replied wearily. He was beginning to feel his age and was very tired. From the corner of his eye he saw that Prakash was watching him anxiously.

'Did you come to this party in the hope of meeting your niece? How did you know about it? I sent out the invitations and I certainly didn't send one to you,' said Kenneth slowly. He could not remember seeing Morrison's name on the guest list that was given to him by Perkins and had no memory either of ever seeing the policeman at any of the previous cocktail parties.

'I came because someone took the trouble of sending me an invitation. At that time I had no idea your wife was my sister's child, but the sender of the invitation tipped me off that the circumstances of her death need reinvestigation.'

Kenneth leaned forward and said, 'I didn't send it.'

'Well someone did and it was postmarked central London,' Tommy told him.

'And why did it say you should reinvestigate my wife's death?' was Kenneth's next question.

Tommy stared at him, focusing hard as he used to do when grilling suspects, looking for a give-away flicker of guilt. 'It was an anonymous letter, made up of letters cut from newspapers. It said Sonya had been murdered and asked me if I knew who she was,' he said slowly.

'And you didn't?' interrupted Laura.

He turned towards her, 'No, not then. But I made it my business to find out.'

'It must have been a shock,' she whispered.

Tommy's eyes softened as he looked at her. 'It was. I'm still wondering how whoever sent it knew I was in charge of the investigation – and also that I was Sonya's uncle.' He turned his head to look again at Kenneth and asked sharply, 'Swear you didn't send it, Mr Richards!'

'I didn't. I swear I didn't,' Kenneth's voice was vehement. 'But I sent out the main body of invitations, although *not* yours. The other committee members sent out some on their own initiative, and people were asked to circularise their friends so we could get a big turn-out . . . Perhaps it came from one of them.'

'If it did, the sender is probably here now watching us,' said Laura slowly. Her voice trembled as she stared around the crowded room.

'That's very possible. Whoever took it upon themselves to write to me had inside knowledge. But what motive could they have for starting it all up again? Was it revenge against you or me, Mr Richards? A desire for retribution, or just a wish to cause trouble? Whoever did it and why, they'd want to know if I responded, so they probably *are* here now,' Tommy said.

'But I don't understand. It's as if someone's trying to bait a trap. Why?' Laura asked looking around in confusion.

Kenneth took her hand. 'I've told you not to worry. It's all long past,' he said softly.

The loving look she gave him was so like an expression that Tommy remembered on the face of his sister that he felt a physical pang of sorrow.

He, too, was moved to reassure her so he said, 'You've no reason for concern, Laura – if you don't mind me calling you that. The only person who should be worrying is the person who killed your mother – if anyone did. An Indian woman who talked to me about the case said that the guilty person carries the knowledge in their heart and in time conscience will force them to speak.'

With a sigh he passed his untouched glass of wine back to Kenneth, 'Thank you, Mr Richards, but I have no taste for more wine. Perhaps you won't mind if my friend Mr Rao fetches me a whisky. It's better for an old man of my age. Can I ask you a favour? Will you act as my messenger and ask some people to come over one by one and talk to me about Sonya? After all, I've come a long way to clear this up – not Sonya's death, because nothing can be done about that now, but I want to know who is bringing it up again after so long.'

Kenneth stood up and said, 'Just tell me who you want. I'll bring them to you.'

TWENTY-NINE

B efore he undertook Tommy's commission, Kenneth led
Laura across the room to Roly who put his arm round
her and asked, 'Hey, this is a great party. Are you feeling
better?' His enjoyment of parties was infectious and made
her smile at him as she said, 'Yes, I am, but something
strange has happened. I've been talking to that old man over
there. He knew my mother. In fact he was the policeman who
investigated her death and he's come here tonight because
someone wrote and told him her death was not natural, but
that she'd been murdered. It's rather unsettling . . .' Her
voice trailed off as she indicated Tommy. She did not feel
capable of adding that the old man was her newly discovered
uncle. She'd tell Roly that story later.

Defensively he glared across the room and said, 'What
rubbish! Your mother died of a heart attack. Let me get you
a brandy to make you feel better. I'll be the one to stay
sober and do the driving after all. You look as if you need
a drink.'

She'd lost count of the drinks she'd consumed already
but leaned gratefully against him, taking strength from his
dependability and the faith he had in her. 'Thanks Roly. Get
me that drink. I can always rely on you,' she said.

When he was off at the bar, she suddenly felt weak so
leaned her back against the wall between the windows,
and was held upright by its solidity. All around her were
chattering people, who looked happily oblivious to any
dramas being played out among them. Is anyone else going

through the mental turmoil I'm suffering, she wondered? Is there another person desperately trying to cover up confusion? By the law of averages there had to be someone, she supposed.

Suddenly she felt that she was being stared at. Turning her head to the left she found herself looking over the sea of heads at John Carlton-Grey. His eyes were the same pale piercing colour that she remembered and they still had the capacity to cut right into her. It was the first time she'd seen him since four days before her mother died, the first time since that terrible row. She shuddered and swiftly turned her head away but she was too late. He was coming towards her. When she felt his hand on her shoulder she looked down at his long fingers – a musician's hand. She remembered his skill at playing the violin, and at other things as well. Her body stiffened and every muscle went so tight that she feared she might snap.

'Laura,' he said softly.

She stood very still and said nothing. 'Laura,' he whispered again, his head close to her ear, 'I'm very, very sorry. I never got the chance to tell you that.'

Turning her head she found herself staring straight into his eyes. Close up they were not so arresting now, but looked pouched and weary, the eyes of an old man.

'It's too late to be sorry, far too late,' she told him.

Just then Roly appeared with her brandy and she accepted it gratefully. More than ever now she needed the artificial boost it could give her.

'This is an old friend of my mother's – John Carlton-Grey,' she told her husband, 'and here's his wife, Barbara.' The ever vigilant Barbara was walking towards them too, smiling in a remorseless way.

'Carlton-Grey!' cried Roly happily, 'Any relation to Nigel? I used to ride against him in point-to-points in Ireland when I was a lad.'

John smiled his gentlemanly smile, 'Yes, Nigel's a cousin, a bit distant though.'

'How is he?' asked Roly, who could always be relied on to defuse any tense situation, often without realising it.

'He's very well. He inherited a title and sits in the Lords now instead of on a saddle.'

Roly laughed, 'Old Nigel was a devil to race against. Not above shoving you overboard if you got too close going round corners. We once had a punch-up about it in the weighing room at the Curragh.'

John laughed, too, and said, 'Next time I see him I'll tell him. What's your name?'

'Roly Gomez, I'm married to Laura here.' He slipped his arm round her waist and she leaned against him. Barbara was smiling, too, now but stiffly as if she was anxious to get her husband away.

John allowed her to steer him off in another direction, saying over his shoulder 'I'll tell Nigel, Roly Gomez still bears a grudge, will I?'

'No,' shouted Roly, 'I was the one who did the shoving that time.'

Then he turned back to Laura and said, 'The colour's coming back into your face. The brandy's working. How do you feel?'

'I just wish this bloody party was finished,' she said, looking around for Alice, whom she spotted scuttling from group to group, more animated than she had been for years. She certainly didn't want to go home yet.

'Can you see Kenneth?' Laura asked Roly, who nodded and pointed to the old policeman sitting by the wall. Kenneth was leading Julia Whitecross towards him.

Almost dispassionately she studied the impassive looking old man. How strange that he's my uncle, she thought, how strange that we are united by blood but have never met until today. Is it as strange for him as it is for me? All of a sudden she was gripped by a desire to talk to him again so she began making her way towards him, saying to her husband as she went, 'I must speak to him again.'

Before she could reach Tommy, however, Dee Carmichael appeared and spotted him, running towards him, bending down and saying, 'Hello, Inspector Morrison. Do you remember me? I was married to Ben Carmichael – the rugby player.'

Tommy smiled and held out a hand, 'Of course I remember you, Mrs Carmichael. How good to see you again. I heard about Ben and was very sorry. But there's someone else here tonight who I know will be delighted to see you, too – it's Prakash Rao.'

He waved a hand to his left and she turned to look where he pointed. Prakash, who'd been off fetching another whisky for his employer, was shouldering his way through the throng. She gasped in amazement.

'Prakash! From Walkeshwar Road. What a surprise to see you here.'

'He's my bearer and my friend,' Tommy interrupted, 'I couldn't have got here tonight without him.'

Prakash had been one of the servants that Dee missed dreadfully as friends as well as helpers when she returned to England so many years ago.

'Prakash,' she exclaimed again, in obvious delight, holding out her hands to him, 'It's wonderful to see you again.' She remembered him as a leggy youth, but he had grown into a dignified and elegant man who looked like a university professor instead of a household servant. But, she thought, he'd always been very patrician, even as a boy.

He was smiling as he said, 'Mrs Carmichael, it's good to see you, too. I've told the Inspector many times how you saved me after I stabbed that cook.'

She laughed as well, 'Gosh, yes, I'd forgotten about that. You came to our house that day, didn't you, Tommy? I remember other things as well, Prakash. We used to garden together, didn't we? And you rugby tackled a thief who was trying to steal our laundry and sat on his head until the police arrived. My children will be so pleased when I tell them I've met you again.' The Carmichael children had all loved Prakash for he played games with them, carrying them around on his back and taking their lunch boxes to the kindergarten school on Malabar Hill.

Tommy was watching this exchange indulgently but it was obvious that he wanted to continue with his own conversations and Kenneth Richards was hovering nearby, trying to introduce Julia. Tactfully, Dee and Prakash stood aside to let her in. She was at her most patronising when she smiled down at the old man and said, 'Kenneth says that I must remember you from Bombay but I'm afraid I don't. I hadn't much to do with the police.'

'I was Sonya Richards' uncle,' he told her.

She looked taken aback. 'Really?' There was a pause during which he could tell what she was thinking: He's obviously Anglo-Indian, and she was, too. What's he doing here? She'd drunk enough to ask him outright, 'Did you come all the way from Bombay for this party?'

'Yes, in a way I did,' said Tommy, 'And I'm happy to find that I have a beautiful relative who is here, too.'

'You mean Laura? Didn't you know about her?' asked Julia curiously and slipped into the empty chair by his side, prepared to gossip more.

'No. I didn't even know I had a niece called Sonya until a few weeks ago,' he said.

Julia was enthralled. 'Really? How did you find out about her?'

He ignored her question and said wearily, 'I believe you and my niece Sonya knew each other well. I'm curious about her. Describe her for me, please.'

'She was *so* nice, we were *such* friends . . .' Julia began to gush.

'Mrs Whitecross, spare me the hyperbole. I haven't enough time left to cut my way through it. Tell me the truth. Tell me what she was really like,' Tommy retorted sharply.

She gaped at him, taken aback by the word hyperbole, unsure of what it meant. Her mouth was still slightly open when he continued, 'For how long did you know her?'

'Three or four years, I think. Is this official? Are you asking me these questions as a policeman?' She gathered her wits and wanted to know.

'I'm asking as her uncle. I never knew her, but she was my sister's child and I was in charge of investigating her death, although I didn't know who she really was at that time. I'm very much afraid I let her down,' he said slowly.

She was filled with animation again. 'You mean there might have been more to the death than was said at the time. I've always thought that, too.'

Leaning closer, she looked round to see if Kenneth was within earshot. He wasn't so she half whispered, 'Inspector Morrison, it is my belief that your niece was murdered by her husband. He insured her life for a large sum of money and he was already sleeping with the woman he's married to now – that's her over there, the thin one. She's called Alice. They might have been in it together.'

'That's very interesting,' said Tommy, 'How do you think they did it? She was alone on the train. She was perfectly well when the bearer took in her morning tea but dead in her locked compartment two hours later when the train arrived in Bombay.'

Julia lowered her voice even more, 'I've thought a lot about that. She was taking heart pills, you know. Her doctor had started her on them not long before she died and I remember my friend, Andy Parnell, who was a ship's doctor with Anchor Line at the time, warning her to be very careful and never take too many of them. They could kill her if she overdosed, he said.'

'But to overdose she would have to administer the pills to herself. It would be suicide then,' said Tommy.

'Not necessarily. They were capsules, you know, those little things that look like torpedoes. I have to take some myself for my arthritis nowadays. If you shake them there's never much powder inside. I can't imagine why they have to make them so big – one standard size I expect. All the killer would have to do was open a capsule and put in more powder, maybe the contents of three or four other capsules. She'd never notice, she'd just swig it down. I always think of that when I take my own medication. I shake them up and look to see if they're full or not. Sonya wouldn't think, would she?'

'But the person who gave her the pills on the morning she died was her servant and I'm certain he didn't kill her,' said Tommy slowly.

'Servants! He might have been bribed. You can bribe a native to do almost anything,' said Julia tactlessly, 'but I suspect her husband, because he doled out the pills and gave them to the servant so they could control how many she took. Andy warned Kenneth about the danger of Sonya overdosing. I was there when he said it, at a lunch party. She came on to the party, straight from the hospital and showed us the pills she'd just been prescribed, shaking them out into her hand. They were green and black as I remember. She asked Andy what they were and he told her to be careful with them.'

'Who else was there?' The old man's voice was sharp.

'Let me think – me and my husband, no, he wasn't there but Belle Bolitho was with her husband, and Tricia Keen with some man or other. The party was at Tricia's that time because we took turns in having curry lunches at each other's houses on weekends. It must have been a Saturday and not a Sunday because the hospital dispensary was open. Her daughter and Kenneth would have been there, and maybe the awful Alice as well because she'd begun hanging around him about that time. There would be one or two others but I don't remember their names.'

Tommy sat back in his chair and looked hard at her. 'I don't suppose you killed her, Mrs Whitecross, did you? You seem to have it all worked out very neatly.'

Julia's eyes flew open. 'Me? Of course not! Why should I kill her? I wasn't interested in the man she thought she was in love with—'

'She was in love with someone else – not her husband?'

'*Nobody* in my set was in love with their husband,' said Julia sweepingly.

'Who was the man she cared about then?' he asked.

She looked away shiftily before she said, 'I can't remember actually' so he knew she was lying and wondered why, because she'd been so full of information up to that point. But it didn't matter. She'd given him the lead he needed.

'Thank you very much,' he said, standing up in order to encourage her to go. She got up as well.

'If you find out who did it, will you be able to charge them with murder?'

'No. I'm retired now and anyway I'm afraid that murder would be very difficult to prove now,' he said. As she was turning to go he stopped her in her tracks by saying sharply, 'One moment, Mrs Whitecross. Did you send me a letter telling me that Sonya was my niece?'

She managed to spin round quite sharply on her walking stick and stared at him in obvious astonishment before she said, 'A letter? Why should I do that? I've never even heard about you until tonight.'

THIRTY

Things were going even better than she hoped! Buzzing like a bee because a real drama was being enacted in front of her eyes, Julia hurried back to her group of friends and said excitedly, 'You'll never believe this. That old man over there is an Indian police officer who's trying to find out who murdered Sonya Richards! And he's her uncle too. Isn't it amazing?'

Tricia, who was standing on the edge of the group holding Farquhar's hand, turned on her heel to look at Tommy and said, 'Wow, fancy that! Sonya was murdered you say? We always thought there was something funny about that though, didn't we? He's a handsome old boy, must have been a stunner when he was young. Who's the Indian with him?'

'God knows, probably his lover,' said Julia disparagingly, 'I saw Dee Carmichael talking away to him as if they were old friends, but she's always been peculiar. She liked the Indians better than the Brits when we were in Bombay.'

At that moment Kenneth pushed his way into their circle and said to Tricia, 'I wonder if you'd come and talk to Sonya's uncle who's sitting over there. He's very anxious to speak to her friends.'

'Darling, I'm thrilled. I know he's a policeman. Julia's spread the happy news, haven't you Julia? I'd love to talk to him, although I don't think I'll be much help,' she cried, letting go of Farquhar's hand and telling him, 'When I'm away, sweet, fetch me another little drinkie.' Her ebullience was beginning to wear off a bit and she needed bucking up.

Tommy watched her approaching and weighed her up. No fool this one, he thought, not like the woman before her.

She slid into the chair by his side and said, 'Hello. I'm Tricia Keen and I've been told you're Sonya's uncle and Laura's great-uncle. What a good-looking family!'

He smiled slightly at her flattery and said, 'I'm sorry I never knew my niece but it's a great surprise to meet her daughter. Laura seems to be a nice person.'

'Yes, she seems all right now but she was a bundle of trouble when she was young,' said Tricia.

He raised his eyebrows and said, 'Teenage rebellion, I suppose.'

'She was only out in Bombay for a little while before her mother died. It hit her hard and afterwards she went out of circulation. Then Alice had her sent home again,' said Tricia.

'You knew them all well?' asked Tommy.

'Quite well,' she replied cautiously.

'Tell me about Sonya,' he said.

'I'll try. What exactly do you want to know?'

'Anything, everything.'

'That's a tall order. We went to the same parties, we knew the same people but she was closer to Belle Bolitho and Julia Whitecross than to me. I've never been much of a girlie person and I didn't play bridge like they did.'

He frowned, 'She played bridge?'

'Yes, with a gin bottle on the table I'm afraid. They were very keen.'

'You need four people to play bridge. Who was the fourth?'

'Sometimes Andy Parnell, sometimes John Carlton-Grey, other times anybody they could rope in – even James, Julia's husband, but that didn't happen often. I think they tried to teach Laura as well but she wasn't up to their standard.'

'Mrs Whitecross said that Sonya was warned to be careful about over-dosing herself with her heart pills.'

'Yes, I remember that. We speculated about it after she died.'

'You don't think she killed herself, do you?' he asked.

Tricia was surprised and wrinkled her forehead. The skin felt taut after her cosmetic surgery. 'No. I'm pretty sure she didn't. She had her ups and downs like everybody else but she wasn't the suicidal sort. Apart from not getting on with Laura, things were going her way at that time so she had no reason to do herself in.'

'Mrs Whitecross tells me you all suspected Sonya's husband of arranging her death,' Tommy said carefully.

Tricia looked him in the eye. 'People talked. They usually do, don't they? But Julia doesn't like Kenneth and she does like making trouble. Personally I don't think he has the guts to be a wife murderer. If he had, he'd probably have got rid of Alice, too, long ago.'

Tommy leaned back in his chair and she took the opportunity to stand up and say, 'If you'll excuse me now I have to go to the little girls' room. I'll be around till the end of the party if there's anything else you want to ask me.'

In the cloakroom, she shut herself in a cubicle and smoothed out the five pound note again. After she snorted the drug, she felt better almost immediately and set out in search of Farquhar. Their charade was going very well and had everyone fooled. It took her a little while to find him because he was at the back of the room, standing in a corner beside a huge urn from which a leafy plant sprouted. Beside him was an animated, happily chatting man, Dee Carmichael's gay friend Colin. Their heads were together and they were laughing, obviously enjoying each other's company. Tricia paused as suspicion hit her. Bloody hell, she thought, trust Gene! She knew her brother frequented gay clubs and so she should have asked more questions about where exactly he met his friend Farquhar. Not that it mattered really. It would be a pity if they didn't end up in a hotel together, for she hadn't enjoyed a fling for some time, but he must not be shown up in his true colours before her friends.

She marched up to the happy couple and said, 'All right Farquhar, back to work. Let's go and annoy Marian. She's always disapproved of me and I wouldn't want to let her down.'

Tommy's spirits were slumping. I haven't got to the bottom of this yet, he thought, perhaps I never will. Bombay to London was a long way to travel on a wild goose chase, especially at his age.

He looked up and saw that Kenneth, anxious to be co-operative, was advancing on him with another woman in tow. 'This is Sonya's friend, Mrs Belle Bolitho,' he said. Belle, looking solemn, lowered herself into the chair by Tommy's side and stuck out a hand as she said cautiously, 'Pleased to meet you.'

She had keen, intelligent eyes, Tommy noticed, but looked apprehensive. Could she be the one who sent him the mysterious communication that started this whole thing off?

'You know about Sonya Richards being my niece?' he asked.

She nodded and added, 'And that you're the policeman who investigated her death. Yes, I know. It's a long time ago now.'

'People seem to have quite accurate memories about it though,' he said.

She nodded. 'It was a sensation at the time. Sonya knew a lot of people and everybody had their own theory about how she died.'

His eyes were fixed on her face as he asked, 'What was your theory?'

'I think she died of a heart attack. She'd been told her heart was dodgy, but she went on drinking heavily and smoking a lot. She was rather a careless sort of person, you see.' The last sentence was said carefully as if she didn't want to hurt him.

Tommy remembered the half empty bottle of gin, the tonic bottles and the stubbed-out cigarettes in the dead woman's sleeping compartment.

'For how long did you know her?' he asked.

Belle frowned, 'About three years, but really well for the last two.'

'Did her behaviour change at all during your friendship?' he asked.

She nodded. 'Yes, it did. After Laura came back from England before she died, Sonya was a bit tetchy. They didn't get on well, but often that's quite common between girls and their mothers, especially if the mothers have been used to getting all the admiration. They can be resentful if their daughters start to outshine them. I've always been glad that I only have a son.' Simultaneously they both turned their heads to look in the direction of where Laura stood beside her husband, talking to a group of people.

'The daughter is a beautiful woman,' said Tommy softly.

'She was then, too, but so was her mother,' said Belle.

'Were they alike in nature?' he asked, and the reply was a nod of the head, 'I think they were underneath. Sonya was very fiery. She flew into terrible rages sometimes, and didn't think before she spoke. Laura was slower to anger, but I always felt that it was simmering away underneath and might be even more dangerous if it was let out. She kept secrets better than her mother, though.'

'How long did Laura live with her mother and Kenneth before Sonya died?' he asked.

'About six months I think. She wanted to leave school, and Sonya agreed at first, but later on, she was keen to make her go back to finish her education, she said, but I think she just wanted rid of her. It was only six months, but that was long enough for the tensions to build up.' She was trying to tell him something, he knew.

'They quarrelled,' he said as if he was making a statement and not asking a question.

'Did someone tell you about that? It was awful. I thought Sonya was going to kill Laura. We had to hold her back,' said Belle.

He said nothing, just kept his eyes on her face. From years of questioning people he knew that silence always brought forth words. One or other of the protagonists would have to say something and it was never Tommy.

Belle talked on, 'It was in the flat that Julia rented that it happened. I blame her. She made sure they were both there at the same time, although she knew they were getting on each other's nerves already. I'm sure she did it deliberately – she said she didn't of course, but it was exactly the sort of thing she likes doing.' Belle sounded dejected, suddenly regretting the past.

'Tell me the circumstances,' Tommy gently urged her.

'I don't want to get anyone into trouble,' said Belle.

'You won't. The case is closed. I'm only interested because Sonya was my sister's child, and because someone here tonight has taken the trouble to make sure that I was told about her,' he told her.

Belle leaned towards him with her hands knotted tightly in her lap. 'It started just before the monsoon broke – you know how terribly hot and steamy it gets. You really think you're going mad. Julia rented an air-conditioned flat in Marine Drive from some people who were going home on leave. It was lovely . . . we all used it.'

'But you had your own flats. What did you do there?' he asked.

Her eyes shifted away from his. 'Played bridge, that sort of thing.'

'Why not at home?'

229

'Well my flat wasn't air conditioned.'

'I'm sure Mrs Keen and Mrs Whitecross had air conditioning,' he said, and she nodded, saying, 'They did, but they wanted to be away from home.'

'What else did you do in the flat?'

'Oh God, I suppose you know already. We met men there. We were very stupid. It began as a sort of lark really. We made assignations and met them there.'

'For money?' He kept his tone neutral so as not to alarm her but he knew the truth because of what the Bombay servants said.

'Yes,' she said. After a pause she went on, 'We didn't do it very often, just if we picked up people in one of the bars. Tricia and Julia didn't need the money but they liked the idea of being high-class tarts. The money came in handy for me because my husband wasn't a high earner and he didn't mind . . .' Her voice trailed off.

'What about Sonya? Didn't Kenneth mind?'

'He didn't know. She didn't take on just anybody like we did. She mainly used the flat as a place to meet her lover.'

'I heard she had a lover. Who was he?'

Belle looked across the room and motioned with one hand to a man standing with his back to them. 'That's him. His name's John Carlton-Grey. It was going on when Laura came back from England. Sonya was mad about him.'

Tommy looked across the room at John who was standing beside his well-bred looking wife. He had one arm round her shoulders, the model of uxoriousness.

'Did Laura object to her mother having a lover?' he asked.

'She didn't know at first.'

'So what happened?'

Belle pulled a face. 'He got his eye on Laura, of course. He always preferred young girls to mature women. He seduced her, quite deliberately, and she fell for it completely. I think she needed to believe that someone cared more for her than for anyone else in the world and he has a silver tongue, that one. She agreed to sleep with him and asked Julia if they could use the flat. She'd no idea her mother had been using it, too. Just as she'd no idea her mother and John were lovers. Sonya didn't suspect Laura either – as far as she was concerned, she was just a rather annoying kid who was cramping her style.'

Tommy allowed an expression of distaste to cross his face. His heart was heavy because he had not expected this. 'It ended in tears I take it,' he said.

'More than tears, blood as well. Julia, the bitch, sent Sonya a message that John wanted to meet her in the flat at the time she knew he would be there with Laura. Then she rang Tricia and me and asked us to go there for a game of bridge. I remember it was two in the afternoon – siesta time. We should have known she was up to no good because she always liked her sleep.

'Tricia and I drove there together and the place was silent when we let ourselves in – we had our own keys. We were waiting for Julia when Sonya arrived and was not at all pleased to see us. She went into the bedroom to wait for John and that was when she found them hiding in bed together, stark naked. I'll never forget the scream she let out at that moment. It was like a banshee.'

Tommy shook his head, imagining the scene. Belle stared into his face as she went on, 'John did a runner of course, but Sonya set about the girl, hitting her with anything that came to hand. There was blood gushing from her nose by the time we pulled her mother off. I took Laura home and she told Kenneth that she'd fallen off one of the polo ponies that she sometimes exercised on the racecourse. Julia never turned up at all and that's how I knew she'd planned it.

'The very next day Sonya announced she was going to Madras to visit her friend there. I never saw her again and the next time I saw Laura was at her mother's funeral service. She still had a black eye. We didn't speak to each other and we've not seen each other until tonight.' Belle sounded weary.

Tommy took her hand and said, 'Thank you very much, Mrs Bolitho. I think you are probably the only person who's told me the truth. You didn't send me an anonymous letter saying my niece was murdered, did you?'

'No, of course not,' said Belle, 'Because I don't think she was murdered. I think she died of pique.'

THIRTY-ONE

When Prakash saw Tommy rising stiffly to his feet, he rushed over to help him and walked beside him into the centre of the crowd. Tommy knew where he was heading. Turning his shoulders sideways, like the old rugby player he was, he carved a way through until he was standing beside John Carlton-Grey.

'Good evening. We haven't met before but I am Tom Morrison, the uncle of the late Sonya Richards, who I believe you knew,' said Tommy.

His stiff, formal way of speaking surprised John who raised his eyebrows as he said, 'Hello, Mr Morrison.'

'Detective Inspector Morrison,' said Prakash from behind them.

'Retired,' added Tommy. Then he said, 'I wonder if you'd come with me into the hall so we can talk without being overheard.'

'What do you want to talk to me about?' asked John with a note of disquiet in his voice.

'About my niece and her daughter,' was the reply.

'All right,' said John turning to face the door.

'I'm coming, too,' said Barbara firmly.

'I'd rather you didn't, darling,' he said.

'I am coming,' she said in a tone that brooked no opposition.

The three of them went into the hall and sat on the bench recently occupied by Kenneth and Laura. Prakash remained standing by the door leading into the party room.

'Let's have it,' said John, wishing he could light a cigarette at that moment, but Barbara had forced him to give them up ten years ago.

'You were the lover of my niece, Sonya Richards, at the same time as you seduced her daughter, Laura,' said Tommy coldly.

Barbara showed no reaction at the mention of Sonya's name but her head shot up and she stared at her husband in surprise when Tommy mentioned Laura.

'Oh no,' she sighed.

'Yes,' said John.

'You were present when the mother attacked the daughter and might have injured her severely if she hadn't been pulled away,' Tommy went on.

'Yes.'

'Tell me how you got into that awful situation,' said Tommy. For a moment John wondered what would happen if he told this old man to go to hell, but there was something about Tommy's implacability that made him answer.

'Sonya was very handsome, and very keen. She hounded me down, really. I told her it was only a casual affair as far as I was concerned, but she insisted it was the love of her life. She was determined we should both get divorced and go away together. I was powerless.' The excuse of the committed philanderer, thought Tommy, who had heard many different men say exactly the same thing.

'So, she was obsessed with you. What about her daughter?'

'She was like her mother, really – determined.'

'Are you sure? Wasn't it you who was determined to seduce her, no matter what? She was little more than a child after all.'

'Come on, she was all woman and a beauty. Still is. She was throwing herself at me. It was hard to resist. She arranged everything. She said she'd never been to bed with a man and wanted me to be the first.'

Barbara cringed, but stayed silent.

'And you were caught in bed with her by her mother?'

'Yes. That was a bad business.'

'Did you try to placate the women?' asked Tommy.

John looked hard at him, 'I bolted, wouldn't you?'

Tommy did not answer that, and only asked, 'Did you see either of them again?'

'Sonya tried phoning but I wasn't at home to her. She went to Madras either the next day or the day after. I never saw Laura again until tonight. I've just said to her that I'm sorry.'

'Rather a belated apology,' said Tommy dryly and stood up. This whole business was tiring him out and he doubted if he had the strength to see it through. Walking back to the door where his servant was waiting, he said, 'Fetch me the doctor. The one over there talking to the woman in silver.'

Then he went back to sit in the cool hall watching the straight back of Barbara as she walked towards the front door, pursued by her husband. 'Wait darling,' he was saying.

She turned round slowly and stared at him, 'I'm going home. You can please yourself what you do but if you want to go on eating, you'd better come with me.'

'But they've not drawn the raffle yet,' he protested, 'We might win airline tickets to the Caribbean.' He knew he sounded stupid but thought he could appeal to her desire for a bargain.

'Bugger the Caribbean, bugger the airline ticket. I could buy my own airline if I wanted to. I'm going home,' she said and stalked out of the door, followed by John who knew she was dangerously angry because he had never heard her use the word 'bugger' before.

Andy Parnell came into the hall as the Carlton-Greys were leaving. He looked from them to Tommy and said, 'Your friend said you want to see me. Are you ill?'

Tommy shook his head as he replied, 'I'm all right. Sit down. I want to ask you some questions.'

'Right, fire away. What do you want to know?' said Andy, sinking on to the bench. He was very tired and wished he was on his way home.

'You were involved with Mrs Whitecross and her friends in the late 1960s,' said Tommy.

Andy nodded, 'Yes, I suppose I was. I was young and wild, although you probably wouldn't think it to look at me now.'

At least, thought Tommy, he's not blaming the women like Carlton-Grey did.

'Do you think it possible that my niece Sonya Richards could have killed herself by taking too many heart pills? She'd had a terrible row with her daughter, you see.'

'Too many pills would probably have killed her and she knew the risk because I warned her and her husband about it. I don't think she overdosed deliberately, though. She wasn't the type. Sonya would always bounce back. If too many pills killed her, I don't think it was done accidentally because, after she died Kenneth told me that he had given her servant only enough pills for her to have two a day while she was away. There were none left when they took her body off the train.'

Tommy nodded and asked, 'Was there any other way that a heart attack could be induced in her?'

'Yes, but how? Someone could have injected her with a substance to make her heart stop, but she was alone in a locked cabin. It's a mystery,' said Andy.

'Mrs Whitecross thinks someone filled her pill capsule with double or treble the approved dose. Would that have killed her?' asked Tommy.

'It's a distinct possibility. Her heart was dodgy. But if someone did that, they got away with it, didn't they?'

'They did indeed,' agreed Tommy sadly.

Andy stood up and offered the old man his arm, so they walked back into the party room side by side with Tommy thinking that now he had probably found out how the killing

– if it was a killing – had been done. However, he was still in the dark about who had done it or who had taken the trouble to alert him to the whole unsavoury business. Was it only to point out to him that he had failed as a policeman in a case that had a direct connection with his own life? He was even beginning to doubt his original conviction that the anonymous letter writer was among the party guests. Surely whoever it was would be forced to approach him in some way before it was over?

The vigilant Kenneth saw them re-entering the room and came rushing over to say to Tommy, 'Sit down Inspector Morrison. If you want to speak to anyone else, you might have to wait a bit because they're going to draw the raffle any minute.'

Just then a woman walked up behind him and said, 'Won't you introduce me to your friend, Kenneth? I don't think we've met.'

Kenneth looked glum as he told Tommy, 'This is my wife, Alice.'

To Alice he said, 'This is Sonya's uncle, my dear.'

Alice's eyes went as round as glass marbles in a look of surprise which Tommy could not decide was real or pretended. 'Sonya's uncle. Good heavens. I never knew she had an uncle, did you Ken?' she said.

'I don't think she knew either,' said Tommy. Madeleine certainly would not have told her.

'I suppose it's all part of the great Sonya mystery that's designed to keep Laura and my husband happy and shut me out,' said Alice nastily.

Tommy said nothing, but as he listened to her, he wondered if she was the sender of the mysterious message. She was a likely candidate, but he doubted if he could force the brittle woman to admit it.

He turned to Kenneth and said, 'Do you think that Laura will speak to me again after the raffle's over? I don't want to upset her but I'll be leaving soon, and there's a few things

I'd like to say to her. We will probably never meet again after tonight, after all.'

'I'll ask her,' said Kenneth, half turning and trying to locate Laura in the crowd. She was away on the other side of the room and he could see the top of her dark head rising above the others. As he made his way towards her, Marian and Peter were appealing for silence so they could start the raffle.

Ignoring Alice, Tommy went to sit down and as he did so, Arthur Perkins, who had been watching the comings and goings around the old man throughout the evening, walked over and bent down towards him. There was unmistakable glee evident on his face, although he tried to hide it.

'Are you finding it upsetting being faced with an unknown relation?' he asked concernedly.

Tommy looked up, saw the glee, and knew without a shadow of doubt who had sent him the anonymous letter. 'How did you know about the link between me and Sonya?' he asked.

'What do you mean?'

'I mean why did you send me that anonymous letter telling me that she was my niece and that she had been murdered?'

Arthur was silently congratulating himself: Who could have believed that old Pip's files, and my own memory for scandal, would have turned up so many secrets?

'I didn't say she was murdered. I only said she might have been,' he said smugly, not denying the charge that he was the sender of the anonymous letter.

'It doesn't matter now. You got me here. And even if I find out that she was unlawfully killed and who by, there's nothing I can do about it. All you'll have succeeded in doing is putting people in fear and bringing me grief. Perhaps that's enough for you,' said Tommy wearily.

Perkins' face darkened. 'I think Kenneth Richards did it. I wanted to take the wind out of his sails. Pip Leyland, the man who kept the party index file, thought so, too. He'd been friendly with some ex-Siam railway men who told him about Richards' collaborating with the Japs and betraying his Colonel, Tony Anstruther. Pip knew Anstruther – the Japanese crucified him, you know. He hated Richards, and said so in his notes.'

'You were never on the Death Railway. You can't set yourself up as the conscience of the world,' said Tommy, but his mind was registering with shock the name of the dead colonel – Anstruther was the name Madeleine had given to the father of Theresa's child. Would this web of coincidence in which he found himself ever be unravelled, he wondered?

Perkins hissed like a venomous snake, 'What's wrong in exposing those useless people? Look around – look at that woman Whitecross and her friends, look at the cuckolds, the loose women and the seducers, look at the drunks, look at the rugby bores who couldn't tell the difference between opera and bawdy songs, look at the people who only had big jobs because of their family connections. They disdained me, they laughed at me because I'm small and never played rugby. I wasn't part of their macho society.' All his old frustrations came flooding out in a tide of bile.

'How did you know I was Sonya's uncle?' Tommy cut into this tirade.

'She told Belle Bolitho about the papers she received when the woman who adopted her died. I knew Tom Bolitho, he was friendly with some of my friends. He talked about it one night. I remembered the mother's maiden name particularly because that was the same time you were in charge of the case concerning my friend.'

'Was Mrs Bolitho's husband homosexual?' Tommy asked bluntly and Perkins shrugged, 'He liked to dabble.'

'Why did you wait till now before you started to meddle in all this?' was Tommy's next question.

Perkins straightened up. 'Because this is the last cocktail

party. It was now or never. Richards annoyed me badly at one of our meetings and I decided to spike his guns. Even if he didn't kill her, starting an investigation, making you or the police ask questions would worry him, wouldn't it?'

'But what if he didn't kill her?' Tommy asked.

'Whoever did it would be worried . . . if they're still alive. Nemesis, you know, like a Greek tragedy,' he smirked.

The crêpe-like eyelids dropped on Tommy's eyes in a gesture of dismissal. 'Mr Perkins,' he said, 'You are a very unpleasant man.'

THIRTY-TWO

Peter frantically clapping his hands did not stop the crowd yelling at each other, so he climbed up on to a chair at the end of the room and began shouting. 'Attention, attention!' he called to the noisy gathering, 'We're about to draw the raffle. Have you all got your tickets?'

There was a ragged cheer from a group of men near the bar. 'California here I come,' called out one of them and his friends began singing, 'Cal-i-for-nia here I come – right back where I started from . . .'

'Hush,' said Peter severely, 'I'm going to ask Marian to draw the winning ticket. Are you ready darling?'

She was hoisted up on another chair beside him and raised the grey topper above her head. 'The tickets are in the hat Peter wore when he got his gong,' she cried and a few dissidents in the gathering gave deep groans in an effort to take the wind out of her sails, but she blandly ignored them.

As Peter held the hat, she dipped her fingers in among the folded tickets and ruffled them around a bit. The room fell silent and eventually her hand re-emerged with a scrap of yellow paper between the thumb and forefinger. People drew in their breath as she unfolded it, screwed up her eyes a little because she didn't want to put on her spectacles, and said very loudly, 'Number one hundred and seventy-four.' Then she held the winning ticket up above her head.

The room rustled as people started looking at their tickets. Sounds of disappointment could be heard but no one whooped in joy.

'One hundred and seventy-four!' shouted Marian again, more loudly.

There was more checking, more disappointment, but still no claimant.

'Perhaps that ticket holder has gone home,' said Peter, despairing because they had not kept a list of names and numbers. They'd have to stage the draw again and he felt that would be an anti-climax.

'Does no one have one hundred and seventy-four?' pleaded Marian for a third time and then, suddenly, from one of two men standing close together by the potted palm, a hand shot up and a voice called, 'Gosh, yes, I am sorry. One seven four. That's my number.'

Like one person the whole crowd turned and stared at Farquhar. Tricia, on her way back from another visit to the loo and feeling very peculiar indeed, gave a wild whoop before she cried out, 'Darling! What luck! Where will we go?' and rushed through the crowd to embrace him.

A mutter of disappointment ran through the onlookers. 'Trust Tricia,' said some people who knew her well.

'Who the hell is that fellow anyway? Was he ever in Bombay?' asked others as if residence in the city should have been a qualification for entering the raffle.

The vitality of the party began ebbing away. People started drifting towards the door, some of them making arrangements to go on for dinner, others looking sad because they realised that there would never be another occasion like this. Most of them would never set eyes on each other again. The next time they heard of these old acquaintances they would probably be reading their death notices in the newspaper.

Tricia's legs buckled when she reached Colin and Farquhar and they both put out a hand to hold her up. Her hair was wild and her make-up smeared.

'I feel awful,' she muttered, 'Don't let the girls see me.'

Farquhar looked at Colin and said, 'She brought her own

car but we can't let her drive home like this. She's been snorting something, I think.'

'She can come to my flat to sleep it off,' said Colin.

'I've gotta go home. Jim'll kill me if I don't,' moaned Tricia who was being held up between them like a rag doll.

'We'll take you home, don't worry,' said kindly Farquhar. To Colin he said, 'I've a mini in the Sloane Street car park. If you drive it, I'll drive her Jag to Virginia Water. Then we can come back together in the mini. I've got this marvellous air ticket. Where will we go?'

'Let's start with Jamaica. After that I think perhaps Provence, so you can paint and I can look after you,' said Colin, laughing and looking boyish again. His dreams were coming true.

Then he remembered Dee. Where was she? The crowd was thinning out and he spotted her talking to a couple he did not recognise. She was looking dejected so he said to Farquhar, 'Wait a minute. Grab hold of Tricia. I've got to clear this with my friend, Dee.'

He rushed over to her, took hold of her arm and whispered in her ear, 'Darling, I know you'll understand but I've met the most wonderful man. This is it – after all those years, it's happened to me at last.'

She understood what he was telling her. 'Don't worry about me. I'll get a taxi and go home to Kate's. It's not far. I'm a bit tired anyway. Oh Colin, I do hope it works out for you. Good luck.' And she kissed his cheek.

'I'll whistle up a taxi for you,' he said, 'Do you want to go now?'

'Yes, I'll just say goodbye to Inspector Morrison and Prakash – he used to work for Ben and me, you know. I never thought I'd ever see him again! This has been quite a party,' she said.

With Colin beside her she walked over to where Tommy was sitting with his hands folded on top of his walking cane.

His face was sombre. Prakash stood beside him, looking anxious.

Dee held out her hand to him first and said, 'Goodbye Prakash. Meeting again has been wonderful. I often wondered what happened to you after we left Bombay.' To Tommy, she said, 'Goodbye Inspector Morrison. Are you going back to Bombay soon?'

'Tomorrow, I'm afraid,' said Tommy.

'I'm sure Prakash will look after you well,' said Dee, who suddenly began feeling very emotional and feared she was about to weep for some reason she did not understand. Perhaps it was because the old man looked so desolate.

'He will. He is my best friend,' said Tommy solemnly.

Colin, sensing her sadness, gently held on to her arm as they went into the marble hall. People were crowding out of the door, but a distraught looking man was standing by the porter's desk arguing about something.

'I can't let you in,' the porter was saying, 'That party is all but over. Look, they're all going away. The room was only booked till eight thirty and it's eight twenty now!'

'Damn and blast!' said the man, turning away. In doing so, he almost bumped into Colin who was concernedly ushering Dee towards the door. She looked miserable and he was wondering if he should take her in the mini to Virginia Water as well and then give her dinner to cheer her up.

'Do you want to come with me?' he asked but she shook her head and said, 'Heavens no. I'm fine. I just need a taxi.' As she spoke she stepped towards the door and had to dodge to avoid the latecomer who was also heading for the exit.

'Oh my God. What are you doing here?' she gasped.

He looked at her, ran his eyes up and down her finery, and then gave a broad grin.

'Hello Queen of Sheba. I'm sorry my plane was late but I came to tell you that I love you and want you to come back,' said Algy, getting straight to the point.

'I love you, too,' she gulped and, sobbing, put her arms out to hug him.

They clung together in the middle of the departing throng for what seemed like ages before she stood back and asked, 'How did you get into the country? What if they come looking for you?'

'Don't worry. I flew in from Lisbon this evening and I'm going back to Gib on the last plane tonight. I bought two tickets in the hope that you'll come too,' he told her. His face was solemn now.

'What time's the plane?' she asked.

He looked at his watch and said, 'Ten fifty-five. We've just got time if we go now.'

Her whole attitude was transformed. Animated and laughing she turned to a surprised looking Colin and said, 'This character is Adam Byron, the man I live with. You said you'd whistle up a taxi, didn't you? Do you think you could do it now?'

Colin ran into the forecourt and by good luck picked up a cab immediately. He held the door open while Dee and her mystery man got in, but she leaned out to kiss him and say, 'I'll write and explain everything. You'd like him . . . He's not a gangster or anything bad but he shouldn't really be in London because some people are looking for him. I've got to get him back home as soon as possible. Good luck, darling. Be happy!'

He shook his head in bewilderment, staring after the taxi. While it drove away, he could see them hugging each other on the back seat.

THIRTY-THREE

K enneth did not forget that Tommy wanted to speak to Laura again, but the drawing of the raffle delayed things and it was not until people began drifting off and the crowd was very much less dense, that he took her across to the old man. She was reluctant to go. 'He reminds me too much of my mother,' she protested. Her speech was slurred because she'd been drinking much more than usual and her head was swimming.

'It's hard for him, too. He didn't even know he had a great-niece until tonight. Be nice to him, darling. He's going back to Bombay tomorrow; he's old and he doesn't look well,' said Kenneth.

So she went and sat on the chair beside Tommy, very conscious of the hovering presence of his servant. The old man took her hand and said, 'I hope I haven't disturbed you too much by digging up the past. When I was sent that anonymous letter saying your mother had been murdered, I felt responsible because I'd been in charge of investigating her death. It was worse when I looked into the case again and found out who she was. It's all been a profound shock.'

'I understand. Do you think she was murdered?' whispered Laura. Her face was very white and there were dark smudges under her eyes.

'Yes, I'm afraid she was. I even have a good idea how it was done,' he told her.

She stared at him, eyes wide and frightened like a cornered animal.

'How?' she whispered.

'By filling one of her heart capsules with at least three times the normal dose of Digoxin. These capsules are easy to open. Whoever did it knew she was taking the minimum number of pills away with her . . . All they had to do was load one of them. It was a lottery as to when she actually took the dangerous one. She could have died on the way to Madras, or in her friend's house, but, as chance would have it, the last pill she took was the one that killed her. Very simple. It fooled the coroner, as well as me,' he said. He was still holding her hand.

'Kenneth didn't do it,' she whispered urgently.

'I know,' he said and lapsed back into one of his waiting silences.

'It could have been a natural death,' she said.

'It could. It will stay on record as that because this murder is impossible to prove. The only thing I can do is to make the killer aware that I know what they did. Taking away someone's life is a mortal sin. My sister Theresa, your grandmother, had a tragic life and I'd like to know that whoever killed her child feels remorse.' His voice was infinitely sad.

Tears were running down Laura's cheeks. 'Oh yes, yes indeed,' she said brokenly.

'Do you feel remorse?' asked Tommy gently.

Her face convulsed and she gave a terrible sob as she gasped out, 'It was because I hated her so much. It was because of John. I really loved him but she was stronger than me and I knew she'd win in the end. I remembered what Andy said about the pills. I did it without thinking because I was so angry . . . As soon as she left I wished I hadn't and when we heard nothing for three days, I thought she was safe. But then they found her on the train. I collapsed. Everybody thought I was overcome with grief but it wasn't that – it was terrible guilt, it's always been terrible. I've never been able to forget it, but I don't want Kenneth to be blamed for anything because he's been so good to me. I think he knows, although he's never said a word – not a word.'

With a sudden surge of energy, she wrenched her hand away from his, jumped up and stood looking down at him. He stared impassively back up at her. She was so like Theresa that he felt pain strike deep in his gut at the sight of her. Suddenly she opened her handbag, pulled out a small bunch of keys and ran for the door.

Kenneth, who was standing a short distance away watching anxiously, ran after her calling out, 'Laura, Laura, wait for me.'

She pelted through the hall, scattering some people who were saying their farewells. Out on the street she found the car and jammed the key in the lock and as she was climbing in, Kenneth wrenched open the passenger door and got in beside her, grabbing her arm in an effort to stop her reversing off down the road. But she shook him off as if he was a troublesome insect.

He was sobbing, 'Laura don't. Stop. Don't, my dear, this'll blow over. No one will do anything to you. I won't let them. I'll say I did it.' He felt it was essential to get through to her because although she did not erupt into anger often, when she did, she went out of control.

'No you won't. No you won't. You've had enough trouble in your life already,' she screamed, pressing her foot hard down on the accelerator. With a terrible roar, the huge car leapt backwards. Other cars coming up had to drive on to the pavement to avoid being hit. Suddenly she slewed into St James's Street but found herself facing the wrong way against the one-way traffic.

Roly emerged from the club just as his car sprang into action. He pressed clenched fists to his temples, moaning, 'Oh Christ, oh Christ!' as he started to sprint down the cul de sac. He reached the main road, in time to see the Mercedes barrelling off down the hill, scattering the up-coming traffic.

Drivers were sounding their horns and shaking their fists at it but it went faster than ever.

Roly was a very fit man and he started to run down the middle of the road, yelling 'Laura!' as he went. At the bottom of the road, the car swung to the left, still going against the traffic. Laura was driving far too fast and it took the corner on two wheels, teetering out of control for a moment before it disappeared.

The breath was rasping in his lungs and he had a stitch in his side but he kept on running, although he knew there was no chance of catching her. He didn't care if he was killed, he had to follow. Then he heard it – a terrible splintering screech and a loud crash, followed by what seemed like an eternity of silence. Sobbing, he rounded the corner and stared along Pall Mall. A hundred yards in front of him a column of smoke was rising from a jumble of cars. Roly put both arms over his head and howled like a dog, 'Oh no, no, Christ, no!'

A taxi drew up alongside him and the driver got out. 'Here mate, get off the road. Come and sit in my cab. What's happened?'

Roly looked at him with tears running down his face. 'My wife's in that,' he sobbed pointing to the crash. The man took his arm and said, 'Come on mate. Get in. You don't want to see it. I'll phone for an ambulance and the police.'

But Roly would not go. He stood weeping and catching his breath for a few seconds, then started to run again towards the wreckage.

The white Mercedes was on its roof, its wheels in the air. One of them was still slowly turning. Other cars were slewed across the tarmac, some with their bonnets sprung open, and others with their boots pushed in. Miraculously, though people were staggering around shocked and bleeding from cuts, no one seemed to be seriously hurt.

No one, it turned out, except the people in the Mercedes.

It lay at the side of the road because as it hit the pavement, it had turned completely over. From the distance it looked deceptively untouched, but as Roly ran towards it, he saw that the roof was pushed in and completely flattened like a crumpled cigarette packet.

The taxi driver was running beside him, and he shouted at some men crowded round the car, 'My wife's in there. Get her out!'

One of them came towards him and pushed him in the chest, saying to the taxi driver, 'Don't let him look in there. There's nothing can be done. We're waiting for the ambulance.'

'Get her out, get her out,' shouted Roly, beside himself and fighting to reach the car.

'They're both dead,' said the bystander in a terrible voice.

Roly didn't listen. He fought his restrainers and threw himself at the wrecked car but when he knelt down and looked in at the mutilated bodies he knew what they said was true.

A police car and an ambulance came screaming up, to find Roly Gomez sitting on the pavement with his head on his knees weeping like a child. The bodies of Laura Gomez and Kenneth Richards were recovered when the fire brigade arrived with cutting gear. Miraculously, they were the only fatalities.

Tommy and Prakash came out of the club, walked up to Piccadilly and got into a waiting taxi to take them back to Kensington without knowing anything about the crash. They had to leave their hotel very early next morning to catch the Bombay plane, but as they waited in the departure lounge, Tommy opened his newspaper and in a column down one side of a middle page, spotted a short item:

'**Pile Up In Pall Mall.** *A woman and a man were both killed last night in a pile up involving seven other cars in London's Pall Mall. They were named as Laura Gomez, 38, and Kenneth Richards, 70. Police said they were driving against the traffic when the accident happened.*'